De-Evolution

JOHN LARS SHOBERG

MOON PHAZE

MoonPhaze LLC

Dedication Page

Dedication:
To Trudy

ISBN 978-0-9863301-5-5

Print 1 - November 2020

MoonPhaze LLC, 613 del Pilar Dr., Groveland FL, 34736
MoonPhaze.com

Dedication Page

Contents

Prologue

The winds were so strong that as the door to the colonial administrator's office swung shut, several sheets of paper blew off his desk. One landed upright; the field report he had received that afternoon from Clarence Knowles on the creature everyone was calling a Jabberwocky, because of its pieced-together appearance.

> "Without an actual physical specimen to examine, this report is conjecture, based on interviews with the few eyewitnesses who have encountered the creature. Various accounts place it between 2 and 3 meters in height when standing on its hind legs, but able to gallop through the forest at high speed when on all four. It has a muzzle like the wolves found in the woods just north of Petersville, but the rest of its facial features are a jumbled mess of conflicting descriptions. Its fur appears to be a patchwork of types and seems to vary throughout its body. It appears to have claws on only one of its forelimbs or hands, accounts vary about whether it is the left or the right forepaw. It is able to scale trees by means of a web-like line it shoots from one of those paws, usually the one without the claws. They—though at this point no one has seen

more than one at any one time—seem to be stalking our encampments, but run from any encounters with a human colonist.

"Recommendations: Until we know more about these creatures, I would recommend avoiding all contact with them. Further, I believe it is essential to organize a scientific investigation of them to determine if they pose a threat to our settlements."

Chapter 1

Mudslide

"There'll be no damned Communists on my colony." If they got out of this alive, Jeff was going to ram those words down Howard McCurtel's throat.

Damn it, just because the man was the self-appointed colonial governor, did he have to build his home so far away from the main settlement and commandeer so many of their initial resources to do it? Jeff Martin had been driving the only vehicle Petersville could spare up this canyon for three hours now. Three very long, very hazardous hours. And doing it as fast as was safely possible. Which meant he was barely crawling up the canyon road. The rains that had caused the flooding in the Rockefeller basin had finally let up, but not for long. The only satellite they had available for weather surveillance showed that this was merely a respite. More rain was coming in from the North Carnegie Ocean. How did McCurtel get the right to name everything after his damned heroes?

The car began sliding again. He managed to regain control by dropping his speed another kilometer per hour. If it weren't for Marsha and their three kids, he would have left McCurtel to his fate.

No, that wasn't true. Human life was still the most important resource the colonists had on Belenius 3, and Jeff knew he would fight to save every one out here without regard for his personal feelings. The irony of the situation didn't escape Jeff; here he was rushing out to save the very man who blocked every safety rule Jeff had tried to institute. Blocked them in the name of his beloved free enterprise.

Rounding another bend along the mountain trail he was traversing, the lights of the McCurtel place finally came into view. McCurtel had bragged that building his home halfway up the canyon wall, tucked away from the drop-off into the Rockefeller's flowing river, would offer him sufficient protection from any possible flooding. Well, maybe he was right about that, but according to the old FEMA reports Ron Bales had dug out of the ship's database and shown Jeff just five hours ago, there could be another problem.

He pulled into the drive. It was the longest drive Jeff had ever seen, and paved, no less. They had arrived in a generation ship. Everyone now living on Belenius 3 had been born in space; the original settlers, their ancestors who left Earth, were long dead. This waste of land and ferro-plastic shamed Jeff's respect for the plans those ancestors had made for everyone now here.

He switched off the electric motor, jumped out of the five-passenger transport and ran up to the ten-foot tall double doors that would attempt to deny him entrance. It was starting to rain again, just like Ron had predicted.

Without missing a step, Jeff burst through the doors and hollered, "Howard, Marsha, Billy, Tommy, Sarah! Everyone out of the house now!"

The children began to make their appearances at the top railing separating everyone from a two-story fall to the floor of the cathedraled living area. Howard rose from the sofa where he and his wife were calmly listening to a recorded symphony in the great room. The colony had only two satellites orbiting and McCurtel had to use one of them to beam entertainment to his out-of-the-way homestead. Then he had the audacity not to answer his message monitor in this emergency.

"Jeff, what gives you the right to break into my home?" Howard demanded, then looking past the intruder, noticed the door. "And close those doors. In case you haven't noticed, it's raining outside."

"Howard, for once in your life, don't argue with me. Everyone has to get out of this house NOW."

"I will do no such thing," Howard responded. As his wife emerged from the great room, she slid her arm around her husband's waist. Instead of reciprocating, Howard McCurtel folded his arms in front of his chest in his 'I'm not taking any bull' stance.

"Howard, if you had been monitoring developments in the colony you wanted to govern, you'd know we have major flooding throughout most of the lowlands. Emergency crews have been sandbagging the Rockefeller River trying to save Petersville!"

"I just got a report two hours ago from Harvey Fenderman." That guy reported everything to McCurtel, exactly the way McCurtel wanted to hear it. "You had everything under control. I was planning on giving you a bonus once this was over, but after this behavior..."

Jeff didn't wait for him to finish, "The rains have already saturated these mountains. Even your precious Lynch Canyon is filling up."

"That's the Merrill Lynch Canyon!" His voice showed the offense he took to the slight most colonists were using at his naming conventions, "And we're high enough up to be protected from any possible flooding."

"It's not the flooding we're worried about. We tapped into the historical database and found old United States Federal Emergency Management reports about something called mudslides. And according to the soil analysis we did when you built this place and the rainfall estimate of the last week, this area is ripe for one." As if to emphasize Jeff's point, rocks began pelting McCurtel's roof. Several of them thudded to the ground, but at least one gave off a crashing sound of shattering plastisteel and glass.

Jeff turned and ran to the doorway. Several large boulders were now sitting in the driveway with one of them perched on the remains of the transport he had driven up in.

He turned back into the house. "That was only the beginning. The rain has washed away the ground holding the rocks above us. But the real danger will come when the soil loses its consistency and begins flooding down the mountain. Howard, you have to get your family out of here."

Damn, he knew that look on McCurtel's face. "There is nothing wrong. How many times have I had to save this colony from your over-protectiveness? We will be perfectly safe. Our home has been extremely well constructed. If anything, you have cost this colony a valuable transport. But we can simply deduct its cost from your pay. The walk back to Petersville should inspire you to think more carefully before you react." More rocks pelted the roof while he talked and a loud crunching sound came from outside.

Jeff dashed out into the now-pouring rain to see what had happened this time. McCurtel and his eldest son, Billy, followed him out a few seconds later. The front of his garage had been collapsed. While the boulder had missed his two electric runabouts inside, it was sitting in a position that neither of them could get out of the structure.

"Is there a problem now?" Jeff turned his frustration loose. "You need to get back in that strong house of yours and let Admin know our situation."

Billy, the oldest of the McCurtel children, was visibly frightened. He looked to his father, who nodded his agreement. Billy ran back into the house to place the call. Then it hit Jeff; it was very quiet inside the house.

"Howard, didn't you have music playing when I got here?"

"Beethoven's Fifth from the ship's archives, why?"

"Because I can't hear it anymore."

Billy came sprinting out of the house. "Dad, the sat link is down. I can't get a carrier signal."

Jeff looked up at the roof of the McCurtel house. It had a satellite receiver mounted to the roof. Or at least it should have had. He could just make out the mounting brackets, but the dish was gone. Tapping Howard on the shoulder, he pointed up.

"We're cut off up here. We have to get you and your family down to Petersville and safety."

Billy began clinging to his father's arm, but instead of making him see reason, it must have hardened his decision.

"No, we can all stay right here. We're safe and once Admin discovers we're out of contact, they'll send someone up to look in on us."

"Howard!" Jeff said with exasperation, "Don't you get it? I'm that somebody. I'm all that's left. Everyone else is off fighting the floodwaters. We're on our own." Rivulets of water began to flow over everyone's boots. Throwing his hands in the air, Jeff added, "Let's at least get back in your house, if you won't leave."

He wouldn't have believed the rain could come down any harder than it already was, but by the time they got back to the McCurtel front door, Jeff made a vow to never make such unfounded assumptions again.

"Howard, you're tracking mud all over the foyer." As Mrs. McCurtel spoke, Jeff looked down at his boots. They were covered in mud. In the dark, Jeff had assumed the liquid flow was rain. But it was more than that, it was free-flowing, liquid mud!

"Howard, we have to go now!" Totally ignoring any mud he might be tracking, Jeff sprinted up the stairs two at a time to get the remaining McCurtel children. "Tommy, Sarah, get some walking shoes on and get downstairs now."

McCurtel was waiting for him when he got back down. "What gives you the right to order..."

Marsha grabbed her husband's head in both her hands and turned him to face her. From the frightened look on her face, you could see she at least was getting a grasp of the deteriorating situation. "Stop that, Howard! We're cut off out here. If Admin thought enough to spare Administrator Martin to come up here to warn us, **they** must take the threat seriously. And if they thought it was serious enough to bother **you**, then I'm scared." She hollered upstairs, "Kids, get your hiking gear and hurry!"

"But, honey..." he went on.

"Don't **honey** me. We're leaving with Jeff and we're leaving now."

Jeff had never heard Marsha use that tone of voice before. Howard's shoulders drooped as he resigned himself to the inevitable. Jeff had to bite back his smirk when McCurtel turned back to him.

The kids were down in minutes and everyone hustled out the door. The rain had not let up. Now Jeff silently thanked McCurtel for the paving resources he had squandered in building the driveway to his place. Otherwise they would never get through the mud to the main road.

Even with the paved road, they never made it. Halfway down the driveway, a series of loud crashing and splintering sounds came from the direction of the house. With the last of the solar-powered yard lights, they saw the McCurtel home being swept off its foundation and crushed in a sea of flowing mud. A sea that was heading for the main canyon basin, and they were directly in its path.

"Everyone. Quickly gather as close to me as you can." Jeff began opening the pouch he wore on his belt and mounted a small box over his belt buckle.

"Jeff, this is no time for a group hug. We have to outrun that mudslide."

"Get close to me, now! I have a rescue field, but only a personal one." Rescue fields were developed for use in case the survival suit you were wearing developed a leak while you were in a hostile environment, like the vacuum of space. Jeff was hoping it could handle the reversed pressures of this mudslide.

The children looked to their mother and as she moved next to Jeff, they did also.

"Oh, all right," exclaimed McCurtel, realizing he had been outvoted again, and moved in as close as he could.

Jeff pressed the button activating the field. McCurtel had to duck a bit as the back of his hair was singed when the field usurped the space it had been occupying.

Jeff was still facing the oncoming mudflow as he exclaimed, "Brace yourselves..." but before he could utter another word, the force bubble was swept away with everyone in it.

Their bubble flowed along with the mudslide, rolling as it was pushed along and tumbling everyone inside of it. The field was designed to keep things in, like oxygen, without converting it into ozone. So there was no electric discharge on the inside, no one got electric shocks as they bounced along in the spinning bubble. Several times, Jeff felt the rocks in the terrain underneath him as they pushed against the field. Each time wondering if the force field had reached its limit, but each time it recovered and rolled on.

They were carried down from the canyon landing McCurtel had built, over the edge of the landing and fell towards the swollen river below. As they fell, the field generator finally gave out, about six feet above the river's surface.

Since they had been tumbling within the protective bubble, they were flung out at various angles.

Jeff hit the water feet first, sank well below the surface without ever touching the bottom.

He fought his way back up with the river's current continuing to try to pull him under. It took all his strength just to keep his head high enough so he could breathe.

An eternity passed before he felt a solid object brushing past him. Reacting more than thinking, he grabbed hold of whatever it was. He found himself anchored to one of a series of boulders jutting back to dry land. Well, at least solid-looking land.

He pulled himself around the rock until the flow of the river held him tightly against it and he wouldn't be pulled off. He could now begin looking for everyone else.

The rain had stopped again, and the clouds were finally starting to thin. With the little light breaking through from Belenius' twin moons, Jeff was able to see a large struggling mass flowing towards him in the river. He stretched himself between two of the boulders, allowing the river to hold him firmly against them, and grabbed whoever it was before they went further downstream. It nearly pulled him from his perch.

He still had his right leg stretched between the two boulders when a not quite floating and very massive something smashed into his leg. Despite all the noise of the river and his focus on holding his struggling victim, Jeff could still hear the snap of his leg.

He did not scream.

He could not allow the pain to distract him.

He had snagged Howard and now he had to get him out of the rushing current and onto the safety of the rocks. It was during the latter, when intense tearing pain radiated from the middle of his lower leg when he tried to reposition himself that told him it was most definitely broken.

"Howard," Jeff yelled into McCurtel's ear. "Are you, all right?" His words revealed his pain.

McCurtel coughed several times before he was able to cough out, "Fine, no thanks to your damn bubble. You're paying for a new haircut." But he kept a strained grip on the rock that saved him from continuing downstream.

Jeff looked up the river, down the river and onto the far bank. Marsha and Billy had been clinging to each other when the field died. Tommy was protecting his little sister. They had probably been thrown in a different direction. Jeff hoped they were on the far side of the river, the Petersville's side, the tamed side. That was when Jeff saw the light.

On the far bank of the river, somebody was signaling them with a flashlight. That meant at least one of the others had made it. He finally noticed that it was winking in code, the old Morse code Jeff had taught most of the older boys. And since Billy was one of the ones he had taught, it had to be Billy sending the message.

"...safe? Mom and Bill here. No sign of Tommy and Sarah, though. Will head for town. We'll anchor there so you can focus on finding them. Repeat. Dad, Mr. Martin, are you safe? Mom..."

He took the flashlight that was still clipped to his belt and acknowledged Billy. Jeff felt relief that Billy remembered enough survival training from his ship lessons to not make himself another victim.

"Well, Howard, it looks like Marsha and Billy are safe. So I guess it's time for us to get out of this river and back to town. We'll have to get a search organized to find your other children."

Jeff looked to his side of the river. They had to cross over five boulders; six, if you counted the one Howard was clinging to. *Not impossible*, thought Jeff. There was merely a span of one to three meters separating each of them. He turned back to McCurtel and saw the blank look of terror on his face. Between the other man's rapid panting and the chill of the river, Jeff knew he had to solve this problem fast.

"Howard, I need your belt." Jeff shouted over the river.

"No way. This was the first belt my tanning factory turned out last year."

"You nitwit. Forget your souvenirs. I need rope. Since I didn't bring any, I have to use the next best things. Our belts," Jeff shouted back. Jeff simply turned to face the oncoming fury of the river and let it hold him against his rock while removing his belt.

McCurtel, seeing Jeff begin stripping his off, resigned himself to removing his own. He was only able to force his death grip loose on one hand at a time to remove the belt. But a one-handed grip on a slick, wet boulder was not enough to keep McCurtel from being torn off by the river's flow. Jeff stretched out of his perch just enough to grab one of McCurtel's flailing arms and pull him back before he slipped away.

"Damn it, man. Be careful," Jeff hollered into McCurtel's ear before turning his head to release the built-up scream his leg was giving him. Holding McCurtel tight, Jeff inched himself back into balance on the rocks and grabbed McCurtel by one of his trouser pockets, holding him while McCurtel finished removing his belt.

Jeff looped McCurtel's belt around McCurtel's wrist using the belt buckle as a cinch and told him to hold onto it. With the two belts buckled together, Jeff had a leather strip that he hoped would be long enough to span the gaps between the rocks. Finally he pulled McCurtel over to the rock that was supporting him.

"Howard," Jeff shouted over the noise of the Morgan, "I'm going to work us to shore. You stay here. When I'm secure on the next one. I'll pull you over." He watched as McCurtel gave him short quick head nods to acknowledge what he had said. "Just make sure you hang on until I tell you to let go."

Jeff thought they only had to get past three more boulders before the pitch of the canyon wall would allow them to walk out the rest of the way. Well, let Howard walk out, anyway. Jeff turned around and inched his way out from his perch, trying to grab the next boulder. He was short by a foot. Ignoring the pain in his broken leg, Jeff braced his good leg for a strong upstream push and launched himself for the next boulder.

He felt his fingers just touching it as the river tried to sweep him past. He kicked with both his legs and got just enough hold on the rock to pull him up to it. Each kick had been a burning stab he had to ignore, but at least he had crossed the first gap. He hollered at McCurtel, then pulled him across when Jeff finally convinced him to let go.

The next boulder was close enough for Jeff to touch it before having to launch himself again. Though it still took several tries to convince Howard to relinquish his relatively safe position.

A tree limb the size of Jeff's wrist spanned the distance between the next two boulders and Jeff inched his way across using it. McCurtel was easier to convince this time.

"Howard, try to stand up," Jeff suggested after giving his boss a moment to recover from their last crossing.

McCurtel slowly turned his head in recognition that Jeff had spoken but with a completely blank look informing Jeff that he was past the point of comprehension. *So much for walking out,* Jeff thought.

Once more Jeff braced himself before realizing that he only had to move the tree limb to span the next crossing. Once he was across, he felt for the bottom with his hand and found it. He pulled McCurtel over. McCurtel must have scraped his knees towards the end of the crossing, since he rose from the water to stand next to Jeff, who was still floating.

"Don't stop, man," Jeff shouted McCurtel into awareness. "Get out of this river." As soon as the thought penetrated his mind, McCurtel made a run for dry land, scrambling as far as he could from the water. Jeff had to settle for crawling up the bank.

Jeff took several moments to catch his breath. Then he remembered that they were on the far side of the Rockefeller. The side the colony only last year established as off-limits because of the danger of wandering in it. They were in jabberwocky country.

"Howard," Jeff began as he pulled himself further up the embankment. The pain in his leg tore all his speaking breath away from him. He had to wait for it to subside before he could continue. "**Damn**, that hurts." He was breathing hard with every sentence. "Howard, I think my leg is broken." A couple of quick breaths. "You're going to have to splint it." He tried breathing deeper and relaxing out the pain. "Find a couple of stout," deep breath, "branches, about a meter long." Long slow breath. "Good strong ones, okay?"

"Jeff," a new and different look of panic was expressed on McCurtel's face. A look that told Jeff everything he needed to know. The man was thinking about bailing on him. "I think it would be better if I went off and, ah, got help. Send people back, people who could fix you up."

"Howard. HOWARD! Listen to me. We're about half way up Lynch Canyon on the wrong side of Rockefeller River—the jabberwocky side! As long as the river current is this strong, Admin will never be able to get a boat up to us. That means an air rescue. And for that, they will need a clearing large enough to set down in. We're going to have to find one, then get a signal to them. Otherwise, they're just going to be looking for our bodies in Buffet Bay." Jeff had just slurred McCurtel's place names three times and the man hadn't responded. McCurtel was scared!

"Splint your leg? I can't—don't know—we have med units for that type of thing," he said.

The man had never so much as bandaged a cut, thought Jeff. Shipboard life had been too easy, what with the medical regenerator units they brought along. McCurtel had even installed one in his precious home as 'My right as the major shareholder and governor of this colony.' Just one more thing lost to this storm.

"Howard, just find those sticks." Jeff had to get his leg immobilized; every time he moved, he could feel the sharp, tearing pain. A pain he couldn't react to or he'd spook McCurtel into bolting.

While McCurtel stumbled through the early growth forest of the canyon wall, Jeff pulled himself further away from the river. Three distinct times, each one louder than the last, he heard McCurtel run into something and curse the rock, rock, and branch. At least that was some reaction and that showed Jeff that McCurtel was recovering from his paralyzing fear.

After about fifteen minutes, McCurtel finally returned with several sticks for Jeff's inspection. He picked two that were about an inch thick and three feet long. "Now comes the hard part," offered Jeff. "You're going to have to straighten my leg and secure it in place with those sticks. Despite any screaming I may do, you **have** to straighten that leg."

McCurtel's face went blank again as he managed to get out, "I've never done anything like—you've got more experience in this than I—why can't you just—I'll get you anything you need." Jeff had never heard this degree of uncertainty being expressed by the Belenius Governor before. It was the first social response he had heard from Howard since they had been kids onboard the spaceship.

"Howard, listen to me." If McCurtel— *No, maybe it was time to think of him as a person.* If Howard could maintain this attitude, Jeff just might be able to coach him through it. Definitely not the 'My way or the highway' of Howard's old self. "While the process is not difficult, I can't do it myself. I need someone to ignore my pain and set the bone, then secure it in place. I can tell you what to do, step by step, but you have to do it. For me, Howard, you have to do it for me. Do you understand? Are you up to the challenge?" Jeff put some cheer into his voice but moved slightly in doing so. He grabbed a deep lungful of air and held it. He was hoping Howard wouldn't notice.

"Jeff, you need a med unit," Howard said timidly. "I could just..."

"No, Howard! You are going to set and splint my leg, then we can walk out of here."

"But if I could get Dr. Parker, he'd know what to do."

"Howard, sit yourself down facing my leg." Jeff waited before moving again, since Howard wasn't. "**Now, Howard!**"

Howard jumped at the force Jeff placed behind his last statement. Force that was amplified by the scream Jeff had been holding back.

Now that Howard was in position, Jeff twisted himself around until he was sitting up with both his legs straight out in front of him and propped up with his arms behind him.

Once he had again mastered the pain, Jeff said, "First take my leg with both your hands **and**," Jeff winced with the pain as Howard found his grip.

But Howard immediately let go. "Sorry! I knew I couldn't do it. You need a real doctor."

"Howard, let's get one thing straight right now. You're going to cause me a lot of pain while doing this. Pain beyond my ability to hide. But you're going to have to ignore it and do what I tell you. Even if I scream for you to stop. You **have** to do it. There will be no doctor, no med unit, only you. I need you to do this if I am to survive. Can you understand that?"

Howard sat there for a long second and then nodded.

"Good. Now take my leg in both your hands and press tightly. **OOWWW!**" Jeff screamed as Howard got his grip, this time not letting go. Jeff had to take in several deep breaths before he could relax enough to continue. "Now. Without moving your fingers, rotate your palms clockwise. **OOOWWWWW!**" More deep breathes. "Just a little more. Wait. I'm not going to be able to tell you when to stop, so stop when my foot is straight up and down. Okay, go ahead." Jeff gave into the pain and screamed loud and long while Howard worked his leg into position.

Howard held his leg straight for a couple of minutes before Jeff could recover enough to give him the next set of instructions. "Take these two sticks," Jeff said as he reached out and took a couple of three-foot length of branch. "Place them on either side of my leg. Then wrap them as tight as you can with our belts. I mean tight. The splint has to make my leg unbendable or it's no good."

Jeff again let the pain subside after Howard had wrapped his leg and asked, "Just a little tighter, please." Panting as Howard pulled the belts one notch more.

It had taken them over an hour to get Jeff ready to travel. But with the help of a couple crutches that Howard had actually trimmed himself from some of the longer tree branches that had fallen, Jeff was ready to walk out of here with Howard.

Unfortunately they wanted to go in different directions. With all the water that had come down the canyon, Jeff wanted to get as far away from the Rockefeller River as he could. Inland would offer firmer footing. But after just saving his subordinate, Howard was pumping himself back into his old self and wouldn't have it.

"You're the one who said we need to find a clearing," he threw back at Jeff.

"But the bank is going to be unstable, possibly undercut after all this rain."

But now that he was back in a situation he could understand, Howard straightened his back and said, "I'm the Governor and I say we stay by the river. Otherwise, the good citizens of Petersville will not be able to rescue me."

"Us!"

"Yes, I meant us."

There are times to stick to your guns and there are times to give a fool his head. Jeff just hoped he could pull them out of whatever situation Howard landed them in.

For the first time in over a week, the sky actually cleared up. Among the stars, the twin moons of Armstrong and Aldrin, named by the ship's astrophysics navigator before Howard could get a chance, were casting a rather eerie light into Lynch Canyon. Not a lot of light, but from their positions—one directly overhead and the larger one angling off towards Petersville—they were creating dueling shadows on everything. So with the roar of the river on their left and the stillness of the woods on their right, the two men walked down the bank of the river.

Jeff was much slower than the overweight Howard because he had to concentrate on where to plant his crutches before swinging forward. Howard, on the other hand, meandered like this was a walk in the park, staring all over the place. At one point, he must have thought he saw movement on the far side of the canyon. He raised both hands to his mouth and shouted across. "Marsha," then even louder, "Marsha."

Jeff thought it was a damn fool thing for him to be doing, but he had enough trouble just keeping himself moving. He almost failed to notice that Howard, who was not paying attention to where he was walking, stepped right off the edge of a washed out ravine. As the big man began falling, Jeff jumped with his left leg and made a diving grab, catching him by his jacket before landing belly down. Jeff had just barely kept the two of them from falling into a feeding stream for the canyon river. *Where is all this water coming from?* Jeff thought.

"Howard, I can't pull you up. I don't have the leverage." Jeff damned his broken leg again for making this impossible. "You're going to have to climb up yourself."

Again Jeff saw fear crippling this once fiercely independent man. But this was not a situation that Jeff could extract them from by himself. He had to make Howard see that only Howard could save them both.

"Howard, you have to grab my arms. I need your help to save you."

A small voice was emitted from Howard's lips. "Don't let me fall."

The drop would have only been fifteen feet, but the stream would have swept him back into the river with no chance of further rescue. Jeff pulled him a little closer to the top but couldn't hold it. Terror registered in Howard's expression as he fell back down the inches Jeff had pulled him up.

"I won't let go. But we have to work together to get you out. Grab my arms." When he got no reaction from his fear-paralyzed boss, Jeff switched to a more commanding tone. "Now, man! Grab my arms, **now**!"

That got Howard moving. He grabbed Jeff's arms just above the elbow but froze again, just hanging there. The change in load dynamics caused Jeff to start slipping. Sliding over the edge.

"Climb man, climb! Or we're both going into this ditch."

"I can't," came a faint voice.

"If you don't climb, we're both going to die. I'm not letting you go. **Now climb**!"

As if jolted by the last words, Howard began making his way up the side of the ravine. Digging his feet into the soft wall and moving one hand to Jeff's shoulder then the other. Jeff tried to dig his left foot into the soft ground to anchor himself but he was still slipping. Finally Howard made his way onto the top of the ditch; Jeff shifted his position and pulled them both further away from the oblivion that Howard had almost plunged them into. They both just lay there panting for several minutes.

"Well,... we can't... go that... way," Jeff said in short spurts, trying to control his breathing. "What were you... shouting at, anyway?"

"I thought... I saw... Marsha and... the kids," Howard said.

"Well, I don't see them now," Jeff said and silently hoped that nothing else had heard Howard's bellowing.

"There's not much of a clearing here, is there?" Jeff commented after a few more minutes.

"You could have just let me fall!" Howard said like the thought had just occurred to him.

Damn the man, thought Jeff. "No, I couldn't! You still don't understand, do you? Everyone in this colony is important. More important than any resource we brought with us or have found here. Together we make up the most valuable commodity on Belenius 3."

Howard just gave Jeff a blank look. He had never been at a loss for words about how he wanted this colony run. But tonight had been a bit hard on him. He had lost his precious home, his family was walking away without him and a crippled underling had just saved his life. For the third time! All that Jeff could read into Howard's blank expression.

"Life, it's all about life, Howard. Every human life on this planet is irreplaceable. If we die, all the stuff we brought, everything we have found here will still be here, but there will be nobody to use them. Nobody to care about it. And without each other, we won't survive to tame this planet. So yes, to me everyone's survival is **all** that matters. So I'm going to go right on fighting for every single person's continued existence." He hadn't meant to go into his usual sermon, but Howard needed a shock to get him moving again.

"Maybe..."

"No maybes. You're just as important to my survival as I am to yours. Now try and get up, we have to find a way across this ravine."

They lost a few minutes while Howard again foraged for downed branches strong enough to replace the crutches that had gone into the ravine during the rescue. Then they moved along the ravine and into the tree line. Obviously, the river never got this high, at least in the lifetimes of these medium sized evergreen trees growing here. About a kilometer in, they found a fallen tree that looked long enough to span the ditch.

"Looks like a lightning strike," Jeff thought aloud, "at least it's not rotted." Then turned to Howard. "If we move it across the ravine, we might have ourselves a usable bridge."

"Easy for you to say." Howard was sounding more like McCurtel again. "You won't be able to help."

"I can get down and help push. Don't worry, I'll do what I can."

Despite the slightly lighter gravity of Belenius 3, a log is still a log, and when it's big enough to be useful, it has a lot of inertia. They moved it. With a lot of sweat and cursing, but they did move it. Jeff tried to counterbalance their end by sitting on the log, but it still dropped just enough to stick into the far side of the ravine just below the top, instead of going all the way across.

Jeff sat down on the end and tried to bounce on it a couple of times. This was a big mistake; the pain from his leg decided to reassert itself. After taking a moment to relax,

Jeff decided that at least the log was buried deep enough to hold their weight.

"It seems solid enough. I'll go first." He tossed his crutches across to the other side, then laid face down on their bridge. Slowly he pulled himself across, dangling his useless leg over one side. Once he got to the opposite bank, he sat up and rolled up onto the far side. The log had settled a bit during the trip, but it still seemed solid enough.

“Okay, your turn,” Jeff called across the ravine.

The defiant look on Howard’s face told Jeff that the man was planning to one-up him. Howard stepped out onto their bridge and began walking across it.

Jeff saw the bank begin to crumble under the torque Howard was placing on the log. “Sit down, man. You’re over-stressing the bridge.”

Instead of heeding Jeff’s instructions, Howard just walked across faster. As the bank increasingly gave way, he almost broke into a run.

Jeff dropped flat to the ground reaching into the ravine. “Jump man, **jump**!”

But the bank gave out before Howard could effectively leap to the bank. Jeff was again holding his boss above that swiftly flowing stream. The log they had used for a bridge was rapidly sailing down into the river. This time it required less effort to get Howard to safety.

Howard helped Jeff up and handed him his crutches, when they heard a branch snap behind a tree to the north west of them.

Most of the indigenous species of this portion of Belenius had been surveyed and cataloged. While some of the predators could present a danger to the human colonists, none really posed an active threat, choosing to hunt smaller game than man. But one species had eluded their efforts to record it, something large. Someone had referred to it as a jabberwocky—the few glimpses of it led to descriptions that could only be an amalgamation of native fauna—and the name stuck.

Both men turned towards the sound and saw the jabberwocky approaching.

Jeff braced himself on his right crutch and rotated his grip on the other one to fend the creature off.

Howard took off in a run.

"Howard, don't," Jeff cried, but all he did was attract the jabberwocky's attention. He leaned hard on the crutch supporting his right side, the side with his useless leg, and buried it into the soft soil. Then he raised his other crutch like a great sword to assail his attacker.

The jabberwocky wrapped one large paw around the twig Jeff held and tore it from his grasp. Jeff fell backwards, dropping into a seated position, and took a two-handed grip on his remaining crutch. Without having to worry about falling over, Jeff had the balance to keep the beast at bay.

"Howard, I could really use some help out here," he shouted, hoping there might be someone within hearing range.

The stalemate between man and beast went on for just a couple minutes before Jeff hit his opponent a little too hard and broke his weapon. Shifting his tactics, he tried to use the point created when his crutch broke to ward off the monster. Never having seen a spear before, the jabberwocky didn't see it as a threat and just clamped its paws around it and pulled it away from Jeff.

Thoroughly unarmed and immobile, Jeff closed his eyes and waited for death. Just as the five hundred-pound creature leapt at Jeff, Howard came running from behind a nearby tree, driving his shoulder into the airborne beast. Since he had no friction to overcome, McCurtel was able to drive it a considerable distance away from Jeff.

Jeff opened his eyes when he heard the creature hit a bush. While he was shocked to find Howard getting off the ground next to him, he knew they had no time for formalities. "Thanks, man. Find us some weapons, quick."

The jabberwocky was stunned for a moment by the unexpected attack, but it quickly recovered and turned to look at its new attacker. Howard had only enough time to grab a stout branch and throw it to Jeff.

The beast, now focused on its mobile opponent, leapt. Howard dodged and ran over to where Jeff sat. "You're right. Every member of this colony **is** important for its survival."

"Not now, Howard! Find yourself a weapon and keep moving."

While the creature chased Howard around the trees, Jeff worked his way back to the ravine's edge.

"Howard, run it over here." He saw the puzzled look on Howard's face but also saw that he was going to do it. Jeff got to the edge and planted himself.

Jeff waited for the struggle to come to him, and when the jabberwocky was close enough, he hit it. Hard! He snapped the branch across the jabberwocky's back and tore a piece of fur, exposing white skin underneath.

It turned to Jeff and roared out its rage, then prepared to leap once more upon its unmoving attacker.

As it did, Jeff shouted to Howard, "Jump at it again." Jeff also planted the remains of his branch in the dirt, leaned back, catching the jabberwocky in its chest. He pushed the lever he now had on it to force the beast over the ravine's edge. Having Howard add his weight to the effort caused both man and beast to sail over.

But Jeff was ready this time. He grabbed Howard's leg, saving him from a headlong plunge into the ravine. The jabberwocky—with no rescuer—fell into the ravine and was washed out into the raging canyon river.

"You... came... back," Jeff said as he tried once again to breathe normally.

"It's not easy to sit back and watch a friend get killed. It is a struggle out here, isn't it?"

Jeff nodded while calming his rapid breathing.

"I'm beginning to see your point of view. We might have to work with each other to get this place tamed, make it safe for everyone. So I guess we'll just have to be communists for awhile."

"Howard, I wish you could get over this label fixation of yours. We don't have to tag everything so concretely. We just need to work together until we're producing enough excess for there to be an economic pie for us to use to create our dreams."

"I'm sorry. I've been a bit greedy, haven't I?"

"Howard, you had a dream, your dream, just like everyone else. That's why we're here."

"I'm going to have a lot of thinking to do."

"Then we'd better get out of here so we can get back to Petersville and find you and your family a new place to stay. You know no one disagreed with your naming our first city after your great, great grandfather. They all read his mission statement, they all agreed with his dream; you just lost sight of it for a while. It's good to have you back. Now let's find me another crutch and get home."

"Do you think the rest of the colony will ever forgive me?"

"I think they'll all just be glad to have you back. Now grab that branch over there and see how strong it is. Once we find a large enough clearing, I can summon help." Jeff patted his lower pant pocket to feel the flare gun still there.

Chapter 2

Rescue

Dawn was breaking over Petersville as the shuttle gently grounded itself. Clinton Jordan, the generation spaceship's last formal pilot and now the colony's best flyer, brought the ambulance-configured shuttle down without raising any dust from the hard packed soil of Landing Pad Two. Like her brother, Landing Pad Two was a large earthen oval demarked by a ring of eight-inch logs harvested from the surrounding forest. Right now, living quarters were more important to the community than paved parking lots, so that was all they had for an airport.

Reversing the artificial gravity technology from their generation ship had been simple enough. They used that technology to construct several sets of gravidic thrusters that allowed their small fleet of shuttles to station themselves at any altitude within Belenius 3's gravity well. Electrically powered turbines drove the shuttles laterally. Plans called for many more as the colony grew. Each shuttle was constructed using modular parts. One drive section, or driver, consisted of a plasti-steel box with a seat for a pilot and co-pilot, along with the controls for the unit. Its metal six-by-ten-foot tang allowed it to connect various modules on the back, converting the shuttle into a family transport vehicle, or a sky crane for construction, or even a cargo van to carry supplies. Right now, it was configured with the ambulance module for the rescue of Jeff Martin and the Governor.

Gravitational propulsion used the invisible gravity waves surrounding truly massive objects for up and down motion. With no downward air currents to disturb the dirt of the landing site, Clint and Howard opened their separate doors on either side of the driver, and jumped onto the landing site.

Logan Rogers, the deputy colonial administrator, and Mary Danforth, who had been in the Town Hall Situation Room having coffee with him when Jeff's flare had been spotted breaking the early morning darkness, ran across the landing field to meet the shuttle. They got to the back of the ambulance about the time Clint got around and knocked twice on the double doors. An audible click announced the doors had been released from the inside and pushed slightly open. Clint reached up, tossed the left one to the side where it found its latched-open position and pulled the right one open to the same point. Mary reached in and grabbed one corner of the gurney stretcher and began pulling it out as Ron Bales, who had been inside caring for Jeff on their trip back, pushed.

"Has there been any word on my family?" Howard stood fidgeting next to the gurney as it was removed from the ambulance, not knowing how to help.

"Marsha and Billy arrived minutes after we saw your flare. They told us everything that happened. She's a strong woman, kept pushing us to get moving and pick you guys up. But we've neither seen nor heard anything of Tommy and Sarah." Logan reached for the other side of the gurney from the one Mary already pulled on. "Get over to the clinic. Marsha's waiting there with Doc Parker for you guys."

"I need to see if there's anything more on the kids." He headed left, towards Town Hall.

Clint thought that was the least forceful statement he had ever heard McCurdel utter, almost like he was asking for permission. There had been something eerie about his conversations with Howard flying back. But the man still had to get medical clearance. "Howard, the clinic's over there." He pointed off to the right of the landing pad. Clint was waiting for the gurney to emerge from the ambulance, to grab the fourth corner of it as he yelled at their colonial governor. "You'll see Dr. Parker before you do anything else. Or so help me, I'll knock you down and drag you in myself."

"That's not your call," Howard started saying.

"But it is mine," Logan jumped in.

Now that sounds more like our Governor. Clint thought. *Why did you always have to force McCurdel to do something, even when it was the right thing to do?*

Howard just grumbled and changed direction.

"I didn't think he'd listen to you guys," Ron jumped off the back of the ambulance holding his corner of the gurney.

"That was too easy." Clint engaged the latch that fully extended the gurney's legs. "Something must've happened out there."

"I can't wait to hear Jeff's story on this one," Ron said. He began pushing on the gurney, "From what I could tell on the trip back, the extent of Jeff's injuries are that broken leg you see splinted. Howard hid from me by riding shotgun, I didn't get a chance to triage him. I'll leave that to Simon."

As Clint, along with Ron, guided the gurney forward. "Way too easy!"

They lifted the back then front of the gurney over the log that defined the actual landing pad and the blanket shifted off Jeff's leg.

"Looks like you got a good splint applied," Logan added.

"That wasn't me. Howard actually applied that," Jeff added quietly. They bounced over a partially uncovered tree root, not having seen it coming in their rushed walk. "Yeoh!"

"Let's see if we can avoid breaking that leg any further," Logan said.

Ron guided the gurney around a couple more exposed tree roots to avoid bouncing Jeff's leg any further, but the barely exposed ones were hard to see in the early morning light.

They rolled up to the sliding doors of the temporary medical facility. Mary had to pull the doors apart, the automatic mechanisms were still sitting in their boxes waiting for a couple more parts to be 3-D printed. Right now it was just a ten-room, two-story building, holding all the medical equipment they had scavenged off their ship, with a lot of empty land surrounding it staked out for future expansion.

Dr. Simon Parker, who had gotten his medical training from computer instructors during the final leg of their spaceflight and the late Dr. Mylor, was inside, still pulling his left arm into his lab coat with steam still rising from the coffee cup sitting on the reception desk.

"Have a seat, Howard. I'll get to you in a minute." He met the incoming gurney and began inspecting the injury.

"Marsha, how could you leave them out there?" Howard stood in front of his rising wife and seated son, who was staring into his own cup of hot beverage.

Dr. Parker picked up his coffee cup as the gurney moved towards the exam room and jerked his head towards the man he knew was going to be an uncooperative patient. "Howard, I told you to have a seat. You can argue with your wife after I've cleared you."

On the tiled clinic floor, there was no need for all four of them to guide the gurney. Logan let his corner go and went over to save Marsha. "Hold on there, Mr. McCurdel. Your wife had a hard decision to make. And she made the right call. It took me over an hour to convince her to stop blaming herself. If she and William had gone looking for the others in that storm last night, we'd have two more victims right now in need of rescue."

"It's all gone. I've lost everything." Howard dropped into one of the chairs and began sobbing into his hands. "Everything."

Dr. Parker pushed open the door to the Exam Room as the gurney approached. "Stop the gurney." Jeff propped himself on his elbow so he could look at Howard. "Howard, you've got a community backing you up here. We'll find your children. They're precious to everyone, not just you and Marsha. But right now, **we** need to get to the autodocs. Let Logan get the search organized. He's the best tracker we have."

"Get him over to the autodoc," Dr. Parker ordered, as he let the door to the Exam Room fall shut behind them.

Logan dropped his hand onto the Governor's shoulder as he walked to the door. "Howard, I'll be in Admin once you're cleared. We'll find them!"

Then he turned to the Governor's son. "Hey, Bill, want to give me a hand?"

The boy was out of his seat, deposited his empty disposable cup on the desk, and leading Logan out the door.

* * *

"Wheel it as close as you can," Dr. Parker said as the gurney and its navigators approached the autodoc exam bed. As Howard opened the door to enter the room, "Outside." Dr. Parker pointed back to the Waiting Room.

"But I need—" was all Howard got out.

"You need me to give you a medical clearance. We still don't know all the diseases this place has waiting for us. Take a seat, **out there**, and wait!"

Howard let the door fall shut as he left.

* * *

The Exam Room consisted of a long plastic bed along the north wall that was their operational diagnostic unit, their Exam Bed. Four more just like it were against the far wall, ready to be installed when a real hospital was built. In the center of the room was the Operation Bed, the actual healing table. It was programmed to perform hundreds of routine procedures, so a doctor could focus on rare, but critical ones.

Jeff was wheeled over to the diagnostic unit. As it bumped along-side, he began to climb onto the bed. Mary slapped her hand on his chest. "Lie still. Let us transfer you over."

He dropped back onto the gurney with his hands behind his head. "You're the boss."

With Dr. Parker and Ron stretched across the bed, they all grabbed a corner of the sheet Jeff was on and lifted him onto the exam bed. Simon went over to the computer monitor and initialized the unit. "Okay, the rest of you, out of here," he said, looking over the top of the unit.

After the door closed, he gave Jeff a visual exam while his sensors warmed up. "Good splint," he pulled on one of the belts. "Very tight," then unstrapped them and dropped the sticks into a nearby trash container. Taking a scalpel, Simon cut away the pant leg and looked at the injury. The bone hadn't broken through, but it looked a bit odd. "But it doesn't feel like you got the bone in quite the right place. Can you rate the pain for me?"

He began massaging Jeff's leg to feel for the break until Jeff yelped.

"Five." Simon kept massaging up and down the leg. "Yeoh, no, seven," Jeff got out through a lot of forced breathing.

"I'd say closer to eight from the look on your face. You have a habit of underestimating your injuries, Jeff." He stepped back to push a virtual key on the computer screen. The bed Jeff was on slid into the tunnel, the diagnostic portion of the unit. With a couple more keystrokes, Dr. Parker was looking at images of Jeff's broken leg. "You have a couple of fractures in your tibia and a small portion of your fibula is crushed. How did this happen?"

After the machine spit the bed back out, Jeff turned to the doctor and propped himself on his left elbow. Now that he was outside the tunnel, he could talk without an echo. "It felt like a rock hit me while I was pulling Howard from the river. I had myself braced across a series of breakwaters when it smashed into my leg" Jeff tried to turn his head a bit more to see the image.

Dr. Parker pulled the monitor around to show him. "We'll have to put in a pin connecting the two portions of your leg while the bone sets and regrows. Afterwards, I can dissolve it and your body will flush out the remains. But then, you're familiar with nano-building materials. You're going to be off your feet for at least a month." He cleared the screen and brought up the Operation Bed's interface. It was a few keystrokes to enter his diagnose and program the treatment. Then we wheeled the bed out of the Exam Machine and over to the Operations one.

"Now just lay back," then he sent Jeff into its tunnel. "I'm going to put you out for this. Otherwise your pain levels would be a twenty, on **your** scale."

"Someone's got to monitor the search," Jeff's voice echoed out of the tunnel as he drifted off to sleep.

"That's what you have staff for, young man." Simon monitored the autodoc for about five minutes before deciding he could move on to his next patient.

"Your turn, Howard," the doctor said as he opened the door to the waiting room. He pulled open a drawer and extracted a rod-like device while he waited for the governor and his wife to enter and take seats. Holding the rod by its wider end, he began passing it over Howard body. "No apparent cuts, but some bruising. Roll up your sleeve."

Howard offered up a moment's resistance but complied with the instruction. The doctor then poked the end of the rod into the inside of Howard's elbow. "Ow, I hate that."

"But it beats the old method of having to draw a tube of blood to check for poisoning," Simon replied. He held the wand up to read its results. "It looks like you're clean."

Simon backed up to allow Howard to get up. "But I want to see you again tomorrow." He took the rod over to the bench with the other handheld examination equipment, placed it in the small brown box labeled sterilizer, and pressed the green button on top. The unit hummed for a moment then dinged. "I heard you guys encountered a Jabberwocky. We still know nothing about them. I want to be sure there's no lasting effects from that encounter."

"Sure, Doc. Right after I find my kids." He rolled down his sleeve, fastened the button on his cuff and headed for the door.

"I mean it, Howard. I won't authorize you leaving Petersville until I know you're clean." Simon turned back to his patient in the autodoc as Howard walked out of the room.

"By the time I get to Control, that fuddy-duddy will have a stay on my file," Howard said in a low tone as he left. As he crossed the waiting room, he saw that Bales was still waiting. "Ron, with me."

Ron started to get up, thought better of it and sat back down. "I'm really sorry about your kids. But Logan told me to wait for Jeff. So if it's all the same with you..." He picked up one of the training manuals that passed for reading material in the clinic.

"What's the point in being Governor if nobody is going to do what you say?"

Marsha had to stop to pull the doors shut again as Howard had broken into a jog towards the Command and Control Building, aka Town Hall. It was a bit of a mislabel to call it a building, since it was a module unloaded by the colony ship when it landed. More like a Quonset hut, a two-story Quonset hut. The colonists agreed that a real town center would be built after all the new residents of Belenius had their own dwellings. They were hoping to start construction by the end of this current solar cycle. Automated construction factories were kicking out building materials, home construction was moving along at an increasing pace. Next cycle, once they had mapped the planet's seasons, they planned on starting their first crops. Their cloned livestock appeared to be doing well on the planetary flora.

Entering the Situation Room of Town Hall, Howard found Logan, Nancy Flannigan, Diane Brown and Harvey Fenderman bent over the virtual display of the central planning table. Banks of computer monitors were mounted along the walls with work stations in front of them, over a dozen in all. They had satellite, radar, and remote aerial monitoring camera data wherever they looked and it could all be fed into the Big Board, the table they were all huddled around. And everything could access the ship's database that was waiting to be transplanted after housing was completed.

"...and we have nothing from satellite imaging?" Upon hearing the door open, Logan stood up to greet Howard. "We just got your temporary clearance from Doc Parker. Glad to see you up and around."

Howard marched over to the table, stared down at the virtual map displayed on its surface, then stood back up and glared at Logan. "What's the status of the search?"

"We're glad to see you too, Howard," said Nancy.

"Nancy, he's just worried about the kids." Logan then turned to Howard. "No bodies have washed up in the basin as yet. We can't find any traces of them using the satellites and the foliage is too dense to send in search drones, but we do have a pair of them patrolling the river, just in case. I'm about to put a couple of teams in the field to look for them, with backups for a round-the-clock search. Once Jeff is out from under the autodoc, I can pass the baton to him and look for them myself. You guys can control things from here while we..."

"I'm going!" Howard interrupted him.

"Not until the doctor clears you, Mr. McCurdel," Harvey timidly injected. He looked into the glare on his boss' face and added, "I can take your place until then."

The crack of dawn and the man had a blue business suit on, pressed white shirt and matching tie, just like he did every morning. The man hadn't spent more than five minutes away from Petersville since The Endeavor had landed here just over a year ago.

"Not dressed like that you aren't, Harve." Diane stood a mere five foot tall but had been accompanying Logan on his survey trips since planetary touchdown, along with several on her own. The wiry blond had completed over fifty forays in the untamed regions around Petersville, mapping the area and cataloging native life forms. Many more than Logan had. And those were just the ones she reported. She'd been known to disappear for weeks on end; rumor said she had build a secret camp about ten miles north of Petersville. Even Logan didn't mess with her.

"You heard the lady," Logan agreed. "Find some proper clothes and we might be able to babysit you on this mission. For Howard's sake."

Harvey looked from Diane to Logan, saw their determination.

Howard broke the moment. "Do whatever they tell you, Harvey. Just keep me informed. As soon as Dr. Parker clears me, I'll take over." He turned around and found an empty office chair, pulled it over to the central table, and adjusted its height so he could see the situation screen.

"Harvey, get to central stores and check out a survey pack, one in your size. Suit up and meet us at Rockefeller Landing," Diane detailed for Fenderman. "We'll march inland from there. Logan, you bring Jeff up to speed and have your team catch up with us. With any luck, we'll have some idea where to start looking by the time you get to the disaster site. Fenderman, why are you still standing here? We leave in fifteen, with or without you."

The Governor's personal assistant looked over to his seated boss.

"Move it, man!" Diane commanded.

"She's the boss, Harvey." Howard folded his arms in front of his chest and sat back into his chair. "You'd better do what she says."

Harvey almost turned on his heels before sprinting from the room.

As the door closed, Logan straightened up and looked from it to Diane. "You're going to have to babysit that one."

"We all started out like that, if you remember, Logan." Diane's eyes were following the lines Nancy was drawing on the e-map of the search area. "At least he'll have enough people around him to correct any dangerous mistakes he makes. Remember that pit bubble you stepped in when we first started exploring?"

Logan looked down at his right foot and remembered stepping on a small round mound on his second expedition. It had collapsed under his weight and his leg dropped out from under him. He was knee deep in a burrow when something clawed through his leather hiking boot. The Doc had grounded him for a month while it healed. He spent the whole time listening to Diane taunting him over their radio link as he sat trapped in the control room. "At least we know where **not** to step now."

"I've highlighted a few clearings on the west side of the Rockefeller." Nancy stood upright as she finished highlighting the areas. Even though 6 inches taller than Diane, she did not radiate the same toughness as the smaller explorer. She was the mother of two children who were born aboard the Endeavor and that her husband Martin were taking care of while she oversaw the construction schedule for the rest of the colony's homes. She had an expert knowledge of ground conditions. "Of course, that assumes the children would have been able to make their way back here on the finished, eastern side. The road up the river ran another twenty miles past your place, Howard, to the weather station on... You know, you never named that hill, did you?"

"It was your weather station," Howard bit back. "Sorry, that was uncalled for. Not everything has to be my way." He stood up and stared at the map, then circled an area just south of a large creek, using red to differentiate from Nancy's green. "I think this was where Jeff and I encountered the jabberwocky."

"If it washed into the basin, we never found its body," Logan reviewed the section of map now highlighted. "Either it got caught by something in the watershed and was pulled under or it managed to get out of the river and moved on. Those guys can be tough."

"And neither have the children. I'm hoping if we scout the river bank, we'll find where they emerged," Diane said. "Nancy, you take a team on the east side, follow the main road up to the weather station. I'll lead the teams into jabberwocky country. Logan, you follow as soon as Jeff's in place to coordinate."

Having decided, Diane walked over to the door and gestured with her hand. "Shall we get moving?"

Chapter 3

Rescue Party

Clint gunned the electric motor of the inflatable power boat they used to cross Buffet Bay, and drove it up onto the mud bank a couple of feet. There was no dock on this side like the one they had stepped off of on the other. Diane inspected their immediate surroundings for tracks before disembarking, or letting anyone else. Several small animals had been here since last night's rain, but no human footprints.

She stepped out of the boat, pulled out the docking line and grounded it just a little further up the bank. "Start handing me the gear, Mike. Mary, secure that side while Harvey ruins those boots."

Mary pressed her palm into the inflatable tube hard enough to slightly deform it, then jumped out of the boat. Harvey worked his way up to a standing position. He wobbled a couple of times before feeling stable enough to climb over himself. He inched himself over to the tube, grabbed the line running over the top of it, pulling it tight to keep from falling, then raised his right leg just enough to clear the side and planted it into the river bank.

"What do you mean ruin my boots?" he asked as his foot sunk up to the ankle in the soft mud. He immediately tried to pull his foot free, pushing his left foot into the bottom of the rubber boat, which cost him all the stability he had worked to achieve.

Mary caught him before he could fall backwards into the river. The woman stood six foot tall and had the muscles she needed to pull him from the creek bank. Being a hands-on construction foreman helped her stay in shape. There weren't enough colonists for someone to just stand around and supervise. She pulled his foot out of the mud and helped him get to more solid footing. "Thanks. I guess I should have moved closer to the front before getting out?"

"Lesson one, Harvey," Diane said as she walked up the bank with the last of the backpacks. She had found a dry, grassy spot to place their supplies. "Look before planting your feet. Mary might not be there next time."

After depositing the last of the backpacks, Diane took out a collapsible walking stick from her own. She extended it, twirled it a few times, then began running through a series of martial arts warm-up routines.

"Thanks for the ride, Clint." Michael jumped out of the boat and tossed the line back into the bow.

"See you in a couple of days." Clint gunned the motor in reverse, just as quietly as before, and pulled away from the bank before turning around and heading back across the bay.

Michael waved him off then climbed up the bank to join the others in sorting through their backpacks. Mary had already claimed the one with the field tents and kitchen, the heaviest one, as she always did when they went on exploratory walks. The rest of the gear would be evenly dispersed between the remaining three packs.

Michael opened his, removed his machete and attached it, sheath and all, to his belt. Mary had already taken hers out and was going through her own loosening up exercises. While wearing her pack.

The beige jumpsuit Harvey had been given was covered with mud as he emerged over the top of the bank. Everyone else had already taken their travel gear out of their packs and stored them in the abundant pockets of their jumpsuits. Diane and Mary had their full-brim boonie hats on while Michael wore his Dodgers baseball cap. Harvey sat on the edge of the grass and was using a twig to scrape the mud off his boots. Diane zippered up the last of the packs and tossed it at him. It landed a foot away from his right side, yet it was close enough to make him jump as it landed.

“What?”

“That’s your pack, Harvey,” she said. “Slip it on and we’ll help you up.”

"Forget the mud, Harvey," Mary called to him as she swung her machete around and dropped it into her belt sheath. "Get your bug spray and hat on before the insects and sun get you. Mike, are the Dodgers still playing back on Earth?"

"The last dispatch we got didn't mention anything. Baseball is a much lower priority than the latest 3-D tool files." He patted his own machete. He knew they weren’t going to need them for a long time, but he felt secure knowing it was there. "Besides, it's only a hat."

Harvey pulled the straps over his shoulder and tried getting up on his own. “This thing’s heavy.”

"Give us your hands," said Mary who was standing on his left as Diane moved up to his right. Diane grabbed his hand while Mary took him by his forearm. They both leaned back and pulled him upright.

"It's still heavy," he complained.

Mary took hold of the pack's shoulder straps. "First you tighten the straps," she pulled the straps as tight as they would go on Harvey. Then she reached around behind him to find the pack's belt. "Then fasten the belt so you're not carrying all the weight on your shoulders."

"Better?" Diane asked with her back to Harvey. She was looking at the path they were about to follow.

"It's still heavy. I still don't have a hat?"

"Fine." She took a step back towards the river, "Let's go."

Mary spun the beleaguered assistant around and pulled something from a pouch on his pack. Spun him back and pulled another beige boonie hat over his head. Michael moved up to him and sprayed him down with his own bug spray. Then he and Mary followed their leader back to the river. Harvey stared at them as they carefully went back down the bank. "What have I gotten himself into? My socks are still squishing," he said under his breath before starting to follow them.

When they got about six feet from the waterline, Diane turned to follow the course of the river and called back without stopping, "Everyone keep a sharp eye out for tracks. And Harvey, follow Mike's footsteps exactly. I don't want you getting stuck in the mud, again."

Within the half hour, they'd stopped five times to explain to Harvey the difference between the tracks of the various species of rodents in the area and their large cat-like predators. Both of which they were not looking for and neither of which would have bothered the children they were looking for.

They were staring down at a set of paw prints, four small round depressions surrounding another three times their size. Even though these were the largest that Harvey had found, "Harvey, these are cat prints. Jeff said the kids had time to get their hiking boots on. So we are looking for prints like this," she pointed to the tracks that the three of them had made through the cat tracks before Harvey stopped them. "Only smaller. If you see something like them, sing out. But stop slowing us down looking at every track the native wildlife has made."

After that Harvey kept his mouth shut, even when he saw the green monstrosity perched in an overhanging tree branch they walked under. He kept his mouth shut as he watched its eyes track his movements.

Chapter 4

Father's Turn

Jeff rolled up to the Big Board. His leg cast, which started above his knee and caused his leg to stick straight out, was too high to go under the table. He was forced to park his wheel chair sideways along it and twist around to stare at its readouts. At least the wooden frame around the flat screen allowed him to lean on the table without affecting the virtual display on it.

A red dot on the western side of the Rockefeller River and a blue dot on the eastern side illuminated the positions of the two search teams. A stationary drone relayed their positions and the board updated them every few seconds. Currently Nancy's team was just north of where Howard's home had been. Diane was moving at a much slower pace.

Jeff turned his chair as he heard the door opening. A ding from the computer against the wall came in also. "Just a second, Howard."

With a quick turn and a couple of wheel spins, Jeff was reading the incoming message. It read, "Howard McCurdel is cleared to return to his duties. Good luck, Jeff."

"Simon just cleared me," Howard announced. He came over to the virtual tap map and checked to see that the search parties were still in the field. "Get a shuttle ready. I'm replacing Harvey."

Without turning away from the console he was at, Jeff keyed the PA system rather than using his personal one, "Clint, report to command."

"Be right there," returned the overhead speaker.

He turned back to face the Governor, who dropped a back pack off his shoulder and onto the floor. "I see you've gotten your supply pack from stores."

"I stopped there on the way over here. They had one in my size waiting for me."

Jeff tried to gauge Howard to see if he was really ready to take on untamed Belenius; he was going to be out there a lot longer than poor Harvey. "I told them to get one ready for you. You have a bit of changing to do before Clint gets here. Swap out those sneakers for your hiking boots, get your jumpsuit on, and let's see the hat they gave you."

Howard went into the Men's restroom and changed into a jumpsuit the same beige color as his backpack, which had been tied to the top of that pack. He pulled up a chair and unzipped his canvas bag. The topmost items were his brown, leather, half-calf, laced boots. After swapping shoes, he pulled out the next item—a purple boonie hat—looked it over and pulled it onto his head.

"I'll have a talk with Bill. That hat's just wrong."

"He wanted to give me a bright orange one."

"According to the safety regulations, that would've been the right color."

"I'm keeping the purple."

"Did he offer you a yellow vest?"

"Is anyone else wearing one?"

"Ah, no."

"He said the same thing. I told him, no!"

"At least use the bug spray."

From a side pouch, he pulled out a pump bottle. "I can live with that precaution," and started applying the repellant. "Jeff, do you think that jabberwocky got to my kids?"

Jeff turned back to the control table before answering. "We've never had a case of them attacking or harming anybody since we've landed. Even in our encounter, it never pulled out its claws. If one has your kids, there's a good chance they're still alive, but I think it's more likely to just watch them from a distance. I'm more worried that the river might have gotten them. There's something else I have been meaning to discuss with you."

"William?"

"Don't punish him, he did the right thing. Marsha would have gone after your kids and we'd have four people to find and rescue."

"Is this another community speech? If so, you can save it. We are stronger together, I see that now. And I trust you. You'll find them. You'll bring them back."

"**We'll** bring them back, Howard. The whole colony is committed to their rescue."

Another ringtone, similar to the old bell tones phones historically had, broke the mood. Jeff wheeled himself backwards to the computer console and answered it. "Command."

Diane was on the other end. "Jeff, we've found the kids' tracks. It looks like they climbed out of the river just north of where you came out, almost directly across from the side road up to the old Governor's mansion. Yeah, we found your tracks a bit earlier. The kids seem to be headed inland, I'm guessing to find a safe place to get their bearings. No signs of blood and their tracks are regularly spaced. I'd rule out any injuries at this point."

"That's good news. How are you guys doing?"

"Harvey's slowing us down but not enough for me to leave him behind. Yet! Though Mary's threatened to dump him in the river a couple of times. He's actually spotted a couple of animals we hadn't encountered before. Mike's got them photographed and cataloged. Sometimes it's good to hold onto a little fear."

Since they were on the speakers, Jeff wheeled back to the Big Board. "Howard's ready to go. It looks like there's a clearing to the northwest about a mile from your position." He moved his finger to show Howard the area he was referring to. "I can have Clint put him down there then pick up Harvey. Do you want Nancy's team to assist?"

"Not yet. From now on, this is a tracking expedition. The ground is drying out, and it'll be harder to find footprints the further we go in. Too many footfalls would just obliterate any trail I might be able to find."

The door to the center opened again. "Clint's on his way with Howard. Good luck. Clint, get a shuttle warmed up. Passenger module, pick up Nancy's team on the way back." Jeff touched a memory stick to the point on the command table where Diane's team was and tossed it to him. "Here is your destination."

Clint pointed his thumb over to Howard.

"He's released to go," Jeff replied.

Quiet descended on Situation Room. Jeff ached to be part of the search, but hoped it wouldn't still be going on by the time he could.

Chapter 5

Change of Personnel

"First time in the woods?" Clint banked the shuttle in a circle around the forest clearing, looking for the most stable spot to put it down. The ground had moved a time or two on his previous landings on this side of the river, he wanted to find the best looking area before exchanging Howard for Harvey.

"I never fancied myself as the outdoor type. But I'm more worried about Tom and Sarah then anything this planet can throw at me."

"Good for you. I don't think Harvey felt that way when I dropped him off." He switched to lower and lower gravity variants until the four landing pads settled into the soil. Then he cut the motors. "We're here. Just listen to Logan and Diane, they'll get you through this. If I were going along, they're the ones I'd want with me." He offered his hand to Howard. "Good luck."

He had been reaching for the door handle, but Howard froze for a moment then swung his hand around and clasped Clint's. "Thanks." Then he got out of the shuttle and walked over to the waiting search party.

A muddy, sweat-soaked Harvey bolted past him and into the co-pilot's seat he'd just vacated. His hat got caught in the closing door and he had to reopen it to yank it in.

Clint had also left the craft, leaving Harvey to sit there by himself. He offered his hand to Diane, then pulled her into a hug. After a moment, he came up behind Logan and Mike, who were talking to Howard, and grabbed them both by their shoulders.

"It looks like you guys left me a little squirrel to haul back to camp."

"Hey, Clint." Mike turned to look at who had grabbed him. "Where's that martini you promised to bring me?"

Logan elbowed his fellow searcher in the ribs. "We still have a long way to go before we can celebrate."

Clint slipped his hand in his pocket, extracted a small pouch from it and handed it to Mike below Logan's line of sight.

Mike had it in his pocket before Logan could notice any motion. "Too bad. I could really use one."

"As I was telling Howard. It looks like they've been captured by a jabberwocky and are traveling with it. On particularly wet soil, we see three sets of tracks moving at a child's gait. At other times, we see a single set of jabberwocky ones in what we think is a running gait. Then after awhile, the children's tracks reappear."

"We think the jabberwocky is carrying them in those intervals," Mary joined in the conversation.

Mike continued the briefing. "Overall they appear to maintain a pace equal to our own. We can't seem to gain on them. But we're not falling behind, either."

"With just enough clues," Logan said, "to keep us going the right way. It's like it knows we're here and wants us to follow."

"Can I get to some dry clothes," Harvey cried from the shuttle's window he had rolled down. "I'm cold, wet, and miserable." the four looked over at the man and returned to their huddle. "Please, I want to go home."

Clint turned back to the shuttle. "You guys should be nominated for sainthood. It's going to be all I can do to not remote-open his door and dump him in the river."

"And you're just going to have to put up with him for a few minutes." Diane slapped him on the shoulder to get him moving.

"Take care, you guys. I'll make another run out to you the day after tomorrow."

As the shuttle lifted off, Logan led Howard over to a spot they had prepared for him. "This is normal for this stretch of forest," he swirled his hand at a patch of vegetation. Then moved Howard to a different one. "This one has tracks and signs of something passing through it." He pointed to several tracks on the ground. "These are native animal tracks and we are not overly interested in them."

Mike added, "But Harvey was so interested in them that we spotted several new sets."

"We're not working with him anymore. Howard's going to be more stable. Right, Howard?"

"I just want my kids back."

"Then stay focused." He pointed to another set of tracks. "These are what your kids are making. They still have their hiking boots on. Those boots are making clear impressions." He then pointed to what appeared to be a human footprint. "The jabberwocky isn't wearing any shoes and its tracks look like this. But when it starts running they get so light we have to look for other clues; trampled grass, broken twigs, anything different from that normal patch of forest I showed you earlier."

"But how do I tell if it's an animal or them making a mark?"

"You don't. Just sing out. One of us will make that call. We're counting on you seeing what we miss."

"I think we've waited here long enough. Shall we get going, fearless leader?"

Howard began to answer, when Logan chimed in. "Diane, you stay on point. Mike follow her. Howard, you're next. I'll bring up the rear. You heard the lady, let's get rolling."

The trail Diane lead them on ran parallel to the clearing that Clint landed in, just inside the wood line. As they reached the western edge of the rectangular area, the jabberwocky's trail turned north. Howard reached out, placing his hand on the rock up-cropping as they made their turn. He stopped for a minute, as a thought nagged at him. "This rock feels awfully pebbly."

Logan gave him a slight push to get him moving again. "Yeah, we've run into hundreds of them. They're no big deal. Keep up with Mike."

They passed several more of those rocks, though they were of varying heights, they all had a pebbly feel to them and looked like they might be evenly spaced. Howard even kicked at a bush where he was expecting one. It was there, just covered by low-growing foliage.

Before the clearing came to an end, Howard kicked against something that made the steel shell surrounding his toes ring.

He turned around to look at Logan.

"Diane, hold on," Logan called up the line. "I heard that, too," he said to Howard.

Logan bent down and began digging around Howard's foot as Diane and Mike came back to see what was happening. Diane got down and helped Logan clear the earth and debris away from what Howard had kicked.

"These clearing are still a mystery," Mike came up to stand next to Howard. "They almost happen at regular intervals, but we can't find any reason why they should."

"I never paid the reports a lot of attention, since they were in jabberwocky country."

"Mike, take a picture of this." Logan pointed to the piece of steel protruding from a segment of rock. "Send it back with the next transmission. It almost looks like rebar. But let's let the engineering gurus decide which of us is crazier, me or this planet."

"That's a new one, Howard." Diane slapped him on his shoulder before taking up point again. "But we still have two kids to find. So let's get moving."

As they left the clearing and moved back into the overgrown forest, Diane kept pointing to various signs along their route; snapped twigs, crushed seedlings, bits of fur clinging to the coarse tree bark. Mike relayed the gesture and Logan would quietly call out "Agreed," to the advancing party as he passed the point. After a half hour of this, Howard began to understand what they were pointing at. Well, at least a quarter of the time.

Two hours, about six miles from the last clearing, they came upon another one. Much like the last one, it was cleared in a large rectangular shape, about a quarter mile on each side, maybe longer than wide. With a grid work of native flora cutting it into sections about 20 yards on a side.

"I wonder what causes this vegetative growth pattern?" Mike said.

"Not our mission right now," Logan called up to him. "Focus on tracking Tom and Sarah."

Howard looked over to see what Mike was talking about and forgot to watch his footing. He slipped on an exposed root and stumbled a couple of steps into the clearing. Until his right foot plunged almost knee deep through the soil.

"Howard." Logan made a grab for him, he caught him by his pack and pulled to keep him from dropping any deeper.

Diane and Mike turned and hurried back to help. They grabbed each of his arms and pulled. His foot offered a little resistance when it came out of the hole he had made, but they easily got him out.

Mike dropped to his chest while Diane and Logan got Howard back to trail. "I can't see the bottom of this thing." He pulled a small flashlight off the clip on his belt and shined the light into the hole. "I can see something about ten feet down, not sure what, though. This thing is really wide. I can't make out its sides."

"Howard, you okay?" Logan set him down to look for any injuries. "Anything hurt?"

Howard's breathing slowed and he shook his head.

"I thought we told you to follow our footsteps?" Diane chided him.

"Give him a break. He slipped. It could have happened to any of us." As Diane started to open her mouth, "Okay, maybe not you."

Mike approached the group. "Looks like another reason to avoid these clearings. They're not safe to walk on."

"So we learned something new, without getting hurt. You aren't hurt, are you, Howard?"

"No, I think I'm okay. Just help me up."

"If he can walk, we need to get back on the road. We've lost enough time because of this stumblebum."

"DIANE," Logan said.

"I'm sorry, Mr. Stumblebum." She turned and began walking north again.

Logan squeezed Howard's ankle. When he didn't squawk, helped him to his feet.

"Don't mind Diane," Mike offered as he held Howard's left arm. "She just gets uber-focused when she gets out here. She'll find your kids, though."

"Sometimes I think she's a better tracker than I am," Logan admitted. "Just don't tell her I said that."

"It feels like it'll hold me up." Howard leaned to put all his weight on his right foot. "I guess we had better catch up with her before this 'stumblebum' causes any more delays."

"I'm liking this new side of you, Howard," Logan said. "You're going to have to tell us what happened the night of the mudslide."

"Campfire story-time tonight." Mike turned and hurried off after Diane.

* * *

They decided to make camp for the night a few hours and two clearings later. Logan and Mike hacked out an open area with their machetes. Howard pulled his off his belt and tried to help out.

"Whoa, there." Logan pushed Howard's hand holding the machete down. "You can't just swing that thing willy-nilly. Aim at the base of whatever you're trying to chop down. Twist your wrist at the last second, bringing the edge of your blade chopping into it."

He let Howard try a few more times. "You know, I think it would be a better idea if you started setting up camp where Mike and I have cleared things?"

"Why don't we just use the clearing over there?"

"Remember what happened earlier? I want to make sure the ground under me is solid while I'm sleeping."

"There is that." He attached his machete back on his belt and began opening his pack. "But how will I ever get better if I don't practice?"

"I'll start teaching you the basics in the morning. Who's got the fire pit? Diane's going to want it set up when she gets back."

Chapter 6

The Long Haul

Jeff placed his hands on the chair's armrest and pushed himself into an upright position. His knee was stiff as he straightened it so he could get the doctor-required exercise in. He pushed against the edge of the Big Board in the Situation Room and made his way to a standing position. He needed to get used to walking again, now that his inflatable plastic cast had been removed. With his lower leg nerves electrically frozen, forcing his muscles to become as rigid as a cast for the last few days of Jeff's recovery, he began a rather exaggerated swing step with his right leg. But it did allow him to get the exercise he needed to fully heal.

"I know you," Dr. Parker had said. "Don't overdo things. I want you sitting for a half hour for every hour you're up. More often, if you feel fatigued."

Having finished a ten-minute rest period, he was up and circling the table a few more times. Forcing as much bend into his knee as his frozen muscles would allow. Then he just gave up and limped his way around the table.

"Why don't they check in?"

The chime on the door attracted his attention. Marsha McCurdel, dressed in the same jeans and pullover shirt she'd had on the day before, with increasingly dark lines under her eyes and a tiredness that radiated from her whole body. It had only been an hour earlier that Jeff had sent her to temporary housing to get some sleep after finding out she had spent yet another all-nighter in the Command Center.

"Has there been any word?" she asked.

"Not since I told you to get some sleep."

"I can't. The not-knowing."

Resigned to the company, Jeff said, "Well, get yourself some coffee, I'm in no condition to carry you over to the hospital if you fall flat on your face. Mary started a new pot before she ended her shift."

Marsha shuffled over to the far side of the room and poured herself a cup. Jeff noticed she didn't bother to dilute it with her usual cream and double sugar but still stirred it with a spoon. She just dropped into a chair alongside the table holding the caffeinated brew and sipped her scalding liquid, oblivious to its temperature.

"Marsha, you really need to get some sleep. That coffee's only going to hold you up so long." He pressed a virtual button on the table and hobbled over to where she was sitting. He had been standing still too long and it had caused his knee to stiffen again. He placed a hand on the back of her chair to let her know he was there for her.

She reached up and patted his hand. "I need my children."

"And we'll find them. But if you don't take care of yourself, they'll find themselves without a mother when they get back."

The chime made him turn to the door again as Dr. Parker rushed in. "You all right, Jeff?"

"It's Marsha." He stood up and took a step towards the doctor to prove he was fine, holding back the winch as he bent his knee in a normal-looking motion. "She needs something to help her sleep."

Simon crossed the room to Marsha and placed his hand on her wrist. "How long has it been, dear?"

"I get about an hour sleep every night. I have to be here when Howard calls."

"No, you don't. That's what Jeff's for. You need to be ready for when they find Tom and Sarah. They're going to need their mother and Howard is going to need his wife." Simon turned to Jeff. "How's William doing?"

"He's working with one of the housing teams. He's really thrown himself into their project. I think it's his way of dealing with the worry."

"A healthy release. Marsha, I want you to come with me. I going to give you a mild sleep agent, then put you in the autodoc for some REM therapy. Besides, making Jeff come over to the hospital with news will be good for his leg." He reached for her elbow to help her up. "Now, come on."

As they got close to the door, the radio signaled an incoming message.

"Howard?" Marsha whispered hopefully.

"Let Jeff deal with it."

"I'll come over after they're done reporting. Now, go with Simon."

As the door closed, Jeff dropped back into the communication's chair and accepted the call. "Go ahead, Logan."

"Nothing new this morning. We've been following them for 35 days now and they still appear to be about an hour ahead of us. We aren't losing them, but we aren't gaining on them, either."

Jeff looked down at the red dot on the electronic map. He flipped the historical settings to display the course the team had been taking in their search. Their current path seemed to be in a straight line to the north west, towards a tall mountain range. And they appeared to have held that course for the last week.

"Logan, I've got an idea. You keep following the jabberwocky as usual. I'll extrapolate its forward path and have Clint fly up to a clearing in front of where it is taking them." He reached over and signaled Clint and Ron to report to Command. "Maybe we can trap it between the two of you?"

"I like your thinking. Signal me when you decide where he's going to put down."

"How's everyone holding up?"

"Howard's doing okay for being out here for the first time. He gets more trail savvy each day. Everyone else is doing their usual."

"So Diane's accusing you guys of holding her back?"

"That's too right!" Logan chuckled.

"If this goes on another couple of days, I'll be able to join you." Jeff raised and lowered his foot. *Unless I can convince Simon to unfreeze my leg so I can go with Clint?*

"I'm still hoping this is over before you get the opportunity to."

"I'll get back to you when things are ready on this end. Command, out!"

A light flashed on the board indicating Ron was on a link. "What's up, Jeff?"

"Ron, I need you to come to Command and take the rest of my shift. Denise is scheduled to come in around 4. Oh, and there's a fish pie in food storage here."

"Who made it?"

"Sam Nichols."

"Be right there!"

Get the right cook and Ron comes running. The door to Jeff's right opened to admit Clint.

"What's up, boss man?"

"Get a shuttle ready, Clint. This time, let's give the search party a treat, couple the camper module onto it. Let me know when you're ready. We're going to put you down a couple of clearings ahead of them."

"Give them a rest night?"

"Hopefully catch that jabberwocky this time."

* * *

Jeff made his way over to the hospital after Bales relieved him in the Situation Room. The idea of getting out into the field again, even if the doc quashed it, was making his trot between buildings an easy one.

He pried open the sliding doors and called, "Hey, Simon."

"Now you woke Marsha. We're in room two."

He quick-timed it across the waiting area and into the right hand room. Pushed open the door and found Simon sitting next to the autodoc that Marsha was laying in.

"Where's your cane?"

"I don't need it. I'm walking just fine." He quickly went over the last conversation he had with Logan. "What we want to do is jump ahead of the jabberwocky and catch him between the search party and Clint's shuttle. But I need your clearance. Can we restore my leg so I can go with him?"

"You should have two more days before I allow any pressure to be put on those bones. Let me have a look." He picked up a 3 by 5 inch paddle with a 4 inch handle and ran it up and down Jeff's healing leg. He frowned at the results it showed. "No can do. It stills needs time.

"But," he put his hand up to forestall what Jeff was about to say. "Promise me you use that cane I gave you and I'll allow you to go with Clint. Just stay in the shuttle!"

"Thanks, doc." Jeff turned and rushed out the door.

Before the door closed, he heard, "That was probably a mistake."

Chapter 7

Closing In

Jeff stared down at the final clearing before the woodlands gave way to barren landscape stretching into the mountains. Even with the heaters going, he was glad he had brought a heavy jacket. It was frigid here compared to the natural warmth of Petersville.

"That looks like our clearing," Clint said. There was almost no external noise in the shuttle cockpit, but they still wore headsets to stay in communication with the Command Center.

"Agreed, set down there. You copy, Ron?" Jeff called into his headset mike. "We're setting down. Let Logan know where we are and give us an ETA for his arrival."

"Roger that. And thanks for the pies."

"Did you eat the fruit pie also?"

"Wasn't that for me?"

Jeff smacked his free hand against his forehead. "No, Mary left that for her shift tonight."

"Oops."

"Just get a hold of Logan."

"Roger, chief."

As they dropped altitude, "Jeff, something over there." Clint pointed with his left hand out his side window, his right hovering over the controls to make any last minute adjustment as they came down.

"Where?" Jeff raised himself slightly from his seat to look across to and out the indicated window.

"It's gone now. Settle back in. I'll be touching down in a couple of seconds here."

Their rate of descent decreased to a slow crawl as nearby treetops came into vertical view of the windows. By the time they were passing the lower tree trunks, Jeff was itching to get on the ground. Fidgeting with but not opening his door.

He barely noticed as the six landing feet of the camper-driver combo connected the earth below. But before Clint could shut down the drive units, the shuttle's back end began to sink.

"That's not right," Clint said as he adjusted the rear gravidic units bringing the shuttle back to level. Then the front end started to drop.

"We'd better get airborne," Jeff suggested. "Logan reported some of these clearings weren't very solid."

"I agree." Clint lifted the shuttle a few feet vertically and set it to hover in place. "I don't think we're going to catch your jabberwocky from here though."

"I think you're right about that." He switched over to his radio. "Logan. Come in, Logan."

"Logan here. We're about 45 minutes out."

Jeff looked over their location. Where they had set down now showed six large holes, each about five times the size of the landing pad that had touched them.

"Something's not right about our location. We can't land here." He looked over to Clint for any ideas.

"We could try that tundra up ahead?"

"If that doesn't work?" Back on the radio, "Logan, we're going up ahead another five miles. Just past the tree line. We'll find a place to set down and wait for you there. If the jabberwocky makes any changes, let us now immediately."

"Okay, we'll push a little faster. See you in a couple of hours."

Clint rose just over the tops of the trees surrounding the clearing and headed northwest again. Jeff got back in touch with Command to get a new location to set down along the jabberwocky's projected path.

Just under five miles northwest, the trees cleared away. But the landscape took a severe turn upwards and they faced landing on terrain that was sloped at a 50 degree angle. It took Clint a few tries before he could find a section level enough to bring the shuttle down, 40 degrees was usually the most it could deal with.

After confirming their location with both Ron and Logan, he shutdown the motors to conserve electricity while they waited. The sun was going down over the tops of the mountain. There wasn't enough light hitting the solar arrays to keep the shuttle flying.

They waited. Jeff sat there listening for anything coming over the radio. Clint climbed out of the cockpit and opened the side door of the camper to go in and check on things.

He opened the vent/window into the cockpit. "Nothing looks like it got bumped around. I'll start setting things up, based on these power levels we're going to have to spend the night here."

"With the extra walking they're having to do, they won't be able to get camp set up before dark. Yeah, I'd get things ready for them."

About an hour later, Clint climbed back into the cockpit. "I put six steaks on to cook. I've set it for slow cook to conserve power."

"I hope we haven't blown our chance to catch the jabberwocky."

"If we miss it here, we'll have flushed it into open territory. We can launch a drone tomorrow."

"Out here, we should be able to use the shuttle to chase it down quickly enough."

"Not with any modules attached to it. We're at the edge of its range right now. We're going to have spend most of tomorrow morning charging this baby to make it back to Petersville."

Jeff touched his monitoring screen to check the power levels of the batteries. They were down to almost one percent. "Is that going to be enough for tonight?"

"I've powered most everything down. Using just the infrared cooker and the heater, we should be okay for another 12 hours. I just wouldn't plan on going anywhere for a while."

Jeff reached over to shut down his controls, but Clint caught his hand before he could touch them. "Don't worry about the monitors. They use very little power, and unless they're running, we can't access the battery power for anything else."

* * *

Jeff had finally had enough of just sitting. He opened the door on his side of the cockpit, brought his good leg to the ground and slowly stretched his other one down to make contact. He reached in back of his seat and pulled out the cane Simon had insisted he use. He walked around the short square front end of the shuttle and stared at a group of trees he expected Logan and his group to emerge from.

He had walked across the front of the driver unit a couple of times to get his leg working again and try to stay warm, when the bushes at the base of the medium height trees rustled.

He rapped the windshield to get Clint's attention and pointed. By the time he looked, the rustling had stopped and Logan's team was not present.

"It must have been the wind. I thought it might have been them." With all the windows closed, Jeff was using his radio link.

"That makes us even on seeing things that aren't there." Clint opened his door and stepped out to join Jeff in their wait.

After a bit, Clint went back into the camper and brought out the portable fire pit. He set it up and went off to get some fire wood for it. All the while telling Jeff to let him do it or he'd report Jeff to Dr. Parker.

Jeff finally gave up. He pulled a camp stool out of a storage locker and sat next to the fire pit keeping watch on the point Logan should be emerging from.

About an hour later, his efforts paid off. As Diane broke through the wood-line undergrowth, Jeff got up from his stool and headed down to meet the rescue team. Logan, who had been bringing up the rear, waved as Jeff caned his way down to meet the party.

But Diane wasn't coming. After she'd emerged into the tundra, she stopped for a moment and turned back. She was headed back into the woods in a more eastern direction.

Seeing her change of direction, Howard followed her away from the encampment.

"Hey, where are you guys going?" Logan hollered at the departing individuals just a second before Jeff had been going to.

Jeff was surprised not by the reason for their departure but by who articulated it. "The jabberwocky's trail turned here. It headed back into the trees for a while."

"Howard?" Jeff turned to Logan as the two men met each other, Mike heading up to help Clint at the camp site.

"He's a quick learner. Looking good," Logan said as he noticed Jeff walking.

"Just don't tell Simon, okay?"

"Not a word." Logan pantomimed zipping his lips shut.

"Their finding a new trail explains why we haven't seen the kids come this way. Just how far are they going to pursue it before breaking off for the night? It's getting pretty dark."

"Diane, we're breaking for the night. We can pick up the trail in the morning." Then Logan repeated himself into his radio in case she was too far away to hear him.

She had been, as her radio response indicated. "Howard and I are coming out now. I'll plant a marker so we know where to start again."

Seconds later, they broke out of the tree line and planted a red flag. This time, Howard lead the climb back to the group.

"Damn, this chase is really getting you into shape." Clint patted Howard on his back. "I've never seen you move so easily."

Howard ignored the compliment and went right up to Jeff. "Any sign of my kids?"

"I'm afraid not," Jeff answered. "But once we can confirm they have moved onto the open tundra, they won't be able to hide from aerial surveillance. It'll only be a short time now.

"From what we've seen, the jabberwocky is taking good care of them. Whenever we see their tracks, there is no overt signs of fatigue in their gait."

"I'm thankful it didn't eat them, but what does it want my children for?"

Jeff allowed his speculation of the last few weeks. "It's taking them somewhere. That very act means we have drastically underestimated these creatures ever since we landed. It is either taking them somewhere to show them something or to someone to show them to it."

"Or its," Logan added. "We've never had any idea of their real population. There could be thousands of them, for all we know."

Mike sparked the fire starter and got a fire going in the fire pit. Clint emerged from the camper with a tray containing six plates, each with a medium cooked steak on it.

"Let's eat." He passed the tray to each of the campers. They in turn pulled a camp stool from their packs and sat down to eat.

"What, no wine?" Mike commented after taking his first bite.

"This is a camper, not a bistro," Jeff quipped.

Then Clint took over. "We've a bit of a power problem right now. We're at the limit of how far this baby can travel. So tomorrow's a charge-up day."

Diane took over from there. "It looks like we're back in the woods again tomorrow, anyway. Have that shuttle ready when we finally get that thing flushed out. It's run out of hiding places from now on."

As the fire died away to glowing coals, they entered the heated cabin and turned out six of the eight beds available to them. Diane and Mike curtained each of theirs off while the rest of them fell asleep fully clothed. Jeff went so far as to leave his boots on, he didn't want to have to deal with them in the morning with his frozen leg muscles.

Chapter 8

Into the Mountains

"It looks like they travelled another hour, around three miles, before heading up into the mountains." Jeff sat in the shuttle's cockpit while it was charging, listening to the reports coming in from the search team.

"Diane, are you still able to track them?" He hated sitting here, this close to the action, and not being able to do anything.

"It's slow going. We'll have to deal with rocky terrain, but occasionally I can find a moss footfall. We can keep going."

"Send Command your location and let's see what satellite imagery can tell us." *It's still too early to send out a drone,* Jeff thought to himself.

"I think Logan's already on that."

"I've got you covered," said Logan over the circuit.

Jeff connected his monitor to the sensor suite back in the Town Hall and pulled up the current satellite feed. Whoever was in Command had already fed the coordinates into the system. Very tiny ants were climbing the hill up into the Thomas Mountains, as Jeff was calling them now. He adjusted the coordinates slightly to look further up the mountain and found three more ants moving higher. Then they disappeared in the boulder strewn terrain.

"Logan. Diane."

"Yes." There was a slight squawk of feedback as they both answered at once.

"I had them, then lost them. Due north of your position." He adjusted the coordinates back. "I still have you. It looks like about a two-mile climb."

"Jeff, thanks," Howard said. "We'll be there in no time."

"Speak for yourself, Howard. How's the shuttle coming, Jeff?"

"You'll probably get to them before we do. About another hour of the charging before we can safely lift off," Clint replied.

"So don't wait for us. We'll follow as soon as we can." Jeff shut down the circuit and turned to Clint. "The area they're heading for is even steeper than here, can you set this down up there?"

He looked at the satellite feed Jeff brought up of the area. "Nope, not the way we're rigged now." He got out of the cockpit, with Jeff following a moment later.

He disconnected the electrical lines that joined the back module to the driver unit, pulled up several levers and pressed a button on the camper between the two units. The camper rose slightly off the ground and Clint pushed it away from the driver. He had to push it about ten feet so that it cleared the driver's metal tang and he could lower the camper back to the ground.

"But I'll have a better chance without the camper attached."

"Does that mean we have enough power to lift off now?" Jeff jumped back in the co-pilot's seat and checked the energy reserves. The batteries were at fifty percent.

Clint got in the other side and looked at the readout. "Not without risking a recharge memory. They're in no danger, we can take the time to recharge the unit properly. We're getting too far away from Petersville to expect help."

Jeff sank back into his seat and grabbed the energy bar he'd left in the cup holder. He pushed another inch of it out of its wrapper. He placed the end in his mouth, closed his teeth around it and jerked the rest away from his face. "I need to get out there," he said between chews.

* * *

Parts of the trail Diane was establishing forced Howard to get down on his hands and knees to climb. But then, so did everyone else, it was that steep. After a bit, they reached a more level patch and made better time zigging up the mountain's side.

In all, it took over an hour to climb to where Jeff had indicated he had last seen the children and their captor. But they made it. They were on a small plateau with over a dozen holes in the mountainside, each large enough to admit the jabberwocky. None of which offered any clues as to which one they may have taken or if they had just pushed on.

"Everyone grab your flashlights and see how far in these guys go," Logan ordered.

After checking one cave that ended a few feet in and another that he could see no end to, Howard's radio came to life.

"Stand clear, down there."

He looked up and saw the shuttle's driver unit descending on them. They all moved aside to allow Clint room to land.

With the smaller shuttle, Clint was able to find enough flat ground to keep the shuttle mostly, but not quite, level. Jeff was actually sitting higher than Clint as Clint was powering systems down. Seeing Jeff's struggle with his leg to get out, Howard went over to help him.

"Thanks, Howard."

"I see why you lost them." Logan pointed at all the cave openings.

"Do we have any idea about which one they took?"

"We just got started searching them when you arrived." Logan used a louder voice, "Anyone find any dead ends yet?"

Diane held up two fingers, Mike said "I got two", and Howard replied, "I got one also."

"With the one I found, that means we have ruled out about half of them. But we haven't seen any tracks for the last hundred yards or so. We've been following your coordinates."

"If we each took one of the remaining caves..." Howard started to say.

"Nobody's going into those caves alone," Logan began. "And do you have any caving experience, Howard?"

He first looked at the ground then looked Logan in the eye. "No, but that doesn't mean I can't do my part. They're my kids, after all."

"Logan's not going to leave you out of the search at this point. Right, Logan?"

"I was thinking about that. You're not a safe spelunker right now, either, Jeff."

"They're my kids!"

"No one's leaving us behind. Logan, what about 2 teams of three? I can always retreat if the space gets too small for me."

"He does seem willing to learn. Okay, Jeff, you go with Diane and Clint. I'll take Mike and Howard with me. Howard, do everything I say, when I say it, understand?"

"Haven't I so far?"

"That's the only reason I'm agreeing to this."

Each team made their way to a different opening. Before they entered, Mike slapped Howard on the back. "Don't worry, old man, this is a first for me, too."

"Enough chat back there. Wait a minute, what did you just say, Mike?"

"I was just telling Howard that I haven't been cave exploring before, either."

"Great, two rookies." Logan took his pack off and opened a side pouch. "I'm hoping you both have helmets in your packs?" He pulled out a flat, flexible disk and pulled it over his head. When he had it covering past his ears, he pressed a button in the left side and a snap of electricity converted the soft material into a hard carbon composite. He finished by buckling it on. "Now get yours on."

He took the two-inch flashlight he had been carrying and attached it into the mounting bracket that had hardened into existence on the helmet's right side. "I want to see three lights shining ahead of me at all times." He threw his pack back on and turned to the awaiting darkness. "Let's move out."

After a few minutes, Howard tapped Logan on his shoulder. As point man, he spun around and blinded Howard for a second with his light before moving it out of his face.

"What?"

"You're leaving footprints in the dust."

"So?"

"He's right, Logan. When we came in here, there wasn't any dust on the floor. But now we're leaving tracks in it."

"Okay?"

"The only tracks in it."

Logan thought about that for a second. "I see your point." He started walking back to the cave entrance. "I guess we move on to another one."

"Nice one. Maybe he'll think twice about calling us rookies again."

* * *

They walked about the same distance into the next cave before Logan froze, raised his hand and clenched his fist. Howard almost ran into him before seeing he had stopped.

Mike tapped his shoulder. "Clenched fist means stop."

"Maybe you guys should have told me that before now."

"Quiet, you two." Logan pointed to the tracks in the dust.

They had hoped to find one set of footprints and two sets of shoe prints, not a myriad of footprints but no small shoe tracks.

"It looks like there may be more of these guys than we thought," Mike whispered.

While his other two searchers bent down to examine the tracks, Howard raised his head, causing his light to creep up the cavern walls. The natural brown and black lines of the rock gave way to lines of many colors. Lines that Howard finally resolved into some recognizable shapes.

"Guys."

"Some of these tracks only have a couple of days' worth of dust over them," Logan whispered.

"Ah, guys." Howard raised his voice slightly but still not to his normal strength.

"What is it, Howard?" Logan stood up and squared around on him. As he did, his light swung onto the spot that Howard was already illuminating. His light swung onto an image that depicted the landing of the Endeavor.

"We may have really underestimated these guys."

Chapter 9

More Rescuers

Logan headed back to the entrance. "We need to get the others." He keyed his radio, "Diane, meet us back at the shuttle. We need to rethink our plans."

He kept walking to the cave entrance and a moment later repeated his request. Coming to an abrupt stop, he waited for an answer that never came. After a minute's inaction, he sprinted for the mouth of this cave. Mike and Howard followed as fast as they could.

"Logan, wait," Howard called out as he saw him round the cave mouth. Howard put on a burst of speed and caught their team leader. "Wait," he gasped out, grabbing hold of his shoulder.

"They're in trouble." Logan turned, grabbed Howard's hand and threw it off his shoulder.

"Yes, but we don't know what kind of trouble," Howard labored to get the words out. He bent over, holding himself up by his knees, trying to catch his breath.

Mike finally caught up with the two of them. "We can't just go rushing in, Logan. Remember your confined space training."

"We don't want to become victims who need rescuing also," Howard finished for him. "I know what it feels like. I know what Marsha and Billy went through, still go through. But we need to get help before we go charging in."

Logan let out a deep breath. "Damn it, Howard, you're right." He took the flashlight off his safety hat and shined it into the cave. "We don't even know if this is the one they went in."

"It could have been a dead end like the first one we explored." Mike moved up to the entrance and shined his light in also. Doubling the beams did nothing to extend their range. "Let me go in to the dust line and see if they went this way. I promise to come right back. You can keep an eye on me the whole time."

Logan took Mike's light out of its clipped holder and attached it to the back of his collar. Then handed him his own. "Now we can keep an eye on you. See if the dust is clear up ahead and get back here. I'll be watching you the whole time. If I holler, it means I can't see your light anymore and you need to get back here immediately." He unclipped the machete from Mike's belt and smacked it grip first into his free hand. "And use this if you have to."

Mike started into the cave. Logan dug in his pack for his spare flashlight, never taking his eyes off his teammate. He shined its light on Mike's back and kept it there as long as he could. Eventually all he could see was Mike's light staring back at him.

"Well, it was your idea, Howard. Get on the radio. Get us some help."

It took about five minutes for Howard to call back to Petersville and arrange for the other two shuttles to be loaded with more volunteers, to come and join them. When he got back to Logan, Mike was exiting the cave.

"They're in there, all right. Once I got to where the dust began to accumulate, I saw the same scramble of footprints we saw in the other cave. Only this time there were shoe prints mixed in." He looked up at Howard approaching, "Some of them were kids' sizes."

Logan turned as Mike looked up and asked, "Well, what about reinforcements, Howard?"

"It depends on how fast they can get moving, but once they do, it'll be a four-hour flight to get here. So late afternoon at the earliest."

"We can't just sit around here singing Kumbaya until then." Logan walked back over to the shuttle and opened the rescue locker in the side of it. He began pulling out its contents and setting them on the ground. He found about two hundred feet of still packaged rope, in four different thicknesses. A few camp stools, a fire pit, a signaling laser, about three days worth of non-perishables, and a fifth of whiskey. "Clint's?" he held it up and asked Mike.

"Clint's." Mike acknowledged.

"Just what're you looking for?" Howard came up behind Mike and picked up the shovel Logan had set aside.

"A gun or something."

"You've been watching too many of those old videos we brought. We didn't bring any guns."

Logan slammed the package of rain ponchos to the ground. "We can't wait a whole day. We have to get after them." He looked over the spread-out items, focused on the fire pit and took the igniter off the side. "Maybe we can smoke them out," he said as he reached for the fuel cans.

"NO!" Howard straightened up, grabbed the igniter from Logan's hand and took on the posture he'd used for most of the last year running this colony. "You will not endanger the hostages."

"I have to agree with the Governor on this one, buddy." Mike moved to stand behind Howard, facing down Logan. "Help's on the way. We just have to sit tight. Once they're here, we'll get them all out safely."

Logan made a grab for the igniter but Howard passed it quickly back to Mike, who stepped out of his reach. When Logan went to go around the Governor, Howard placed a hand on his chest, stopping him. "We wait. Jeff Martin, the man I chose to run this colony and one of the hostages in that cave, told me the hardest thing you can do when people are in danger was to wait for the scene to be safe enough to be of actual help to them. And not become just another victim. I will not allow you to become that next victim. We will wait!"

"Just who do you think you are, giving me orders?"

Mike answered him. "He's the guy in charge, Logan."

"Now are you going to settle down or are we going to have to restrain you?" Howard's eye drifted to all the equipment Logan had already set out. "It looks like we might have enough rope."

Grumbling, Logan went over to the pilot side of the shuttle, got in, adjusted the radio to monitor their reinforcements and sulked.

"Thanks Mike. I don't think I could have controlled the situation without your support."

"I think you could have. Besides, you were right, and he knew it. He just has to stop long enough to see that."

"You think he'll hold a grudge? I don't need that when we go in after our people."

"He'll come around. It's the same thing he's counseled others about." Mike set up one of the campstools and opened a ration packet. He took out a pouch of dried apples, sat down and began eating them. "Want an apple?" He handed up a slice.

Howard grabbed his own stool, and sat next to Mike. "Thanks," taking the slice to chew on.

* * *

The sun rose to the tops of the mountain peaks and began its descent to their left. Howard was pacing behind the unassembled fire pit as Mike kept watch on the cave entrance. Mike was working on his fourth bag of apples when Logan finally left the shuttle cockpit.

"Howard, I don't know what came over you that night a couple of months ago, but I'm glad it did." Logan walked up to Howard and stuck out his hand. "You had the guts to stop me from doing something I would probably have regretted for years to come. I really appreciate it."

Howard took the offered hand. Mike walked over to the signaling laser they had set up an hour ago, to give the men some room.

"Thank Jeff when we get him back. It was his doing."

"I will. Can you forgive my stubbornness?"

"Been there. How soon are the reinforcements getting here?"

"Mike," Logan hollered over. "Make sure that thing is working. The shuttles should be here in a few minutes."

Mike hopped off the back of the shuttle where he had mounted the laser on the roof. "It's at full strength. They should be able to snag its signal with no trouble.

"In fact," Mike looked overhead as the first of two shuttles with passenger modules attached began their descent.

* * *

Everyone in the colony of adult age had been trained on the operation of the shuttles. Any three of the people present for the search would be able to get them back to Petersville. The remaining twenty made up the rescue team that was going to brave the Jabberwocky den.

Logan broke the party into two groups of ten, focusing most of the science staff to the second team. Since Clarence Knowles was the colony's expert on jabberwockies, he would be leading it. There was too much they didn't know about them, so much they had to learn. Logan hoped they could give him something to work with once he found the creatures. Knowles' team would go down the other cave and gather what they could from the wall drawings.

Logan, Howard and Mike lead the first team down Diane's tunnel to attempt a rescue. At about the same distance in where they had discovered the drawings in the other tunnel, they found the walls bare. No drawings, no markings, not even any attempts to engineer the walls. But the dust showed tracks moving deeper into the earth.

It got colder the deeper they went. Finally people started to activate their personal heaters to keep their focus on their mission rather than the cold. Ron Bales, as meteorologist, was keeping a check on the atmospherics. The oxygen levels remained the same as they were outside.

"They must have some sort of ventilation system," he concluded.

"What?" Mary Danforth asked as she squeezed through another narrow passage.

Ron, being just past the constriction with a granite corridor a meter wide again, leaned back slightly as she came through and explained, "With all the bodies in this enclosed space, we should be using up the oxygen and increasing the amount of carbon dioxide present. We aren't. There must be some kind of ventilation system down here keeping the air recycled with outside air."

She pushed the last of her hips out of the rocks and into the open area, brushed at little bits of dust she'd rubbed off the rocks. "Oh, of course."

"Logan says quiet back here." Mike relayed the whispered command before turning and catching up with Howard again. Carl Brown had given Mary a shove to get her through and out of the way as he wedged himself into the gap.

They moved deeper for another ten minutes before Carl slipped on a small rock. His shoulder brushed against the cave walls. "Damn." He tapped forward for a stop.

"Logan, Ron," he whispered. "What do you make of this?" He pressed his hand against the rock face. It washed away with a little rubbing. Then he scratched away the dirt to reveal a long layer of ice beneath.

Ron took out his machete and began scraping the wall, soon others followed. Until Howard had to restrain people from crowding the area.

After a few minutes, they had uncovered an ice ring that was a meter wide surrounding this portion of the tunnel.

"Well, that explains why it's colder inside the cave than outside," Ron speculated. "Usually it's the other way around in these colder latitudes." He took out a temperature gun and measured the ice. "Super cooled, also. It's about 40 degrees below freezing." He pointed his gun to the walls ahead of them. "Things should start getting warmer from here on."

"But not if we keep standing around," Logan said as he started moving deeper into the cave.

"Maybe I should have gone with Clarence," Ron said as he repacked his equipment and fell in line with the rest of the party.

On the far side of the ice ring, the tunnel narrowed slightly. Howard pressed his hand against the rock face, it was getting warmer, as Ron had predicted, but it was also smoother than before. He turned enough to meet Mike's eyes and pointed to it.

Mike ran his hand over it also, then motioned back down the line until one of the construction guys got a feel.

"This tunnel has been machined," Bill Flannigan called up. "It's too smooth to be natural."

Logan brought the march to a halt. He huddled everyone as close as he could get them together. "What part of 'quiet' are you people having trouble with? No, shut up!" Three people had begun to open their mouths. "We are on a rescue mission. If you wanted to do exploring, you should have gone with the others. No more talking, is that understood!"

Everyone just nodded.

As Logan was about to get the line of rescuers moving again, his radio chirped. "Now what?" He touched his ear to reply, having set the unit to be touch- rather than voice-activated. "Logan here. What have you got?"

Clarence was on the other end and broadcasting on an open band so everyone could hear him. "From what we can tell, you're walking into a Neolithic city. Expect cooperative effort on their part. And be careful."

"Thanks. You, too."

Howard activated his link. "Harry, we found an ice wall down here that appears to have been machined through. Have you found anything like that."

"Did Ron get any measurements?"

Howard pointed at Ron and mouthed talking.

Which Ron did. "It's how I found it. I'm forwarding them to you now."

"Thanks, we'll check it out."

Another twenty minutes of silent march brought a dim light ahead of them. Logan shut off his flashlight and held up his clenched fist. Everyone stopped as it came into view. He pointed to his unlit flashlight and was rewarded with a whispered, "We're okay," coming up the line.

He turned and whispered to Howard. "Kill your flashlight. Then pass the word up the line for everyone else to do likewise."

Howard turned and complied.

One by one, the members of the group extinguished their lights and the light coming from in front of them grew to fill the darkness. Logan passed the word for everyone to link arms and he moved to the edge of the corner the light was coming around. As he stopped, he felt the others bumping into him. Coming to a halt also.

Chapter 10

The Native Camp

Logan edged his way around the corner. Multiple fire pits provided the illumination for this vast cavern, and without their flashlights, the humans were blanketed in a gray darkness. Other members of the party came around to see but stayed in that blanket.

Multiple fire pits were burning, too many for a quick count. Each one was a stone ring about six feet in diameter with at least one humanoid tending the large blaze. The fire pits were spread throughout the large underground vault, filling its twenty foot height with enough light for them to see the house-like structures built into the side walls.

The humanoids milling through this underground city and tending the fire pits were not the jabberwockies they knew. They were the same five foot height, with two arms and legs, but their fur and muzzles were gone. They had an almost bare skin and fingers that did not end in claws.

"Could they have been wearing animal skins?" Mike whispered into Howard's ear.

"They don't have a muzzle, either," Howard replied. Their facial features had some boney protuberances running from their jaw line to their scalp, but the long snouts were gone.

"Why use such an intricate mask when a small piece of skin could keep away the cold just as well?" Ron said over their shoulders.

"Are we assuming these are our jabberwockies then?"

"Quiet, you three." Logan took a step out of the darkness but hugged the wall as much as possible. "Follow me. Stay against the wall. As much in the shadows as possible." The fire pits had been spaced so that very few shadows were formed, but every so often there was a gap in coverage. It was a race to get between them without being seen.

A few feet in, they ran into an opening in the cavern wall, a six by three foot almost rectangular opening. Logan shoved his flashlight inside to have a look. It was a small room, yet was large enough to hold their entire rescue party. He slid past it, then shooed everyone inside.

There was no one in the chamber, no furniture, nothing to sit on. Just a pile of furs in the far corner from the opening and a pile of what looked like trash in another. Several of the group plopped down on the furs and made themselves comfortable. One even tried to stretch out until he got elbowed in the ribs for trying to take all the space.

"Looks like someone's bedroom," Ron began.

Mike went over to the pile of stuff in the other back corner and began searching through it. He held up one of the stones that had been shaped long and narrow. "I'm finding an assortment of flints over here. They could be tools. Ow!" He dropped it after cutting himself and it bounced off a bone skull in the pile. "They have a good enough edge to be used for cutting, at least." He licked the finger he had run across its edge.

When he picked the skull from the surrounding debris, Mike saw it was only the front part of a snouted beast's skull. The inside was packed full with some kind of moss. He detected a faint but pleasant odor, so he placed it over his face and attempted to breath. There was no impedance to his attempt. He tossed it over to Bill. "Remind you of anything?"

After turning it over a few times and placing it to his face, "Looks like a gas mask of some sort."

"Now why would a Neolithic culture be using gas masks?"

Ron accepted the skull from Bill for examination. "And against what? We cleared this planet's atmosphere before we landed." He passed the skull around for everyone to see.

"Could it be ceremonial?" Ron asked. He shoved the skull away from himself. "Could the moss be some kind of hallucinogen?"

"Are you thinking that the jabberwockies seen around Petersville were on some kind of spiritual dream quest?"

"Pipe down, you guys. This is a rescue mission, not an anthropological one." Logan was looking out the opening into the city. "There must be hundreds of these dwellings. And I haven't seen a physical door on any of them." He turned back into the chamber. "So how are they holding the hostages?"

"Are these even the same people who captured them?" Howard replied. "They don't look anything like the jabberwocky Jeff and I ran into."

"I thought that's what you guys were debating? If not, then the jabberwockies had to have gone through here.

That means they're either working with these people or have an agreement with them."

"Hey, Logan." Mike tossed the skull mask over to Logan when he got the man's attention. "I think they may wear these when they go out."

Logan put the mask up to his face and found he could breathe easily through the moss. "Why?" He passed the mask over to Howard, then turned to continue examining the courtyard.

Howard stared at the front of it. "Now that looks a lot like the face we encountered. But why the deception?"

"And with the numbers they have here," Ron added. "Why have we only seen one of them at a time?"

"Wrong questions. Where are they holding our people? That is what we should be focusing on."

A large crowd of about twenty humanoids were crowded around a central table. Many others appeared to be bringing them stuff that they added to whatever they were working on. Most everyone else sat around the fire pits or walked between them.

"I'm going to try and get to the next dwelling. Wait two minutes, then come over one at a time, spacing yourselves about every other minute." Logan took one last look out the door and was gone.

Mike took his place at the opening and waited. Then when he figured none of the humanoids were watching, he scurried over to the next dwelling.

Soon Howard followed, then Ron, and Bill.

"Same as before." Logan pulled Mary in, then leapt out to make for the next dwelling.

After about ten of these transfers, something began happening in the common area. The humanoids began collecting plates and heading for the various fire pits. In the middle of each of them was a stone cauldron that one of their number was scooping portions out of and depositing on each of the plates.

After the first few had gotten theirs, people were finding stones to sit on and used their fingers to eat. The first ones took theirs to a dwelling on the far side and came out again empty-handed.

"I think we've found our missing people," Logan said. "Unfortunately they're completely across that courtyard."

"And if this is their supper," Mike added, "they may be headed back to these dwellings soon to go to sleep." He pointed with his thumb to the pile of furs in the corner.

"Then you'll need to find a room we can hide in until they do." Logan was out the opening before anyone could react and running for the center of the courtyard. The inhabitants eating their supper were on their feet in a second and pursuing him. He zipped through a circle of feasters and passed inches away from a fire pit, slowing just enough to grab a stick of firewood from inside it.

He ran past another two of them but not getting close this time. He brandished the flaming branch at anyone getting in front of him. When he got to the center of the courtyard and the table there, he knocked aside the bowls and dishes assembled on it, then jumped on it.

The table was ten by three foot, made of the same stone as the cavern. He had solid footing on top of it to ward off anyone trying to pull him off.

"Get to our people," he hollered at the top of his lungs.

"Damn him," Mike said.

"We need to find cover while he's got them distracted."

"The only place we know of is back where we came in. We can wait for them to go to bed there." Howard was out the door and heading back the way they had come in. But without the stealth they had used earlier.

Howard got to the entrance first and waved the rest of them into the opening and back into the blanket of darkness. After the last one had passed him, he looked over to see Logan drop his improvised weapon and surrender to the humanoids. "Now we have another person to rescue." Howard ran back into the darkness with the others to wait.

Chapter 11

The Meeting

Howard and Mike kept watch on the courtyard while everyone else ran through the tunnel as fast as the darkness would allow. Eventually lights began to pop on as the party got far enough away where they felt their lights wouldn't be seen. There they hoped to outwait the natives and emerge to rescue everyone after the humanoids had gone to sleep.

As Logan was being pulled from his perch, several of the humanoids pointed at a far wall opening. They grabbed burning branches from the fire pits and started over to where Howard and Mike were watching.

They didn't wait for thc natives to arrive but followed the others and quickly disappeared from sight. They soon caught up with their fleeing friends.

"Get moving."

"Get deeper into the cave."

"Turn off your lights and use the walls as a guide."

"They're coming, aren't they?" Ron was on his feet faster than the rest and began pulling his friends to theirs.

"If we can get past the tunnel restriction, we might be able to deal with them one at a time," Mike added. He grabbed the last person still trying to get up and pushed him forward.

They cleared the ice ring and were squeezing through the restricting rocks when the torchlight of the humanoids started to come around the last bend they had passed.

"Quickly, everyone push through."

Howard tapped Mike on the shoulder and turned to face the oncoming light.

Mike instead grabbed Howard and pulled him into the gap. Desperation had gotten the party through it faster than Howard had imagined.

On the far side of the gap, they hugged the walls, waiting for the first of the humanoids to come through. Mike had his machete out, holding it flat-bladed, to use as a club if any of them squeezed through.

The torchlight came up to the gap and stopped. Howard peered back through to see what he could. The natives had stopped at the ice ring like it was a restrictive barrier of some kind. Their light flickered a bit as they moved around. Then after a few minutes, they went back the way they had come.

Mike put his machete away and shined his light through the gap. No one was on the other side. "They left." He began to inch his way between the rocks again.

"Either they didn't see us—" Howard began. "Mike, get back here!"

"Why?"

"They may have gone back to get those mask things they wear outside."

Mike saw a glow coming back up the tunnel, killed his light and wormed back to the rest of his party.

"I hate it when you're right," he whispered.

A couple minutes later, a head shorter than expected pushed its way through the gap. "Dad," Tommy McCurdel cried out as he emerged.

Howard reached over and stayed Mike's hand. Then he grabbed his son and swung him into the larger cave section. "Tommy, Tommy." He set his son down and looked him in his face. "Are you alright? Is your sister okay? How did you get away?"

"The Raffie told me you were out here. They asked me to invite you in. Sarah and the others are back in their city, waiting for you."

"The Raffie?" Ron asked.

"That's the name they call themselves." Some noises came from the other side of the gap. Tommy responded with similar sounds.

"Thomas, it that a language? Wait a minute, do they have a language?" Mike asked.

"I just told Lerick that everything was okay. Everything is okay, right, Dad?"

"You speak their language?" Mike continued.

"Yes, son, everything is okay, now." He turned and addressed the rest of the group. "If the rest of you want to wait here, that's okay. But I'm going in." Howard turned to the gap and began to push himself through after his son.

On the far side was a party of Raffians, about five in number. Each of them bore a flaming branch but nothing that looked like a weapon. One of them stood holding his hand out, palm sideways, towards Howard as he came through.

"Don't worry, Dad. I told them that's how we greet each other." Howard took the offered hand and shook it. The surprised Raffian went along with the motion for a second and then reacted enthusiastically to the offer of friendship. Howard finally got him to stop after a couple of minutes.

* * *

Sarah ran up to her father as the rescue party emerged into the Raffian city again. "Ack vac," she said as she leaped into his waiting arms. He pushed her into the air and gave her a quizzical look.

"It's 'Hello, Father' in their language. She's picked it up a lot better than I have," Tommy responded.

Howard set his daughter down. He dropped to one knee to look her in the eye. "I missed you, peanut."

"They took really good care of us, vac. Tommy and I had great fun living in those old dugouts."

"Dugouts?" Howard looked at each of them.

"The whole area between here and home is pitted with thousands of holes in the ground, holes with lots of garbage and sometimes even plastic toys," Tommy explained.

"I'm just thankful the two of you are safe. Your mother's worried, you know."

"Then she and Bill are okay?"

"And waiting for you back in Petersville. Can we check on the others now?" Howard instinctively looked up at the native identified as Lerick. Out of the corner of his eye he saw the rest of the rescue party emerging from the cavern entrance.

Sarah said something to the native, who responded just as quickly. "We'll take you to them," she told her father.

Howard stood up and took both his children by their hands. They lead him to the centermost fire pit, one that was just in front of the central table.

Jeff was leaning against the stone table. Logan and the rest of the hostages were sitting around the fire pit facing Howard as he walked towards them.

"Despite our best efforts, we seem to have made some new friends, Howard." Jeff said as the party approached. He hop-stepped over to his rescuers.

Logan stood up to consult with the colonial leaders as Jeff continued. "According to your kids, the Raffians have been watching us ever since we landed on their planet. They kept fearing that we would eventually march north and seize this safe zone. I don't really know what they are referring to. Since we never did, they've assumed that we are ignorant of the danger."

"What danger?" Logan and Howard said in unison.

"That's the problem. They only know that outside their cave is dangerous, not why it is dangerous. Sarah says they have no words to explain the problem to her."

Logan tapped his radio link. "Clarence, can you hear me, Clarence?"

"Loud and clear. Want me to keep this public?"

Logan looked at the others, who nodded agreement. "Yes. We've made contact with the indigenous species. A sentient species. I need everything you can tell me about those paintings you've been studying."

"I'm just getting a bit of their history. We're filming as much of it as we can find, it's going to take me some time to understand what's drawn here. I'll probably have to do a lot of computer analysis."

Jeff looked at the time. "Get what you can but meet us at the landing site in twenty minutes." He turned to Tommy, "Tommy, I need you to ask a few of them to accompany us back to Petersville, where we can continue our investigations."

Tommy relayed Jeff's message to Lerick. The reaction was not one they had expected. The native made warding signs with his hands and backed away from the party. "Shum, shum."

"I'm afraid that means 'No', Uncle Jeff. Since we got here, they don't like to go outside if they can avoid it. And then they have to wear special masks and furs."

"Well, we need to get back," Jeff decided. "Tell them we have to leave them for awhile, but that we should return in a few days. Tell them we want to be friends."

"Sure thing, Uncle Jeff. I want to tell Bill everything we've done." He turned and began talking to Lerick again.

After they had finished, Lerick spoke loudly, and several natives hurried into one of the dwellings. After a moment, they emerged with several of the snout masks and gave one to each of the party members. Tommy demonstrated how to put them on.

"Place it over your nose and mouth. Then grab the leather straps and tie them behind your head. There is an upper set and a lower set."

"We don't know what we're breathing through these things," Diane announced as she dropped hers to the floor.

"It's hegimoss, Ms. Flannigan. It'll clean the air, make it safe to breath." Sarah said clearly through the snout of the mask she now wore. Sarah bent down, picked up the fallen unit and handed it back to Diane.

"Safe from what?" she asked.

"Evil spirits," Tommy explained, "At least, according to the M'cron, their high priest."

"Well, I don't want to run afoul of their evil spirits," Jeff said as he strapped his mask on. "Just strap yours on, at least until we get to the shuttles and are heading home."

Chapter 12

More Information Needed

The carcass of the Endeavor rested about a mile north of the original encampment and far enough east of the main river flowing down into the ocean to keep the area from flooding. An easy walk to either, but a quick jaunt by shuttle. Carl Brown, the ship's engineer, had four gravity units ready to mount on the chassis that Clint and Mike had already constructed. Getting to the initial settlement, now a construction factory, and on to Petersville was no problem.

With the focus on building living units for all the families living on Belenius 3, time had not been taken for things like a research laboratory for amateur anthropologists like Ahmed Zahakis. He had his chemistry lab, his first profession, where he'd been busy overseeing the formulation of new concrete mixes using the volcanic ash they had discovered a few hundred miles to the east. He'd read something about ancient Romans using a special volcanic ash that made their concrete last for millennia and he was hoping to replicate their results.

Clarence Knowles had to take him up to the computer suite of the Endeavor to give Ahmed a good look at the pictographs he'd recorded. He fed the files into the main computer and used the projection system to display an enlarged version of the cave walls.

A representation of the walls filled the twenty foot long room. Ahmed was running his fingers along the images, not touching the light beams that made them up for fear of distorting what he was seeing. He had worked his way from the earliest images, that of an object similar in shape to the Endeavor landing, through a series of images on how to track and kill the various fauna of the planet, and was now up to the skinning and construction of the masks the humans had returned with.

"This is what I find unusual." Ahmed kept looking at the paintings. "You say that these paintings," he pointed at the images of the mask construction, "are older than the hunting ones?"

Clarence, who was sitting in front of the computer console, called up a color diagnoses of the pigments. They were then displayed next to the image the color sample was taken from. "These two colors are made from the same paint. Yet the degradation of the mask construction inks are considerably greater than the hunting images."

"Do we know how much greater?"

"Without a physical sample of the paint, we can only guess."

"Never a good..." He froze for a second, then began pointing to an image of a log spanning a body of water. "Harry, look at this."

"Looks like a log across a ravine."

"But the log? Can you run a color analysis on its pigments?"

Clarence turned back to the computer and punched in the request. The analysis wasn't as quick as the last time, but it finally came through.

"That's a new one. It offers two possibilities. The first is a color it has never heard of. Something not in its known palette. The second is that there is a layer of brown pigment over the top of a white pigment."

"Let's go with the latter. We know where the Raffians could get a brown pigment, but I think the white layer looks too bright to be a Neolithic white paint?"

"Wait a minute. Additional analysis says that the brown layer is a raw earth umber; you're right, they'd have easy access to that one. Just dig up some of the oxides in the dirt. Iron oxide is all over the place. But the white is a titanium compound. Where would they have gotten that?"

Ahmed keep staring at that image of a ravine crossing. "Where indeed?" He spun around and sped over to the computer terminal. He quickly punched in a series of commands while Clarence, who had slid his chair aside for him, watched.

"You're asking it to analyze all the colors? That'll take a couple of days, at least."

"A necessary step, my friend. And if I'm right, well worth the time."

* * *

"I'm telling you, Ron, there has to be something in the air." Jeff vigorously walked around the Big Board while he addressed the colonial meteorologist.

"Just because the natives wear a dumb mask?" Ron kept turning his office chair around and around, trying to keep up with Jeff.

"You didn't see the fear in their eyes at the mention of leaving the protection of their village. It terrified them."

"Will you stop moving?" Jeff stopped on the far side of the room and walked straight back to his friend. "Thank you," Ron continued. "I swear you haven't stopped moving since Simon released your leg."

"It feels good to be walking again."

"But really, we checked the atmospherics before we landed. Everything is clean. This is a pristine planet. It's just superstitious mumbo-jumbo."

"Or something we don't know to look for. Humor me, run your analysis again."

Ron threw up his arm, got out of the chair and headed for the door. "Well I guess that's job security."

"Thanks," Jeff said to the closing door.

"Can we at least get my equipment moved down here," Ron said before the door closed behind him.

The chime in Jeff's ear beeped, his communicator identified the caller, "Ahmed Zahakis".

"Ahmed, what can I do for you?"

"We need to go back to the Raffian village."

"I thought Clarence got images of everything?"

Clarence spoke next, Ahmed must have them on conference setting. "Not everything. There was a lot I didn't have time to record."

"And besides, we need to go back and confirm some things."

"Like...?" Jeff tried to draw out his question.

"We'd rather not say until we have further confirmation."

"Extraordinary claims call for extraordinary proof."

"How soon do you want to go?" Jeff dropped into the chair Ron had vacated.

"We're ready to leave anytime."

"We've got an analysis running that will take a couple of days—"

Before Ahmed could finish his statement, "A couple of days?"

"Yes, so we have the time available. Should we walk down or can someone pick us up?"

"No, wait there. I'll send someone up."

He disconnected them and sat back into the chair. "Maybe Ron needs to look at the air in the Raffian village and see if there's anything different up there," he said quietly.

"Maybe we should get a sample of that moss before it goes into the masks," Diane Brown said as she entered the back door of the Situation Room. "See if it's collecting anything out of the air?"

"Good idea. Get a shuttle ready. I'll have Ron meet you at the pad, then collect Clarence and Ahmed up at Endeavor before flying up to the village. Use the long range module this time."

"I had to say something." She turned and left by the door she'd entered.

"Damn," he said. "I was thinking of taking Ron up myself. Just to get out of here."

Chapter 13

Peaceful Exchange

Diane brought the shuttle down on almost the exact spot Clint had landed a week earlier, when they first came to the Raffian village. A light snow was beginning to fall in these upper altitudes. The air was getting even colder than when they were first here.

Ron buttoned his collar as he stepped out, went around to the side of the module and pulled out a large black case, heavy enough he had to use both hands to move it. In the rush to get going, he'd forgotten to bring a gravity sled.

Ahmed pushed his vacated seat forward and climbed out. He turned and took the recorder that Clarence passed to him before stepping past the banks of batteries mounted along the walls of the module. Once out, Clarence led the way to the cave with the paintings in it.

Diane had to spend a few extra minutes aboard, shutting down all the systems. Even though they had massive battery backup, there was no sense in wasting power with all the cloud cover obscuring a solar recharge.

She pulled the power fuse from out of the dashboard and pocketed it. Then climbed down and walked over to where Ron was struggling with his case. She reached down, grabbed the handle with her left hand and lifted it away from the meteorologist. "Either get on a construction crew or get to the gym. Where do you want this thing?"

He paused for a few seconds, catching his breath. "As close as we can get it to the Raffian village. I'd rather not use the sampling equipment if I can get the unit into the area."

"I think I can get it past the constriction, but you'll have to be on the other side ready to take it."

"I should be able to do that."

"The largest gap, the only one I can remember that would be big enough, is over your head. But you know how fragile these things are." She tossed the case up a couple of inches without letting go of the handle.

He followed her into the cave and squeezed through the gap. Then he turned and looked at the opening she had been referring to. Yes, the case would pass through it easily enough, but it was just at the limit of his reach; seven feet, if he stood on his toes. He did not look forward to trying to lower it safely to the ground.

As the black case appeared at the top of the cave, Ron stretched as far as he could, trying to reach it.

"Get out of my way," he heard Diane say as she, too, started to emerge through the gap. "Move it or lose it." She had secured the case in the upper opening, then climbed into the gap herself. She had inched it through by pushing it up and moving it before letting it rest on the exposed rock while she moved. "This thing was too wide for me to pass it through to you. But you still need to get some gym-time."

As they emerged into the village cavern, two Raffians greeted them with extended hands.

Ron took the first one and shook it, then the next. After five minutes of this, he tried to explain what he wanted. "I need to set up this atmospheric analysis station and take some air quality readings."

The Raffians looked at each other without any sign they understood him. Ron repeated himself, only slower this time.

"Oh, we have a problem," Ron said after the third attempt.

"You don't speak their language, do you?"

"As far as I know, only the McCurdel kids do."

"Then we'd better get them up here."

* * *

A couple days later, Tommy came back to the fire pit where Ron was waiting. "M'cron says it's okay for you to test their air. Just put it back when you are done."

"Not a problem." Ron opened his case up, took out the box housed within, started to warm up its sensors and attach the sampling tube. The fully charged battery on the unit should allow him to run his analysis for a good hour before having to return to the shuttle for a recharge. Ron knew that was enough time to run a complete set of tests in triplicate.

As the suction motors of the device began to collect the atmosphere in the cavern, Ron held the tube over his head to his maximum height. After a few minutes of sampling, he set the tubing on top of the unit and withdrew a pipe stand from the case and assembled it. It would not hold the tubing as high as Ron could, but it would hold it at a height of six feet as Ron worked his equipment.

The noise of the motors drew a circle of Raffians over to where he was working. They were chattering amongst themselves as he did so.

"Tommy, what are they saying?" Ron looked up and noticed the crowd for the first time.

"They're wondering why you are making that noise. I know it's your testing equipment, but they don't."

"They're not planning anything rash, are they?" He tried to focus on his readings, but his concern caused him to shift his attention to the boy's ability to communicate with the natives. The boy's ability to know what they were planning to do.

He turned and addressed the crowd with noises Ron couldn't understand. After which, the Raffian with the long staff said something else.

"No, some of them were saying you'd brought evil spirits into their shelter. M'cron is reminding them we are friends from the sky and do not understand the terrors of the land."

"What terrors?"

"They don't seem to have the words to describe their fears, only that it comes from the warmer lands and steals their minds."

"Great! I'm going to need more tests than this thing can provide." Ron opened the sample compartment of his case and prepared all twelve plastic bags he had to collect air samples inside the village.

A half hour later, Diane came back. She dropped her mask at the base of Ron's equipment.

"I can't find that damned moss anywhere."

Tommy, who had gone off to play with the Raffian children, walked up to Diane with one of his playmates. "What's the problem, Ms. Brown?"

"I need to find a clean sample of the moss inside these masks, so we can analyze what it's actually filtering out."

Tommy turned and said a few Raffian words to the other boy, who responded in kind. Part way through their conversation, the boy raised his hands towards the roof, then continued talking while pointing over to one of the dwellings. Tommy placed his hand on the boy's shoulder, like Ron had seen Jeff do many times, and nodded.

"Ank says," Tommy pointed to his friend, "the hegimoss is a gift from their ancestors. It is grown on the ceiling, collected once a year and the masks are made there," he pointed over to the same dwelling his friend had earlier. "If we ask Lerick, I'm sure he will give you some."

* * *

Inside the dwelling were three tables set up for various steps in hegimoss preparation. The first table's bowls were surrounded by piles of the moss harvested from the ceiling. Each of the bowls contained a solution which had a large quantity of the moss soaking in it. The second table had long ceramic sheets in it where pieces of moss were apparently drying out. The third table had a native in front of it, she was shaking a powder over the dried moss and kneading it into balls, before placing them in the large chest they had in the corner of the room.

Tommy tugged on her poncho-like garment to get her attention, then he said something in their language and she responded.

She then reached into the chest and extracted one of the balls, handing it to Diane. Diane accepted the gift, took out her own plastic bag, shook it open and dropped the hegimoss ball into it.

Seeing the size of the bag, the native reached in and got another ball which she handed to Diane also. Then the Raffian said something.

Tommy replied and turned to Diane. "Longa says that should be enough for two outdoor masks."

"Ka-lone." Diane had been taught by Tommy that this was their version of 'thank you'.

Longa shoved out her hand proudly. Diane took and shook it. A massive smile spread across the native's face.

"Now to see if Ron is done with his sampling so we can collect our two art critics and go."

"Don't you like it here, Ms. Brown?"

"It's a fine place. But I like the outdoors. I know Carl wants to build a family in Petersville. But I need to see this place before we do. I tolerate one night a week in our house and he suffers another camped out with me. Eventually I'll settle down, but not right today. I like open space too much."

"I like my new friends."

"Then you go play with them while I talk to the others. We'll let you know when it's time to go." She patted her earpiece before sending him off to be with the Raffian children.

Ron was packing up when she got back to him. She looked over to the sample bag he had loaded up with his air samples. "You promised to return their air when you were done," she laughed.

"I have. Notice over by the wall. One of them is keeping an eye on me. I emptied one of our oxygen cylinders after having Tommy explain to him what I was doing."

"Damn, they take this air thing seriously."

"I just hope we can get some answers after all this. Ahmed and Clarence ready to go?"

She tapped her ear piece. "Ahmed, Clarence, you guys ready to go?"

Clarence came on the channel. "You guys had better see this."

"We're packing up, Clarence. Heading home."

"No, you really have to see this."

"Okay, we'll be over in a few minutes."

Ron was placing his equipment into the proper compartments and closing his case. "They ready?"

"No, they want us to come over and look at something."

"Help me get these samples into storage, then we can see what they want."

She radioed Tommy that they would be leaving in a short time, hefted Ron's case single-handed, then went back out the tunnel to the shuttle. Ron followed with a satchel full of air samples.

Even though the module they brought was simply a power unit, it did contain a food storage and prep facilities. A dining table could be folded down from the outside wall of the unit, if they had been staying long enough to make a meal. Ron took a couple of containers of water out of the refrigerator and replaced them with his samples. He wanted to freeze those samples, but that part of the unit was too small.

"Okay, let's see what the anthropologists have for us." He stepped down from the module and began walking over to the other cave.

Chapter 14

History Lessons

Ron, Diane and Tommy came to and passed the painting of their rocket ship without seeing either Ahmed or Clarence. They walked past pictures of the Raffians snaring small and medium-sized game animals, representations of the stars with lines connecting them like Earth-based constellations, pictorial instructions on how to prepare most of the cave-based growths for consumption and which ones not to use. After a while, they finally came upon the floodlights Ahmed had set up to get good pictures of the paintings they were currently viewing.

Ahmed would point at a new painting, circle his hand around the area he wanted captured and Clarence would aim his camera at it. After an audible click, Ahmed would move on to another section of the wall.

"Okay, what's up?" Ron said to get their attention.

"What's so important we can't get back to Petersville for supper?" Diane added. Clarence turned and took a picture of the three arriving. "Clarence, please."

"Do you guys notice anything different about these cave paintings?" Ahmed asked while Clarence pocketed his camera.

"They're cave paintings," Ron began.

"They're much brighter than the ones back there, Mr. Bales. And they seem to be better drawn."

"I had a feeling Tommy would be the one to notice." Ahmed took a step closer to one of them. "I've collected a sample of the paint for each of the pictures we've taken. But I don't think these paintings are newer than the ones closer to the entrance, the ones further from the village."

"If there's a way into the village from this tunnel?"

"Oh, there is, Mr. Bales."

"Tommy, why didn't you tell us sooner?"

"It's a longer route."

"Are there any restrictions like in the entrance we've been using?"

"No, just longer."

"I've been hefting that case six feet in the air for nothing," he wailed. Diane glared at him.

Ahmed tried to recapture the conversation. "My point is that while these paintings look fresher, I believe they are older than the ones back there." He pointed at the way everyone had been coming in. "Just done with better paints and more practiced techniques."

"Did you notice the subject matter of these images?" Clarence asked.

"They look like the Raffians' houses back in their village."

"Five stories high?"

"And they have clouds over the tops of them, Uncle Clarence."

"Yes, they're depicted as being outdoors, not hidden in a cave." Clarence turned and walked a couple of steps further down. "And here we have what almost looks like instruction manuals for building basic industrial equipment."

Ahmed took over the explanation. "The further we go down this tunnel, the more advanced the paintings become. We may be looking at this civilization's Library of Alexandria. The storage of knowledge designed to last hundreds of generations."

"But why like this?"

"It was an intellectual exercise on board the Endeavor while we were studying our professions. How would you design an information storage system that would last through the ages? We change our data retrieval systems too often to store it electronically. Paper, while we can easily learn to read, will eventually decay, crumbling into dust. Carving stone tablets is too time consuming to record the detail that an advanced civilization would need. And languages change too often to make creating something like clay tablets useful."

"Ahmed, come quickly," Clarence had kept walking and now had his hand on a section of the wall. "Feel this."

"That's not granite."

"No, I think they added a sealant to this section of the tunnel."

"Get a sample." He pulled another vial out of his pocket, screwed off the cap and handed it to Clarence.

Clarence then took a sampling knife from his belt tools and began scratching the painting on the rock.

"What are you doing, Uncle Clarence?" Tommy became alarmed at what the archeologists were now doing. "Those are sacred images. Left to the Raffians by their ancestor-gods." He brought his hands together to form a ball, brought it to his sternum and bowed to the painting.

"What's that all about?"

"I'm not sure. A ritualistic warding against bad juju? I'd say we have enough samples, let's not risk taking anymore. I'm going to be doing a hell of a lot of analyses when I get back to my lab anyway."

"Risk?"

"Upsetting the natives. If Tommy doesn't like what we're doing, they might have a stronger reaction. Once we know something, we can come back and get permission."

"But what does all this mean?" Ron looked around, reaching out but not quite touching the images surrounding them.

"Ron, dear," Diane reached over and stroked the side of his face. "I think Ahmed and Harry are saying that the Raffians are a retrograde culture."

"Retrograde?"

Ahmed explained, "We think they're on a de-evolutionary spiral. And we'd better find out why."

"And learn how to communicate with them before we stumble into their social taboos." Clarence pocketed the vial he had dropped the sample into and reached over to take Tommy by his shoulder. "Young man, how would you like to become a teacher?"

Chapter 15

Looking for Answers

"When're you going to move this stuff out of here?" Jeff walked through the open hatch area; the actual hatch had been removed months ago and recycled into new construction material. Most of it had gone into the construction of the camper module for the shuttles.

"I submitted plans for a new lab to the council last month." Ahmed said before turning his attention to one of the teenage interns he had agreed to train. He picked up the bottle the trainee had just set down. "If we put things back as soon as we're finished with them, the next person will have a much easier time finding them. And you could be that next person." He placed the bottle of Potassium Permanganate back between the bottles of Potassium Nitrate and Potassium Sulfate.

"We'll get to them. We still have a lot of people without homes." Jeff walked over to one of the lab benches, leaned against it with his left arm and took a bite out of the apple-like fruit he held in his right.

Ahmed gave a look at his lab assistant, who in turn addressed Jeff, "Mr. Martin, we do not eat, drink, or smoke while in either the wet or here in the instrument lab!"

"Sorry, I forgot." He quickly dropped the fruit into the plastic pouch he had brought it in with.

Ahmed gave his assistant a smile before continuing. "So I will keep working in this increasing diminishing space ship until the time comes when I will have someplace to go."

"We'll get you a proper lab eventually. Construction is moving faster than what we had projected pre-landing."

"I just hope it's not in vain."

"Still worried about those cave paintings?"

"Sir," his lab tech piped up. "I have that paint sample ready for compositional analysis."

"Well let's see what that tells us, shall we?" He led Jeff over to the small metal box mounted on the inner hull of the ship. "Go ahead and inject the sample, John."

The analysis would only take a few minutes so they waited. "So if the Raffians are a de-evolving culture?"

"There has to be a reason for it. This is no getting-back-to-nature religion on their part. Something happened to them."

"From the wall-painting images you brought back, they looked to have quite an advanced society at one point."

"I asked Nancy to dig up one of those rectangular clearings and let me know what she, as a construction engineer, thinks."

"I heard she took some convincing."

"Yeah, you guys do go on about your houses."

"So what'd she find?"

"In her professional opinion, those holes were building foundations and basements. Even the stream beds in the areas look to be some kind of man, er Raffian, made underground structure that collapsed over the decades. She brought back some samples for us to use to determine the date the Raffian decay began. From the paint fragments we've tested already, it looks like about 150 years ago, plus or minus a decade."

"So?"

"So, If the components of the pigments were artificially created, and that's what I'm testing for now, they had to have been made by a society more advanced in the sciences, especially chemistry, than the Raffians we met in that village."

"Meaning?"

"The Raffians are de-evolving."

"Really."

"I know extraordinary claims require extraordinary proof. That's what I am trying to pull together. If I'm right, then Ron's air samples could hold a crucial piece of evidence as to why it happened. If I'm wrong, then I have a lot more tests on his air samples to answer the question those masks pose."

"Is there anything I can do to help?"

"Not unless you can get Francis DNA samples of the Raffians, both before and after this change."

The component analyzer dinged. John grabbed the sheets of paper coming out of the machine as fast as they were spat out. He took a quick look at them. "You were right, Mr. Zahakis. Zinc Chromate." He handed the sheets over to his instructor.

"It's not proof of what I am saying. But it's another piece in this jigsaw puzzle."

"Modern DNA shouldn't be hard to come by, but finding a cadaver from two hundred years ago might." Jeff took his fruit out of his pouch and walked outside where he could finish his pre-lunch snack. And think about the request his chief Chemist had just made.

Chapter 16

Small Vacation

Michael and Mary Black hadn't had a vacation or even a day to themselves since the Endeavor had landed almost one year ago. He felt it was time they got some 'us' time; Mary whole-heartily agreed. Earlier in the month, they had made arrangements to check out the camper module on one of the shuttles for a week. They headed east of the Rockefeller River to explore one of those clearings everyone was talking about. They just couldn't tell the flight controller app which one until they found one that could support the shuttle's weight. And that would be by trial and error.

About a hundred miles east by northeast of Petersville, they found an exceptionally large clearing. Mary was at the controls and set it gently down in the center of the clearing and waited to see how the unit settled.

It seemed to hold firm.

Michael opened his door and stepped down on the long grass that grew throughout the area. His foot held. He tried to scrape the dirt away with his hiking boot. About two inches of dirt moved before he encountered a splintering concrete.

"Looks like we're good here." He called into the door he hadn't yet closed. "I've got broken stone on this side. See what's on yours."

Mary opened her door and repeated Mike's tests. She got the same results. "I'm good here, also."

"Then I think we can get our little oasis set up," he said as he came around the front of the shuttle and grabbed his wife into a hug. He pushed her back slightly, took a deep look into her eyes. "A week to ourselves."

"I'll log your coordinates," said Jeff over the radio. "Have fun, you two."

Mike yanked the earpiece out and placed it deep in his belt pouch, surrounded by discarded wrappings of the candy bars he'd eaten on the trip here.

Mary broke away and headed for the side door of the module. "We've only got about an hour's sunlight left. You'd better get the fire pit started while I see what's for supper." She was inside before he could say anything.

Since the rescue mission a month earlier, shuttles were equipped with long metal poles that could be used to test the ground in a clearing when you landed. Mike got it out and began a survey of the clearing's floor. Vast areas of this one were solid underneath with about two inches of dirt atop some kind of artificial surface. At first Mike had thought it to be concrete but now he wasn't sure.

Presently he did find holes where buildings had been, but only on one side of the clearing, and it appeared to have been a very long building rather than the grid system they had seen elsewhere.

He slung the pole to his back with the strap it had come with and collected fire wood to build a bonfire for the evening. He got the metal fire pit ring out, expanded it to its full six feet diameter and began piling as much wood as he could find next to it. There was enough dead wood in the surrounding forest that he wasn't going to have to break out the axe or chainsaw to keep a bright fire going all week.

After supper, they sat at the campfire in their folding loungers, watching the stars appear as the sky darkened. Michael's hand drifted off his armrest and hung between. Mary let hers drift over to capture his. They just sat there holding hands as all the colors of the universe painted the sky for their pleasure.

"Honey, look, a shooting star," Mary pointed out as a bright dot sped from east to west across the sky.

Several more followed suit. "We must have lucked into a meteor shower on this trip."

"Do you think we can see the Earth's sun from here, Michael?"

"I think you'd have to ask the Endeavor's navigational app that one, dear."

"It's so nice to have all this space. All this clean air, land and water. We're blessed with this chance to start over."

"I don't think Earth was that bad? But all we know about it comes from the videos the original founders of the expedition sent with us."

"All that pollution, uncontrolled weather extremes, sickness; how did they even survive?"

"We just have to make sure we don't make the same mistakes here. We have to build a better society." He pulled up and kissed the back of her hand.

"Those red lights belting the bluish stars up there are just gorgeous." She squeezed her husband's hand and they fell silent for a long time before turning in for the night.

After breakfast the next morning, Mike decided they should take a look under the area he had found to be non-solid when they landed. Mary dug through the supply locker and found electro-plastic helmets, mountable lights, leather gloves, and pads for their elbows and knees. And she insisted they wear all of them.

Michael took the camera out of the charger and slipped it into one of his large pockets. The others he had already stuffed with energy bars.

They hiked across the clearing, Michael probing the ground as they got close to where he remembered the holes being. When his pole slid beneath the ground cover by a foot, Mary unsnapped the shovel from his backpack. She then turned around and he removed hers. They both started digging.

"This isn't working," Michael announced as he once more failed to cut through the interwoven roots that made up the mat that the dirt had collected on over the decades that allowed the small flora to grow over the hole. He turned his back on his wife. "Pull my axe out, would you?"

His axe bit deep, his second stroke severed the first root. He started on the second, then stood upright. "This could take all day. Could you go back and get the chainsaw while I cut an opening big enough for us to use it?"

"Just make sure you've got solid ground under you when you cut through those things. I don't want you falling in before I can get back." She threw that last comment over her shoulder, as she was already on her way back to the camper.

As the fifth root gave way, a portion of the root weave dropped slightly, and sunlight was able to penetrate the depression for the first time in ages. Michael dropped down on his chest and tried to see what was down there.

It was still very dark. All he could see were piles of rot and decay—not what was rotting and decaying, just that something down there was rotting and decaying. "I guess that's why we have to go down there," he said just before hearing something move in the piles of stuff. He saw nothing and the noise stopped just a moment later.

"What's up?" He spun around and flung himself to the right, away from the voice. "A bit jumpy?" Mary held the chainsaw at her side; she was tall enough that it didn't touch the ground. "You want me to run this?"

"I thought I heard something down there," he offered as a defense.

"All the more reason to get this covering off." She brought the saw up and pushed the activator to start its electric motor. She bent down, brought the rotating edge of it into contact with the roots, which severed nicely at its touch. After a few minutes, she let the electric motor die and stood up to stretch her back out.

Michael held out his hand. "Let me give it a try."

"I'm fine." She fired up the unit again and continued cutting. "Just find out how far it is to the end," she raised her voice over the soft whine of the motor.

Michael was back in a minute. "About another thirty feet."

"Damn big hole." She didn't stop cutting.

"You should get there in another half hour. Want me to take over for a while?"

Mary let the motor die and stood up again. "Knock yourself out." She pushed the chainsaw into her husband's chest. "Since it looks like we'll be here for a while, I'm going to get us a couple of chairs." She then headed back to the camper, leaving him to work.

The sun was almost overhead when Michael finally ran into something the saw didn't want to cut. He set it down next to that spot. He walked over to the chair Mary had erected with a small umbrella to protect her from the sun and collected the pole he had stuck upright into the ground there.

Still panting from the sun and work, "It looks like it's time to turn the corner on this thing."

"Let me finish this drink and I'll take over." She picked up her cup from the holder mounted into the chair and poured the rest of its contents into her mouth. "Besides, it looks like you could do with a break."

About an hour later, having taken turns cutting, they had enough of the roots cut that the vegetation fell into the opening, giving them a triangular opening into what was inside.

Piles of debris were scattered about, at least where the sunlight now hit them. Rusted metal was sticking up, though mostly bent into odd angles. Plastic counters, some flat, some at varying angles, were strung on top of and amongst the debris. Piles and piles of dust-like material were intermixed with the plastic and metal. Yet no smell emanated from the area. Whatever would have provided an odor had already done so, and it had left.

It was a good twenty feet down to what looked like a portion of the floor that was solid. So they had to make another trip back to the camper to get the chain ladder. They drove the metal spikes into the gaps of the concrete surrounding the pit and mounted the ladder to the side.

Michael dropped the ladder down, then drove a probing pole into each side of it to act as hand holds for them as they got on and off it at the top. He went down first with his shovel hanging from his belt.

His shoes squished through an inch of indefinable stuff. Using his shovel, he cleared a section of the floor so Mary could have a place to stand when she got down. He was glad she had forced him to wear the work gloves as he began shifting the metal and plastic garbage around by hand.

He finally had a six foot square area cleared by the time she stepped off the ladder. "Tell me again why we're spending our vacation in this hell hole?"

"Because Jeff said I could use the camper if I checked one of the clearings out. So we get six days of laying around for this one day of exploring."

"Okay, but you're fixing drinks tonight." She bent down and grabbed a rusty metal pole and shifted it to the side wall so they could plow towards the center of the room.

Michael heard the slithering again. The mound in the center of the room quivered slightly. "Mary, I don't think we're alone down here."

"I agree," she turned back to the ladder and scrambled back up. Michael held it steady until she got half way up, then began his own climb.

He got his feet up on the third rung when something crashed out of the debris piles and grabbed his left boot. Michael kicked with his right foot trying to get loose of whatever had him. He never got a second kick off.

Michael's hands couldn't take the strain and let go of the rung they were clinging to, and he fell back to the bottom of the room.

Standing over him was a humanoid creature, much wider than the Raffians he had already met and with a snout that was almost a yard long. Instead of fur, the creature had scales all along its back and a smooth underbelly that was showing signs of some kind of outbreak. The hands that it was holding over Michael's head had claws like the Raffians didn't.

"Michael!" Mary cried from above. She had gotten off the ladder and was staring down. She found a stone and threw it at the creature. "Leave my husband alone."

The rock hit it on the head and the creature roared in protest. Its jaws spread a full three feet wide, revealing rows of teeth within.

As it took its attention off Michael and focused on the threat from above, Mary continued to throw rocks. Michael scrambled up and onto the ladder. Climbing faster this time, he got out of the reach of the creature before it could react. Within a couple of minutes, he was out of the pit and disconnecting the chain ladder from its mountings as the creature attempted to climb up.

The creature fell about ten feet onto its back, as the ladder let go. The Blacks headed back to the camper, threw as much stuff as they could into the sleeping compartment and lifted off to return to Petersville.

Their vacation was over.

Chapter 17

Community Meeting

After having lunch in the city's communal hall, Alex and Vicky Notski walked over to the landing field and helped set up chairs for the meeting Jeff Martin had scheduled for this afternoon. Already this issue was costing them a full day off the construction of their new home, having to fly in early that morning so the shuttles could be stored away and the landing field used to hold all the adult members of the Belenius colony. There would not be a shuttle going back north until the following morning. Alex planned on asking to use the last of their ground cars in that case.

They quickly ran out of communal and private chairs and were now setting up benches using planks and logs set on whatever they could find. There weren't enough seats around the landing field to sit the four thousand residents of the colony.

"At least we got our roof up," Alex said as he carried his end of the two by eight he and his wife were bringing over from the lumber mill. "The Clements don't have anything up if it rains later today."

"Bales said there was no chance of rain for today."

"Like he did on that hail storm last week before we even got our walls up. If you recall, we had to replace about half of the flooring we had down."

She dropped her end on the rock they had placed there earlier. "There's nothing we can do about it. Mr. Martin wants a meeting and it's his right to call one."

"This had better be damned important."

Over the next hour, dozens of people came over to the impromptu town hall and finished setting up the seating. There was a raised area in the center; everyone was going to be sitting around it looking inward. Around two, the rest of the community came into the circle and took seats where they could find them. After all the work they had done, the Notskis had to stand with hundreds of others just outside the circle.

Jeff walked up one of the aisles with Governor McCurdel, Clarence Knowles, and Michael Black. They stepped onto the raised dais but had to stand, since all the chairs were being used by the assembled crowd.

Jeff held up his hand for quiet. The people who had been talking to each other quieted down and waited for him to speak. "I want to thank you all for coming on such short notice."

He had to wave down a couple hecklers. "I know we have never assembled in mass since disembarking the Endeavor, but a special problem has presented itself to our colony. Despite all our studies before choosing this planet, we have come to one with at least one—maybe two—native, sentient life forms already on it."

He paused as the crowd reacted to his statement. After waiting for the buzz to die down, he continued. "As some of you may know, the creatures we had been referring to as jabberwockies appear to be the native culture on Belenius or Raffia as they call it. But something happened to them and they have gone down the evolutionary spiral back to a more primitive state. I'd like Clarence Knowles to address what he has found out about them."

Clarence stepped forward as Jeff took a step back and caught his hands behind his back. Clarence then went into detail about what the various expeditions found and the results he and Ahmed had been getting in the lab. "At this point, we have two individual colonists who are able to communicate with the Raffians. Thomas and Sarah McCurdel are trying to teach a few others the Raffian language, including myself, as I think understanding their language will help our understanding of the knowledge painted on their cave walls."

Jeff stepped forward holding his hand up for silence. "And that begs the questions; what happened to them and can it happen to us?"

The murmur from the assembly rose again.

Jeff motioned for silence. "And this is a mystery we have to address. We don't have the ability any longer to move on to another planet. For better or worse, Belenius 3 is our home."

"You've known that for a couple of weeks, what's changed?" came a shout from the crowd. Jeff looked around but couldn't decide who had said it.

"Michael, would you come up here and explain?"

"Mary and I were doing some exploring the other day, and we may have run into another native race occupying this planet. And one not as friendly as the Raffians. We had descended into a unique clearing pit when something crawled out of the debris and attacked us." He held up the hiking boot he had been wearing, the creature's claw marks—while not having gone through the leather of the boot—were still visible and deep. "Something that can do this!"

Jeff placed his hand on the boot and lowered it back to Michael's side. "In the year we have been on Belenius 3, this is the first we have encountered this creature. We know nothing about it. Michael didn't have time to get a picture before it scurried away again. But until we do know more, I am banning all independent exploration of the clearing pits. I will be taking a party back to the Raffian village tomorrow and see if they know anything about it."

Governor McCurdel stepped forward and began speaking. "We will find out what this new creature is and what danger it poses to us. Everyone, keep building like before, and we will overcome the obstacles confronting us."

In the back of the crowd, Alex turned to his wife. "Do you think they know what they're doing?"

She was about to answer when they heard the rumble of thunder coming from the north. "You're not driving in the rain."

Chapter 18

Friendly Visit

Tommy and Sarah jumped at the chance to see their Raffian friends again. Which was beginning to bother their mother; so this time, Clarence Knowles had to take the entire McCurdel family with him on his research mission. Meaning Ahmed and his intern had to stay behind. It was a good thing that Francois Loinet was trained in flying the shuttles, since his DNA samples took precedence over more chemical ones right now.

The Governor sat in the co-pilot's seat so Clarence could brief the children in back. They brought the long range module again today to make sure they could get the kids home by bed time. Marsha had insisted. Clarence and Marsha sat strapped into the seats facing backwards behind the two walls that separated them from the driver, with the children strapped into the bench mounted between the battery racks that made up this module.

"We've found another creature living on this planet. And we know nothing about it. Tommy, Sarah, we need you to talk with your friends and see if they know anything about them. Can you do that?"

"We can try, Mr. Knowles."

"I'll help them, sir," the eldest McCurdel boy added. "They've been teaching me a few Raffian words."

"Thanks. I'd also like a guide/interrupter for those cave painting if you can find one and talk for me. My Raffian isn't very good." He said the last line in his best Raffian.

"You don't grunt enough," corrected Sarah.

"And 'ugug' means bush fruit or berry, not very, Mr. Knowles," Tommy added.

"And that's why I need one of you kids to translate for me." He leaned back into his seat, let out a sigh, and added, "I hope they know what attacked the Blacks."

Around noon, Marsha broke out the snack bars she had packed and passed them out to everyone. Then she tapped on her radio, "Don't forget to eat, Howard."

"Yes, dear."

"Well, you know how cranky you get when your blood sugar drops."

The sound of crunching came through their radio link. "Eating now, dear."

It was a few minutes later that the descent light came on in the module. And a few minutes later that the shuttle landed. Clarence unbuckled from his seatbelt but not faster than the kids.

"You stay seated, until Mr. Knowles tells us it's safe."

He looked at the kids returning to a still position. Then he stood up and took the single step to the side door. The lever pushed up to open and down to secure, it didn't move. "Frank, release the module doors." The mechanism clicked and Clarence slid the door open.

"Almost forgot you guys," Frank joked as he, too, stepped down.

"Sure you did."

He could hear the door on the other side of the module slide open as Howard was letting his family out. "We've got a couple of hours here if we want to get back by Mrs. McCurdel's curfew."

"And you will get us back by seven," she added, coming around the front of the shuttle leading her family to the outside storage compartment, which she opened and began taking out safety gear for her children. After strapping her own helmet on, she thrust helmet disks into the stomachs of both Clarence and Francois. "Make sure you set a proper example for the kids." The two men peeled off the plastic disks before they had a chance to conform to their abdomens.

They made their way to the cave entrance and walked into the darkness. As each of them turned on their helmet-mounted lights, the darkness vanished, but the gloom remained. A few minutes later, they emerged into the cave village of the Raffians.

Since their light had arrived first, several of the villagers were on their way over to greet them. Both of the younger children ran forward and wrapped a hug around one of them as he approached.

"Mommy, mommy," Sarah began to motion her mother over to them. "This is I'mac, he's the one who brought us here and taught us his words."

Howard held out his hand to the Raffin. "I wish you would have come to us first, but I thank you for keeping my children safe."

I'mac recognized Howard as one of the two people he had meet that night long ago. He rubbed his belly where Jeff had planted his spear that first night to toss him into the ravine. Then he used the same hand to shake Howard's.

I'mac squatted down to get eye level with Tommy and Sarah, they exchanged a few words and skipped over to the nearest fire pit and sat on the bench in front of it.

Howard looked over at Billy. "The only thing I could make out was 'tell'. I'm guessing they want to tell each other things."

"And I wish we had time for this. But Howard..." Knowles broke in.

"Right." Howard walked over to where his children were sitting and sat on a log next to them. Three was about all any of the logs could hold. He was separated by a space of two feet from his son, who was sitting on the end of the other log. "Tommy, could you ask your friend for a guide for Mr. Knowles, like he talked about?"

Tommy's head went from acknowledging his father's words back to talking with I'mac. Then back to his father, "I'mac says he'd be willing to talk you through the library."

Clarence stepped between the two McCurdel's. "Library? They have a word for library?"

"Ughulmnol"

Clarence turned to Howard. "Interesting that they would have a word for such an advanced concept."

"Could it be a holdover concept?" Francis injected.

"Now that would make sense. If a library is an important concept for them, they would have insured the word made it down from their more advanced selves."

"That would imply they knew what was happening to them."

Howard got off the log and looked the two men in their faces. "While you two were talking, I'mac got up and left. It looks like he's heading over to that Shaman guy we met last time."

Tommy stood up also. "He's gone over to ask M'cron for permission to enter the library."

"Thanks, son." Clarence looked at the twelve-year-old, then back to the adults. "If he needs permission, it means the library is a sacred place to them."

"So you probably shouldn't take any more samples of it while they are looking."

"Agreed. Ahmed said he had enough to keep him busy for some time, anyway."

"Sarah." Francois knelt down before the ten-year-old still sitting on the log. "I could use your help getting DNA samples from your friends. Are you willing to help me?"

She looked up at her mother standing next to the men. "It's just like we talked about on the way up here, dear. Uncle Frank needs you to talk for him to your friends."

"I'm not going to hurt them, just take a swab from inside their mouths." He opened his belt pouch, took out one of the vials containing a four inch stick with a cotton ball on the end, Opened it and demonstrated on himself what he needed from each of the Raffian volunteers.

Seeing I'mac coming back their way with a man carrying a ceremonial staff in tow, "Billy, you stay with Sarah and me, working with Frank. Howard, you're going with Tommy to this library thing." Marsha was back to family deployment again.

"We'll keep in touch, Ma'am." Clarence said as he took Tommy by his hand and walked to meet the approaching figures.

Chapter 19

Formal History Lessons

Clarence's group walked over to the far eastern end of the wall they had entered the village through and where they found a second entrance into the village cavern. M'cron rattled his staff at the entrance before he would allow any of them to enter.

I'mac said something and Tommy translated. "M'cron is letting the spirits who created their books know we are coming."

"They have a word for books?" Clarence straightened up and rubbed his chin. Then crouched down again to avoid the low ceiling they were passing through.

After a couple of minutes, M'cron raised his arms for everyone to stop and went through the same process, but turning to each of the walls before proceeding. A few more feet, and the wall paintings began. This time, they were in great detail of vast urban cities with large ovals floating between the buildings. Other pictures showed large areas of cultivated land where uniform plants grew taller than the men depicted cutting them down. On the ceiling was a star map showing the Belenius star with nine planets orbiting it. Further on were stars similar but not the same as the ones the humans were becoming familiar with.

M'cron raised his staff, spun once around the gallery pointing with it at all the paintings. He then said something to I'mac, which Tommy chuckled at.

His father tapped him on his shoulder and gave him a puzzled look when the boy turned to look at him.

"M'cron just told I'mac that he would be telling their story. M'cron is going to be testing how well he's learned his lessons."

"Which reminds me, your last learning center report showed more game play then math drill. Turn that around or I'll block your game access," Howard said.

"Yes, sir," the smile vanished from Tommy face.

I'mac turned back to the humans. Looking into Tommy's sour expression, he knelt down and began talking to the boy.

"So, what did he say?" Clarence asked as the Raffian finished.

Tommy replied to I'mac, then said, "He was mostly just trying to cheer me up."

I'mac stood up and looked the adults in the eye but spoke to Tommy.

"He wants to know where you would like to start."

Howard pointed at the cityscape and said, "How about that one?"

Tommy explained what Clarence wanted to I'mac, who then spoke for several minutes before Tommy interrupted him. I'mac then turned to his Shaman who nodded in agreement.

"I had to stop him. He was overloading me with their history. So where should I begin?"

"Where did he?"

"This is a picture of the city of the Gods, our ancestors, er, their ancestors, and what they can become again if they gain a purity of body. It shows the caverns they built, ten dwellings tall. The air bags they used to get between them and," Tommy pointed to a line going up one of the buildings, "the tubes that carried them between the dwellings within the buildings. There was a lot of other stuff but I haven't learned the words for them yet."

When Tommy fell silent, I'mac turned to the pastoral image and began lecturing again until Tommy had to stop him. "I can't even begin translating what he just told me."

"Don't worry, son," Clarence said. "I think that one speaks for itself. Just ask him if that was their food production?"

Tommy tried as best he could to find connecting words and when the two of them finished speaking he turned back to Clarence. "Yes, sir. Back in the days when there was an overabundance of everything."

"Ask him about the one on the ceiling. Specifically why they show nine planets when we only found eight when we arrived here?"

Tommy asked I'mac, who shrugged and turned to M'cron. M'cron said a few words that Tommy nodded his understanding of before turning back to the humans.

"Raffie had eight companions in the night sky, most could not be seen without the help of the ancestral eyes, but they were there. Until one of them fell from the sky."

"I think we need to get to the main reason we're here," Howard cut in. "Tommy ask the Shaman about the alligator people."

"The what?"

"The Blacks found another humanoid race living in the debris of the clearings. We need more information about them. We talked about this in the ride up here."

Tommy spent several minutes trying to get concepts across to either I'mac or M'cron but they didn't understand what he was talking about. Until Tommy mimicked an alligator's snout with his arms. M'cron pounded his staff twice on the ground and motioned everyone to follow him forward.

He took them to an image of several animals behind bars and pointed to one of them with the large snout Tommy had demonstrated. When pressed about men who looked like that, the Shaman repeatedly pointed to the image of the alligator-looking animal, shaking his head whenever Tommy asked about similar creatures.

* * *

Two hours after going into the Raffian library, Howard and his group returned to the main village to see how Frank and his group were getting along.

Sarah and Billy were sitting around one of the fire pits talking with some of the Raffian children, attempting to learn more of the language they used. Marsha was sitting across the pit from them, watching, but looking resigned to not knowing what they were talking about.

She was the first to see her husband and son return. And therefore the first to get up to greet them. Frank had his back to them, looking at some of the flint tools the natives had created and watching how they were chipping off the flint pieces.

"Learn anything, dear?" Howard asked as his wife approached.

"Shum," when she realized what she had said. "Well, maybe a little is sinking in.

"How's our microbiologist doing over there?"

"He stopped taking samples about a half hour ago. Sarah's got everybody coming to him to show him their injuries. He seems to need no translation to administer first aid. When can we start heading back?"

"Tommy, could you ask M'cron if I can look at the paints they used on the cave paintings?"

"Sure thing, Mr. Knowles." He turned on his heel, gave a quick bow to the Shaman and began addressing him in Raffian. The Shaman responded and gestured over to one of the dwellings next to the library entrance. Then he led the way over to it.

Clarence followed Tommy.

"What's that about?"

"I haven't a clue." Howard walked over to the log across from his daughter and sat down. He patted it and added," So we might as well get comfortable. It could be a long wait."

She looked over to where the others were just entering the dwelling. "Shouldn't we keep an eye on our son?"

"I trust Clarence, and one of the natives they're with took care of Tommy for almost two months trekking up here." Howard picked a twig off the ground and tossed it into the fire pit. It crackled and spat as it caught fire. He looked across at his other son and daughter. "I wish I could learn languages as easily as they can."

"Maybe it's time I got back to work. Build a learning program for the computer-teachers."

"Something you and the kids could do together."

"Earn some credits to purchase a new home."

"It was my ancestor who paid for..." He looked into the hardening eyes of his wife and stopped. "Maybe it's time I found some way to earn our keep around here, too."

"Howard, Frank, get over here," Clarence called across the cavern. "You have to see this!"

The remaining adults all got up to see what Clarence was going on about. "Marsha, stay with the children. They don't have an I'mac watching over them here."

As Howard released her shoulders, she nodded her agreement and sat back down. Then he turned and tried to catch up with Francois.

Clarence guided them inside, where they found a log workbench along the near side wall. The workbench contained several clay jars and bowls. Some of the bowls had a dried powder in them plastered to the bottom. "Those look like water-based pigments that have been allowed to dry out since their last use. But over here..." He led them across to the far side wall where, instead of a log bench, there was a glass display case.

Inside the case were several rolled tubes, rolled up indicating the different amounts of whatever was in them. There were also several different sized brushes next to the tubes, some clean, with what looked like hundreds of bristles mounted in them, and some containing dried paint from what they had been last used for. There were also a series of metal sticks with various tips; slanted, straight, diamond-shaped and pick-ended. Against the end of the case was what looked like the remains of a compressor machine and what must have been a spray nozzle. Bits of material were on the case shelf between the two, like whatever had connected them had rotted away.

"When I tried to open the sliding front door," Clarence pointed to the seam in the middle of the glass front with a lock mounted to the side of it. "M'cron stamped his staff on the floor and I'mac reached over and grabbed my wrist before I could touch it."

"They're sacred." Tommy informed his father.

"M'cron told Tommy; they have some kind of ceremony once a year to remember the times when the Gods gave them things like these."

"You mean their ancestors?" Francois asked.

"Yeah, most likely. I wish I could read the printing on those tubes, though. Most of them are faded and what I can see makes no sense."

"You were expecting English?"

"No, but I was hoping for something we could try decrypting back at the Endeavor."

"Then are we done here?" Howard asked.

"If Harry is done, I am," Francois replied. "You ready?"

"In a second." He was still taking pictures of the items in the case. "Just a couple more."

"Meet you at the shuttle, then." He turned to talk softer to the others, who were much closer. "Howard, can you and Tommy wait for him while we get the shuttle ready to head home?"

"Can I say hello to Ank before we go?" Tommy asked his father.

"After we get Clarence pulled away from his artifacts. But make it quick. When it's time to go, I want no argument. Understand?"

"Yes, sir," the boy said over his shoulder as he raced out of the dwelling and across the open area where he saw Ank playing with the other Raffian children.

"I said after... Oh, never mind. They're only kids once. You about ready?"

As the men emerged from the dwelling, Howard saw that Sarah had joined her brother with the other Raffian children. He walked over to where his wife was getting off the log she'd been sitting on. "Give them a couple of minutes with their friends. We'll get the shuttle ready for departure. William, get Frank's sample kit."

"Sure thing, Dad."

Twenty minutes later, Francois opened the pilot's door of the driver after having completed his pre-flight walk around. He buckled his harness and touched his radio link so the people in the module could hear him also.

"I hope everyone had a good time. But buckle in now; we still have a four-hour trip back to Petersville. Remember, this is not a travel unit but a power module, please stay seated unless you need to use the restroom."

"But Mom," Sarah said without using the radio link. "There is no bathroom back here."

The shuttle lifted off the cold barren terrain, angled southeast and headed towards home.

Chapter 20

Clues

Jeff sat back in his chair, letting it fall back until he was almost leaning flat. On the ceiling of the navigation lounge of the Endeavor he was projecting the image of the Belenius solar system they had recorded when they arrived in the system.

He sat up and ran his fingers over the computer controls to call up the image Clarence had recorded on his last trip into the Raffian 'library'. The two images were displayed side by side. Jeff entered a request to superimpose the two images.

He got a jumbled mess.

The first thing he did was center the star in the two images on top of each other. Then one by one, he rotated the time index of their recorded data, since he couldn't time rotate the Raffian cave painting, until the planets depicted in each began to line up. It took a time regression of 250 years to get the two images in as much synch as they were able; the human image was missing a planet between the fifth and sixth planets. The Raffian image showed it to be smaller than the next smallest planet at the far end of the system and between two of the largest ones.

"Could have broken up sometime after this image was painted."

Jeff sprang out of his chair, causing him to bounce through several of the meteors—at least images of them—below the plane of Belenius' ecliptic. Clint had entered the lounge unannounced.

"Could you at least knock?"

"You looked busy." He walked into the center of the lounge, took a chair and got under the projected image. "I wonder if they have any records of what happened?"

"It'll give Clarence something new to look for next time he goes up."

"Listen, boss. Several of us have been wondering how much more time we can afford to give to this purely scientific mystery? We still have a construction schedule to keep."

"I'd put this whole thing on hold if Mike and Mary hadn't run into that new and potentially dangerous predator last month." He sat up straight and turned off the projection system.

"Then maybe we need to send an expedition up to their 'vacation home' and capture the thing? Just for scientific curiosity."

Jeff pulled up the home construction schedule on one of the monitors. While it was loading, "It's too dangerous. Mike described the creature's movements as extremely fast and very aggressive."

"But if we send a large enough team, with sufficient nets?"

Jeff looked down at the computer screen and read the housing list. "Okay, prepare a list of volunteers and the supplies you'll need for me to okay this trip."

"Thanks, Jeff." Clint was out of his chair instantly.

"And Clint, I'm going with you." Jeff was looking at the computer monitor as Clint let the door slide shut behind him. Clinton Jordan's name was at the top of the unfinished construction list.

* * *

Michael Black was on his way to Town Hall to sign up for the expedition, when he passed under the tree Sarah McCurdel was playing in. He didn't give it a second's thought until the thump behind him caused him to pause.

"Mr. Black, could you hand me my climbing claw?" Sarah called down from the six-inch-wide branch she was sitting on.

"Sure thing, Sarah." He bent down to retrieve it. But froze before he actually touched it. It was the same hand that had tried to smother him in that pit.

* * *

Both the McCurdels stormed into the Town Hall's Briefing Room, just left of the Analysis Room, where the hastily called community meeting was being held. Jeff, Clarence, Ron, Ahmed, Nancy, Diane, Logan, along with Mike and Mary Black were already seated in a circle around Sarah. As they came into the room, the little girl bolted from her chair, ran between the Blacks and grabbed her mother, who—seeing her coming—had gotten down on one knee.

"What's this all about?" Howard walked over to where the others were sitting. Stood just outside the circle and placed his hands on his hips.

Mike got up and presented Howard the hand he had gotten from Sarah. It was actually a leathered hand, cut off of some creature with its internals scooped out, then cured. Each of its six fingers had a very strong, sharp claw extending from it.

"Sarah was playing with that. And damned if it doesn't look exactly like the hand of that creature who attacked me last month."

Howard gave it a quick look, then turned to his daughter, who was still clinging to her mother. His voice lost the hardness he had used a second ago. "Sarah, where did you get this?"

She was still crying but wiped away the tears on her mother's shirt before answering. "It was I'mac's. He gave it to me when we got to his village."

"Don't worry, dear, you're not in any trouble." Her mother stroked her hair. Then hardened her voice, "Is she!" More a command than a question.

"We just need to know what it is?" Jeff asked.

"I'mac used it to climb trees. All the Raffians do. It's what I was doing when I dropped it."

"The scratch marks on the trees we kept following when we were tracking the children," Logan snapped his fingers.

"But they occurred so often," Diane piped in.

"I'mac only used it to climb trees once a night. So we could sleep," Sarah explained. She was sounding more comfortable. "He just kept scratching the trees every few feet."

"Damn, if he wasn't marking the trail for us to follow."

"Those guys are cleverer than we thought."

"So what does that mean?" Howard asked as he stood back up to face the others.

Jeff looked around at the assemblage. "We have some more questions to ask the Raffians." Sarah broke into a smile.

"Then you had better make it quick," Ron said. "We're about to hit winter again. And it's won't be as mild up there as we have down here."

Chapter 21

Monster Hunt

"You guys sure you want William flying that thing?" Jeff radioed to the co-pilot of the shuttle Clarence and the McCurdels were readying for takeoff. He was standing on the wooden platform just outside the module hanger, watching them leave.

"I know what I'm doing, Mr. Martin," Howard's eldest son radioed back. "I had a great teacher."

Clint put his mouth next to Jeff's non-radio ear and whispered. "The kid will do fine. He was a quick learner."

As the shuttle lifted straight up and headed north, Jeff and Clint turned back into the hanger and watched the last of the supplies being loaded into the cargo module they were about to hook up.

"Out of the way, guys." Nancy pushed through the two of them as she pulled the cage they had constructed to hold the creature. It was resting on an anti-gravity sled, so she was pulling with her left hand and brushing aside her two male obstructions with her right.

She moved it over to the side door of the module. Ron, who was currently running the forklift, picked it off of the sled and maneuvered it into the hold, secured it to the floor and closed that side door. The rest of the loading could be done from the back and other side door.

"Beep. Beep." Logan guided another sled to the back of the module, this one containing several bags of netting. Each of them had been equipped with inch wide drones on their corners, so they could hover over their prey before being dropped.

"I just hope we don't have any trouble with the drones in the cold."

"Ron said the weather is milder down here, at least for the next month."

"Then we'd better get moving. Bring your shuttle around to the entrance and let's get this thing hooked up."

Clint jogged back out of the hanger and across the field to the hanger that still had three shuttle drivers in it. He went in the side door and looked over the one closest the main door. Finding no visible problems with it, he grabbed the chain and pulled open the hanger door. Across from him was the open door of the other hanger and the waiting module.

He hooked the chain into the hook mounted on the wall to keep the doors from closing while we was maneuvering out. Then got into the cockpit and ran through his checklist before starting the gravity units and lifting off the floor an inch. Using the electric steering turbines, he turned his craft until he was aligned with the door opening and began backing it out of the hanger, then across the dirt lane separating the two buildings, between the two landing pads, and finally up to the connection end of the cargo module.

His unit was making a loud unpleasant noise to announce its movement, getting shriller in pitch as he got closer to hookup. When the two units were within ten feet of each other, right before the tang of the driver slid into the slot of the module, Clint took his hands off the control stick. The two units would do the final maneuvers themselves. Clint waited for the inevitable clunk of connection. Humans had to make the manual connections of the wires connecting the two units, while the computer dropped the pins in place, physically holding the driver to the module. Finally, the green light on his dashboard told Clint everything was ready for him to pull the shuttle out and over to Landing Pad Two.

He touched the radio link in his ear and announced, "Okay, all aboard."

Red lights on his dashboard lit up as the rear and side doors were opened to allow his passengers to enter the module. As they were returning to their green state, indicating the doors had been securely closed, Jeff opened the far door of the driver and got in.

"Everyone's ready," Jeff said.

"I've got one seatbelt light still out."

"You've got one seat empty."

Clint did some counting with his fingers. "Yeah, you're right." He keyed the radio to talk with everyone. "Sit back and relax. We'll be to the Black's vacation home in about an hour."

He punched in three hundred feet to the gravimetric units and rose. Then he pushed the forward drive petal and the shuttle sped west along a route mapped out on the round computer screen in the middle of the dashboard.

Jeff watched as Clint piloted the shuttle straight along the line projected on that screen. Then looked out the windows at the treetops over a hundred feet below, speeding past.

* * *

True to his estimate, an hour later everyone was beginning to unpack the module, stacking the nets on one side of the opening Mike had already cut. Mike and Ron got out a chainsaw each and began cutting away the foliage on either side of the pit. Logan got a third one out and began working on the far end of the pit.

Once it was opened and the foliage drug away from the hole, it was a five hundred by two hundred foot hole in the ground. Parts of the side walls, that had been built with some kind of stone or concrete, were beginning to crumble and cave in. Several piles of debris merged into an almost continuous line of the stuff, with dips and peaks every now and again.

But nothing was moving down there. The full light of the sun shone into the pit, shadows were weak at best, and yet there was absolutely no movement.

"Somebody's going to have to volunteer to go down," Jeff announced. Everyone just turned their heads and looked at him. "We'll put you in a harness and run a line through a winch so we can haul you out faster than you can physically climb back. But someone has to volunteer."

"Okay," Mike finally said. "I'll go."

"Good, grab a class three harness, along with a helmet, and get them on. Ron, Logan, Nancy; get the retrieval tripod set up, string a line to the winch and be ready to hook him up when he gets back. Mary, get the chain ladder ready for him to climb down. Everyone else, get poles ready in case we have to ward the thing off, then get the first net ready to deploy."

Jeff walked over to the first net bag and began opening it. He looked up to see if the others were moving, and while it wasn't as fast as he would have liked, they were carrying out his instructions. He went back to removing the net.

After a few minutes, Mike emerged from the module with a full rescue harness on. Nancy clipped him onto the line with the tripod mounted six feet away from the edge of the pit. Mary gave him a hug before he grabbed the poles mounted on either side of the chain ladder. But before he could place his foot on the top rung, Jeff picked a shovel out of one of the side boxes mounted on the module and threw it down into the pit. It stuck blade end first into a mound of debris close to where Mike would be stepping off.

"Nothing," Jeff said. "It's either a really cool customer or it has moved on. Mike, if it doesn't jump you when you get down there, try encouraging it with that shovel."

"Maybe I can just knock it unconscious?"

"Don't take any chances. I will have my finger on the winch control if anything happens. So don't spook me unless you want a quick ride back up."

Mike stepped onto the first rung and began his climb down. Half way down, a chunk of dirt was broken off by one of his observers and bounced off his helmet. "Can you guys stand back a little?"

It took him a couple more minutes to reach the bottom of the ladder. This time, nothing scurried out of the debris, no matter how much he poked it or dug into it with the shovel.

"I got nothing, Jeff," Mike radioed back to the surface. "What do you want me to do?"

After a few seconds, Jeff replied. "We've got a few hours before we have to head back to Petersville. Come back up, and we'll see if there is another pit it could have moved to."

"This was the only one in this clearing. Mary and I checked before we decided to explore this one."

"Ron, Logan, see if you can find anything Mike might have missed. Everyone else, let's set things up to clear out this pit and see how our friend could have gotten out."

They quickly broke up in teams, Nancy and Clint began breaking out the hardware to convert their tripod into a crane so they could pull the debris out from below. Mary, Diane and Carl assembled the basket for the crane and unpacked the rest of the five shovels they carried on the module. Jeff suited up, dropped his shovel over the side and climbed down to help Mike dig.

As soon as he stepped off the last rung, "Hold it a minute, Mike." When Mike straightened up, "Turn around." Jeff attached the rope coming from the ring on the back of his harness to the ring on the back of Mike's. If they had to pull Mike out, Jeff was going, too.

After a few minutes of digging, Jeff was interrupted on the radio. "Hey, guys, we're sending the basket your way."

"Thanks," he replied. "We should be able to fill it shortly."

"Take your time, Clint's having problems assembling the crane. Ow!"

"It just takes longer than slapping four sides up and hooking them with braces."

"And since you're done with the basket, you can help them put together the crane. Diane, see if you can give Logan a hand. We need them done with their survey so we can focus on this pit."

"I think they're on their way back now, Jeff."

"Make sure we have enough eyes watching for movement down here. I don't want to be caught by surprise."

"I'll get kitted up and join you. I can bring the second basket down and once we get enough space cleared out, we can set it up, too."

"Jeff, why not just burn this pit out? That'll clear it."

"Carl, we need the creature alive." He closed the radio link and added to himself, "if possible."

After an hour with no sightings of the creature, Ron and Carl came down to help clear the debris. They were now able to fill a basket in the time it took the crane operators to haul the other one up and empty it. They were getting a large area cleared.

"Jeff," Mike planted his shovel and leaned on the handle. "What do you suppose this was?"

Feeling it was a good time to take a break, Jeff stood up and leaned on his also. "I never really thought about it." He turned his head to look at everything that had been cleared out and everything that hadn't. "It does look like some kind of basement, though, doesn't it?" He looked over two piles and saw Nancy working. "Hey, Nancy, take a break." And waved her over. "Mike and I were wondering. Just what was this pit for?"

She drove her shovel into a nearby debris pile and sat on a cleared slab of stone. "Why ask me? I'm not an archeologist."

"But you are a construction engineer and we're thinking it might be a basement of some sort."

She took off her work glove and ran her hand over the floor. "This floor has a lot of cracks in it but, in my opinion, it's too smooth to be anything except a poured slab. Possibly a foundation for some kind of building." She stood up as she look over the scale of the pit. "It would have been a very large building."

"Hey, everyone," Ron called on the radio. "Get over here quick. I've found something." As they looked up, they could see Ron waving his shovel over his head to let everyone know where 'here' was.

They had to go around sections of debris they hadn't cleared yet, but when Jeff got over to where Ron was pointing with his shovel, there was a series of steps going into an opening in the floor. A few steps down, it was filled with water, yet the steps could be seen going further.

"I guess we know where our quarry got off to," Ron said as they arrived. Those watching the diggers from above looked down into Ron's tunnel.

"Yeah, it looks like today is a bust. Let's pack up and go home."

"I hope Clarence has more luck."

Chapter 22

Closed for the Winter

"The wind is picking up," Billy said over the radio for his family in back. "If you're not already, you'd better buckle in. We're going to bounce around some."

Running parallel to the mountains as they gained altitude was causing the wind to blow the shuttle to the left and away from where they wanted to go. William McCurdel had to fight the controls to hold her anywhere near the direction they wanted to go.

"Should we turn back, Mr. Knowles?" he finally asked his co-pilot.

"If we do, we won't get back up here for four months. Take us higher, see if the turbulence dies off some."

He set the gravity units for another hundred feet and banked to the left, taking him away from the mountain. The winds let up some, but it was still a fight to go the last twenty miles to the Raffian village. As they approached for a landing, the wind ran against the side of the mountain and tried to blow the shuttle back into the sky. After a fierce fight, Billy managed a safe landing.

Clarence reached over and set the gravitational units for a minus ten feet to anchor them to the ground. "Billy, you can let go now." The boy's knuckles were turning white. "You brought us down, safe and sound." He tried to pry the young McCurdel's hands from the control stick. Billy finally looked over at Clarence and yanked his hands back from the controls. "You did great, Bill. That was the best landing in these conditions anyone could have hoped for." He slapped the youth on his back and opened his door to leave. "Let's get unpacked before the snow really starts falling."

Howard was emerging from the side door of the module. "That was a bumpy ride." As the wind blasted his unprotected face, "I can see why. Everyone get scarves on. It's cold out here."

As Clarence joined him, his family began to hand the backpacks out the door. They both slid one apiece onto their backs and stacked the rest on the ground. "I'd better check on Billy," the elder McCurdel called into the wind.

"Make sure you tell him what a great job he did."

"He landed us? That was good flying."

"And against some pretty stiff winds."

Howard had to work hard to get the pilot door to open against the wind trying to push it shut. When he did, his son was still sitting and staring at the controls.

"Bill, BILL," Howard called to his son.

When the boy finally broke his gaze away from the dashboard and looked at his father, Howard spoke again. "Great job! But climb out of there, we have to get our provisions into the cave. Then we can wait this storm out."

"Yes, let's get away from these winds." He jumped out of the cockpit and fought against the winds to get around the shuttle and collect what he was assigned to carry. After donning his backpack, he took his sister by her arm and helped her fight their way to the cave. Tommy quickly followed, not giving anyone a chance to grab his hand. Clarence waited for the others, then brought up the rear.

They collapsed just inside the cave, to catch a quick break before collecting the rest of their provisions. After the packs were stacked safely away from the howling winds, they readied themselves to head for the Raffian village. As they stared out the cave entrance, the wind began to fill up with the snow now falling from above, making a white curtain across the entrance, obscuring all things not in the cave with them.

"We may be here awhile," Clarence finally said as he got to his feet. "I think we should see if our neighbors have any rooms available." He reached down and helped Sarah to her feet. Howard helped Tommy, while Bill and Marsha got up on their own.

* * *

Before they got to the ice layer in the cave, a party of Raffians wearing masks approached. One held the ceremonial staff of the Shaman.

"Lukco" Clarence said with palms up as they approached. It was the greeting Tommy had taught him.

M'cron said a few words, then held his staff parallel to the ground and guided the humans against the cave wall. The rest of the Raffian party kept heading for the cave's entrance.

"He wants to know what we are doing here," Tommy translated.

"Tell him we have a few more questions."

After a brief exchange between Tommy, Sarah and M'cron, Tommy explained. "Now isn't a good time. He said the harsh times have come, and they are sealing the village against it."

"Sealing the village?" asked his father.

Tommy turned to M'cron and asked. "They seal the cave entrance with snow bricks during the first snow fall. It protects them through the harsh times." M'cron said some more to Tommy. "Unless we wish to spend the entirety of this season with them, M'cron suggests we leave now and return in the emerging season."

Clarence turned to leave, then stopped himself. "There's no way Bill can take off in this weather. I'm afraid we're here for the Winter, everyone. Tommy, thank our hosts for their kind offer, and tell them we accept their generous invitation."

Chapter 23

Planning Another Hunt

"That's right, Jeff. We're spending the winter here with the Raffians."

"Ron's forecasts show the period of current snowfall should end by the beginning of next week," Jeff replied to Howard's radio message. It was the day after his scheduled return and they would only have the satellite in position for another few minutes to complete this call. "We could have another shuttle up there to pick you guys up. And leave the one you took up there until the snow melts."

"No go, Jeff. The Raffians seal the caves during what they call the Harsh season. You guys can forget about replacing our home for a while. Focus on other people's. The Raffians took good care of our kids earlier, they will..."

That was it, the satellite had moved on, Jeff lost the connection to Howard. It would be another twelve hours before it was in position again.

"Nancy, report to Control." He might as well get the changes started. "We need to rework the construction schedule."

"But there's still the problem with Mike's alligator man." Logan had been finishing the design for new machine shop parts he wanted to 3-D print.

"I don't plan on ignoring him, just getting people working on what must be done while we seek them out."

"We?" Logan spun his chair around to face Jeff.

Jeff slid his chair over to a computer monitor, pulled up the home construction list and placed a hold on the McCurtel home. "Get ahold of Diane and Ahmed. We need to plan out a search."

"Construction equipment won't build itself."

"Between Nancy and her brother, everything will get taken care of." The door opened, Jeff spun his chair towards it. "Nancy, we were just talking about you. I've put a hold on the new McCurtel place, they're stuck with the Raffians for the winter. So re-plan construction accordingly. Take Logan, Diane, Ahmed and myself out of the picture, I have a special project for us."

"Well, let me get in here and have a look." She pushed Jeff's wheeled chair to her right and drug another chair up to sit in front of the monitor he had readied for her.

It had been an excessive push. Jeff let it roll to the end of the Big Board, then grabbed the table's edge and redirected himself to get closer to where Logan was sitting. He had to give himself a couple of pushes with his feet to make it.

"They're on their way," Logan said as Jeff bumped into his right shoulder.

Jeff pushed off from his friend and spun around over to the center table. "Let's pull up the satellite map of where

Mike spotted it." With a few keystrokes, he had the most current satellite image of the area projected before them. "Now we know that the creature was in that pit." Jeff used his finger to draw a red circle around the pit they had excavated a few days earlier.

Logan wheeled himself over and stared at the aerial view. "And you let it get away."

Jeff turned from the photo to stare at his friend as Logan grabbed the table's edge. "Without any marks on the walls or debris tall enough for it to climb out?"

"What about the roots Michael and Mary cut away to get into it on their first trip?"

"They threw them on top of the uncut mat of roots."

Logan dabbed his finger on the blue palette, circled the dark section of the cleared pit. "What did you guys make of that?"

Jeff sat back in his chair, causing it to move away from the table slightly. "Without underwater gear, we couldn't risk taking a look. Especially if that was how the creature got away."

"If it really was some kind of reptile creature, it could have been hiding under the water waiting for one of you to come after it."

"Or just hiding. We weren't trying to be quiet."

"They're over there."

"Thanks, Nancy."

They both looked up. Diane Brown had just opened the door, holding it for Nancy, who was leaving. As Diane walked across the room, Ahmed slid through the door before it could completely close.

"Ha, made it." Ahmed jogged over to the Big Board to look at what had people's interest, got there at the same time Diane did.

"It's not like you couldn't have opened it again, you know," Diane said to her left as she placed her hands on the table, leaned over it and looked at the photo. "Why don't you guys render this into a map?"

"We're still trying to figure out what we have."

"As I was saying, we didn't attempt to look under the water but we did poke it with the steel rods we had and those steps continued as far as we could poke."

"So we have a set of stairs," announced Ahmed. "But to where?"

"Either it is some kind of maintenance closet," Diane speculated. "And that seems unlikely, why build a place to store supplies below the lower level? Or it was an underground entrance to the building."

"Wait a minute," Logan began. "Aren't we jumping to conclusions here? How do we know this thing was some kind of building anyway?"

Diane expanded the view to cover all the area from the pit to Petersville. Then she instructed the computer to convert the image to a line-drawn map, like she had suggested when she came in. "If you look at the size, spacing, and locations of the clearings; it begins to look a lot like the city maps from Earth we have stored in the computer." She called up several of the city layouts in memory and displayed them sequentially on the table, going back to the map of Belenius 3 after she was done.

"Yeah, you could be right." Logan began.

Jeff followed up, "I don't believe right angles appear naturally unless something forces nature into them."

"And almost all of the clearings have a right angle depression or feature in them," Ahmed finished the group thought.

"What we can't see from this, is if these clearings have an underground connection. Except here." Diane pointed to the blue rectangle Logan had circled earlier.

"Maybe we could try pumping it out," Ahmed suggested.

"Think about it. If this is an underground tunnel connecting all, or even some of the clearings, it would have a massive volume. Jeff, do we have any pumps with enough capacity to move that much water?"

"She's right, Ahmed. Good idea, but not one we can accomplish."

"We don't have any diving gear," Logan said. "But could we use some of the EVA suits?"

"At least we could test Diane's idea."

"I don't know if they're rated for underwater use," Jeff began.

Diane pulled up some old NASA photos of astronauts training in EVA suits—a bit more bulky than the ones they had—in a large swimming pool.

"Okay, let's try it." Jeff tapped his earpiece radio link. "Clint, prepare a shuttle to take four of us to the Black's pit."

"Any particular module, boss?"

"Use the cargo one. We'll be bringing EVA suits."

Chapter 24

Exploring Underwater

Rather than wearing their suits climbing down the chain ladder, they set up the crane lift over the pit and winched the suits down to the bottom. Clint, as the safety man, helped each of them in turn, checked over their equipment, and secured the rope connecting them to each other and finally to him at the entrance.

Inside their bubble helmets, they would be talking to each other by radio. It was agreed that there would be continuous radio chatter so Clint would know if he needed to haul them out. They had mounted the spare power winch just outside the stairway for that purpose.

"You guys go silent, I'm going to call out three times. On the third no answer, I'm pulling you out."

"And three quick tugs, you do the same thing." Jeff added.

"If I feel three tugs from you," Logan confirmed. "Then we turn around and come back out."

"We've got the plan," Diane who would be taking the lead finished. "Can we get going?" She walked over to the top step and started down. Jeff followed, then Ahmed and finally Logan.

As they dropped below the water level, each of them turned on their lighting systems. They went down a total of twenty-five steps before reaching a level platform. The bottom of the stairs spread into a corridor about twenty feet wide and stretched out of their light's range.

Every step they took stirred up some of the debris they walked through, debris that had floated to the bottom over the course of who knew how many years. "Keep a slow, steady pace," Diane said. "Shuffle your feet. It might keep this stuff down." She slowly shuffled forward and the particles didn't rise as far up.

"What do you think this thing is made of?" Their connecting rope was long enough for Ahmed to shuffle over to the wall and run his gloved hand along it.

"Watch what you're doing," Logan cautioned. "You spring a leak and we're heading back."

Ahmed jerked his hand away, then noticed the burrs protruding from the stone like material. "I see what you mean."

"Clint, you hearing us okay?"

"Roger that, boss man. How's things looking down there?"

"This thing looks like a long hallway. It's completely filled with water. I don't even see any air pockets."

"The tunnel is opening up ahead," Diane called back.

They shuffled a little faster, Logan slowing down when the floating debris in front of him reached his waist. Finally came to where Diane was standing.

Ten feet in front of her, just inside the reach of her light beams, the ground they were walking on dropped off. But the walls on either side widened outside the range of their lights.

"Keep a tight grip, I'm going to have a look over that edge." Diane shuffled over to where the tunnel fell off and shined her light down. "I can see the bottom. Its round, circling away from this point. It looks like it gets five feet deep before starting up again, of course I have no idea how deep any debris filling might be."

"I can't see the other side from here, can you?"

"No. I can see the bottom rising again but not back up to level."

"Ah." Ahmed broke in. "Has anyone looked up?"

"The ceiling's gone from five feet over head to out of light range. This is one big chamber."

Jeff used his left arm controller and called up his laser compass. He pointed his left arm to his left, then his right. His computer measured the directions of the two and displayed the results in his helmet's heads up virtual screen.

"This thing is running north and south, paralleling whatever that pit was back there."

"I don't know how much further you guys can follow that thing. You've already used most of the cable I have up here."

"Right or left?" Jeff pointed to the area above the new pit.

"I don't think it really matters." Diane in the lead turned to her right and proceeded shuffling.

They stayed close to the walls as they moved in a southerly direction. This time, Ahmed kept his hands away from that wall. "What do you guys think all these bits and pieces stuck to the wall are?"

"Did anyone bring any sample containers?"

"I've got a couple of bags, Jeff." Ahmed had a little trouble getting them out and opened underwater. After which he took a screwdriver off his equipment belt and scraped a couple of pieces off the wall and placed them in different bags.

They walked a few feet after Ahmed had finished before Diane called a halt. They had reached a wall preventing them from walking any further. "It looks like we're at the end of the line, guys."

"This area stops, but that pit keeps going," Logan noted as he caught up. "Clint, how much more cable have we got?"

"Not more than ten feet."

"So much for that thought."

"We'll need more equipment to explore these tubes, Logan." Jeff motioned for them to return.

Ahmed tugged at his line connecting him to Jeff. Then he pointed up. "What if we inflate these suits a bit and see if we can find the top of this thing?"

"That's a great idea," Logan said before Jeff could be overly cautious.

"We just need neutral buoyancy, then a couple of arm strokes would carry us up. We couldn't swim in space, but we can here." Diane was already dumping some of her air supply into her suit. Inflating it and lifting her off the floor.

"Don't waste too much air, we still have to get back."

Logan looked at the monitor mounted to his right arm. "Jeff, we've only used five percent. I think we can risk it."

"But not too much. We still have to get back down."

Ahmed began floating up to the height Diane was at. Both were unable to go any higher until Jeff and Logan joined them.

They floated about ten feet off the floor and found their lights reaching a ceiling to the chamber. Another twelve feet and they were touching it.

"That's it guys, you're out of cable."

"That makes this place twenty-two feet tall."

"And look, the tunnel is not all the way to this ceiling."

"I think we need a much more planned out expedition."

"But let's head back. Call it quits for today."

"I can find out what these samples are." Ahmed patted the pouch on his belt.

Jeff released some of the air in his suit and began pulling the rest of them back down. "Clint, start taking up the slack."

Logan was being pulled towards the tunnel they had come down before he landed on the ground. Half an hour later, he was emerging from the underwater stairway.

"You guys have fun?" Clint asked as Jeff emerged.

"You're not going to believe the pictures we took."

Chapter 25

Debrief and Plan

As Jeff approached the entrance to Town Hall, the doors slid open. "People have been busy while we've been gone." He went straight forward and pulled open the door to the Situation Room, handing it off to Logan as they entered.

"Diane, did you finish uploading our images into the computer?" Jeff walked across the room, tossing his hat off to one of the tables against the left wall. While it fell short by an inch, Jeff was already falling into one of the central table's chairs and didn't notice.

"Before we landed." She walked over to one of the control stations, dropped her equipment belt to the floor, sat down and started calling up the files they'd recorded.

The room darkened as the overhead display brought them back into the underwater tunnel they had come from. She advanced the images to the end of it and into the cavern they had found before turning back.

"Can you remove the water and brighten the image?"

With a few commands the water vanished and the chamber they had been in lightened. "Best I can do, any more and I'll start washing out the details."

Jeff got out of his chair and walked over to one of the walls. He reached out and touched one of the spots attached to it. "You got samples of this stuff, right, Ahmed?"

Ahmed had let the door close about the time Diane was draining the image. He patted his sample pouch. "I got a couple of good ones."

"How soon can you let us know what they are?"

Ahmed had taken one of the sample bags from his pouch and was looking at its contents. "It almost looks like it has a square corner." He placed the bag back in his pouch before answering. "It shouldn't take too long. I already have the analyzer set up for the paint runs I had been doing for Clarence."

"In the meantime, Diane, pull up the line plot of the area we covered." The photo image they had been looking at disappeared and a line map appeared in its place.

"Can you bring up the pit?"

The line map of the tunnel went away, to be replaced by another line map.

"Bring both of them to the same scale and reduce to half size. Plot the image on the table."

The line drawings appeared on the table, considerably brighter than their projected views, and merged at the stairway heading underground.

"Now bring up the map of all the recorded clearings and overlap it on this map." A confusing series of images appeared on the table's projection board. "With correct scaling, of course."

The line drawing scaled itself down to fit the clearing satellite image. The larger underwater tunnel pointed between two of the nearest clearings to the one with the stairway. Jeff touched the red palette and reached over to the closer end of the tunnel and drew a line between where they had been to the next clearing. Then he continued that line, connecting about a dozen others.

Logan stared at the map for a minute, then turned to another computer monitor and called up Earth historical files. On the smaller screen, he pulled up a map of the London Underground. As he was looking at it, Ahmed came over to see what he was doing. Diane, standing on the far side of the table, stared across at the image.

Logan pushed himself over to the main table, dabbed himself a green finger and drew a series of connecting circles, anchoring the first one to the underwater chamber. He looked up at the four other people surrounding the table.

It was Clint who broke the silence. "Are we saying that was a transportation system? A subway?"

"I think I'd better get back to the lab and find out what these spots are." Ahmed was out of the Situation Room, letting the door swing shut behind him.

"They had a water-based transportation system?" Logan asked.

"It looks that way," Clint added.

"And if they did, that means all the clearings could be connected."

"And that could be how Mike's alligator creature got out of that pit."

"We need something to explore those tunnels. Something better than our EVA suits."

Clint broke the silence that ensued. "How many escape pods we still have left?"

"Should be a couple of hundred. We've only cannibalized a few dozen."

"You're not thinking..." Jeff began.

"Gravitational units can work in any medium that the object they're attached to can push through. Outfit a few pods with them and you'll have submarines, like in that old movie you guys used to watch."

"We can use the rocket thrusters for propulsion."

"They have an oxygen and food supply for about two weeks. Along with enough communication gear to keep us in touch with each other."

"It might work," Jeff conceded. "It's not like we're actually going twenty thousand leagues under the sea."

"Nor—hopefully—fighting any sea monsters."

"Aren't they too big to turn around in those tunnels?"

"We make a train. Cable them together with the last one on reversed. That way if we get into a jam, it can pull us out."

"I think we have a plan. Let's get started building our underwater subway train."

Chapter 26

News from Afar

In the week it took them to remove, transport, and begin outfitting a three-pod train, along with the two-pod backup, Ahmed finished his analysis.

Knowing Jeff would be welding on the escape pods, Ahmed radioed ahead to let him know he was coming. Jeff stopped his weld, acknowledged the call, turned to see Ahmed heading his way, evaluated how much time Ahmed would take walking over to him, flipped his visor back down and finished the weld. He was pulling the stick out of his electrode before Ahmed could get close enough to hurt his eyes.

"Plastic. A polyvinyl chloride, to be more specific. There were traces of wood fiber imbedded in the material. I'd say something backing up an extremely thin sheet of PVC." Ahmed had found Jeff at their Air Field working on the pod train. He was welding rings between the four thrusters of the pods so a cable could be clipped to it.

Jeff draped the electrode over the power supply, having switched everything off. He removed his gloves and set them down over the electrode, then took off his welding helmet and set it on top of everything.

"It looks like it's time to contact Howard again." Jeff ran his hands against each other and started walking over to Town Hall. "Let's see what Clarence makes of your find."

* * *

"Howard, how are things going up there?" Jeff sat in front of the communications computer in the Situation Room with Ahmed at his side. Clint had seen the two leaving the Air Field and followed them over; he was now sitting on the other side of Jeff.

"Jeff, it's good to hear from you again. It gets kinda lonely up here when very few people speak the same language as you."

Jeff chuckled. "There was a time when you wanted that solitude, Howard." He looked at Clint and mouthed without vocalizing, "There's still hope for him."

"Not any more. Being up here has cured me of any residual capitalist phobias I brought to Belenius 3."

"How are you coming with their language?"

"I'm getting a word or two. But nothing sticks. I can grunt 'Good Morning' to them, but that's only because it is actually a grunt."

"I assume you're trying?"

"Marsha and Billy are doing better than I am. I spend most of my time with Clarence digging through what artifacts the Raffians let us work on."

"Is everyone eating okay?"

"They have some kind of root that grows like crazy in this cave. They know a lot of ways to cook the dang thing.

So, yeah, we're eating okay. I still wish I could go outside. I even volunteered to hunt some meat for the villagers but their Shaman just pointed to their longo root and said it was enough. Or at least that's what Tommy told me he said."

"See you learned a new word."

"What?"

"Longo."

"You don't need to cheer me up. Helping the Raffians is making the time fly past."

"Okay, is Clarence available? I need to talk with him."

"Anything interesting?"

"He can tell you after we lose this satellite connection."

"Hey, Jeff. What you got for me?" the voice on the radio changed to Clarence Knowles.

"We took an EVA suit trip into that stairway of Mike's. It looks like some kind of underground, underwater transportation system."

There was a pause before Clarence replied. "Look for a series of vents near the bottom of the tunnels. Most subways on Earth were below the water table. They used pumps to keep back the water. I'm not saying it isn't a water-based transportation system, but let's rule everything else out before we jump to that conclusion."

"We're getting ready to take another trip down there in a couple of days. We've got several of the Endeavor's escape pods outfitted with gravity units and are going to use them as one-man submarines."

"You guys have all the fun."

"Ahmed has found pieces of PVC on the walls of the tunnel."

"Pipes?"

"No, they looked more like flat sheets, or what was left of flat sheets."

"Get the biggest piece you can and send me a picture next week."

Ahmed reached over Jeff and keyed the satellite mic. "Sure thing."

"Queue up the computer for a download. I have a data packet to send you guys."

Jeff pointed to Clint, who prepared the computer to receive Clarence's file. When Clint nodded, Jeff said, "Go ahead." The download took about a minute before the computer dinged it was finished.

"Looks like our time is about up." Jeff was looking at the track of the satellite they were using to communicate.

"I wish this thing was overhead more than once a week."

"So do I, but we put the thing in a progression to allow us to cover the whole planet every week."

"Well, see you next week, then."

"Bye, my friend." Then he placed the mike in its holder. "I don't think the last of that got through."

"At least they're safe," Clint responded.

"Let's take a look at what's in that data packet he sent us." Ahmed spun around in his chair and began calling the file up on the Command table.

"The Raffians have accepted us into their community as guests. They are not asking us to do community projects, even though Howard keeps asking his children if there is anything they would like us to do.

"The McCurdels have been assigned a home in the northern side of the village and I have one right next to them. Both homes are on the ground level, since I do not have the dexterity needed to climb their ladders. They're simply carved notches in the walls of the cavern leading to the upper ledge. It is amazing how fast the Raffians can scramble up them. Occasionally the older children make a game of climbing by using the whips they carry to wrap around a peg they have driven into the upper walls and climbing up without using the notches.

"Oh, the cord we thought these people projected from their hands before we got to know them, turns out to be a plant-based woven rope, tapered at one end with a wooden handle on the other. Tommy has been telling me about how the Raffian use it and their claws to scale trees very fast. They can even drop one of the large cats we've seen whenever they need to.

"For the winter months, their diet consists entirely of the longo root that grows along the roof of this cavern and all of the side tunnels. They have so many ways to cook this tuber that I have not grown tired of it yet. But I am looking forward to a steak when we get back to Petersville.

"The beds we use at night are made of wood. Obviously brought up from the forest miles below our altitude. But it is patterned on one made of metal in one of the glass cases in their library temple. I wish I had a mattress like the one in the case but I know if they removed it, it wouldn't survive the winter. So I sleep on a bag stuffed with grass and leaves. Something in that sealed case is protecting the objects inside.

"Even though we do not have chores, we have divided up into two groups. Marsha and the children work and play with the Raffians, trying to learn as much of their language and customs as possible. Howard and I spend as much time as M'cron will let us studying the artifacts in the glass cases and trying to interpret the paintings on their 'library' wall.

"Inside the case are several items that look like paper books. I have been working on deciphering the symbols on their spines but they do not correspond to any of the cave paintings. There are painting supplies, like those used on the most sophisticated of the cave paintings, piles of shiny discs with a device they must go into next to them, a myriad of household objects, some the Raffians have copied for their own use, others I can understand but they don't have a clue about, and most of which I haven't fathomed their use. But like I said, a bed, and though I wish mine was more comfortable, I'm glad they don't have us sleeping on the cold floor.

"For it is cold in the village, about 50 degrees. I know it would be worse were we outside. We have enough furs to keep everyone warm. Most of them are patchwork affairs, sewn together with strips of tanned leather. It's surprising, but they don't smell bad.

"Anyhow, we're settled in now. I should have a lot more data on the next transmission. As long as my batteries hold out. A solar charger isn't much good if you can't see the sun. Clarence Knowles, out."

Over a hundred photographs followed his report.

Chapter 27

Submarine Train

Clint lowered the cargo door from the shuttle's driver while Jeff, Logan, Ahmed, and Diane waited to unload it. The ramp hit the ground with a clank as the module's metal ramp hit the concrete of the clearing floor. Logan and Ahmed went inside and powered up the gravity units on the three pods making up the first train. Once they were floating inches off the floor, the two men pulled the lead pod forward and out of the cargo module. The other two pods, which were tethered to the first, followed. Once out—and they came out without losing any altitude—all three were floating a couple of feet off the ground. Logan, Jeff and Ahmed each opened a pod door, climbed up into them and readjusted their units to bring them down to within inches of the pit's floor.

Clint came out of the cockpit after raising the ramp back up. "It's going to take some fancy adjustments to get those things down that stairway."

Jeff closed the door on the middle pod. "Are you volunteering to drive?"

He stopped his forward movement and backed up a step. "No, sirree. I'll stick to the sky, where nothing can come crashing down on me except rain."

Jeff heard the door of the lead pod close, followed by the whine of its sealing mechanism. A moment later, all three pods lifted straight up exactly one inch, then back down exactly two. "Doesn't seem so hard to me," Diane said through the radio link. "Now if Logan and Ahmed can get suited up, I'd like to get going."

Jeff and Clint helped the other two men into EVA suits, then into the middle pod. They stowed their helmets rather than wearing them, to conserve their suits' air supply. They brought them along in case they had to go outside the pod while they were submerged.

"Be careful of the control wire running between each car. If it gets cut..." Clint held open the door to Jeff's rearward facing pod.

"Each pod has separate controls in case we become disconnected." Jeff held up his hand to forestall Clint's next objection. "We have magnetic grapplers for emergencies. And a complete toolbox in the middle pod if we have to stop for repairs."

"At least promise me you'll stay in communication with me while I worry?"

"Will you two stop jaw-jacking," Diane called over the radio.

"I'd better get going." Jeff gave Clint a quick hug and stepped up into his pod. "Keep the home fires burning until we get back."

"The what?"

"Forget it. Just an old Earth saying." He closed his pod door and sealed it. Sitting in the pilot's seat, he toggled the view screen to project what Diane saw. Then he set the controls on remote and let her take them over. "Ready on the back end," he radioed forward.

"Ready in the middle," Ahmed said.

"Clint, can you pull us over into the stairway?" Diane instructed her ground crew.

Jeff saw him wave through Diane's screen, place his hand on the forward loop they had welded onto her pod and begin walking towards the opening to the underwater chamber. It was disconcerting seeing the turn moments before he actually felt his own pod make the same one, in reverse.

He could see Clint line up her pod in front of the stairs, then walk around the side. A minute later, his own pod began moving again. "Getting everyone lined up, Clint?"

"I'll make it easier for you guys to get started down that narrow passageway. Hang on, and I'll give Diane a forward push."

"Let me know when you're about to so I can drop the pods down the steps," Diane acknowledged the plan.

"Okay, I'm in position. Whenever you're ready."

"Pod one descending."

Jeff could see and feel the movement of Clint's push.

"Getting ready to push the middle."

"Go. Pod two descending."

"Your turn, Jeff."

"Clint, are you ready to push?" Diane called back.

"That's what I said."

"Then push. Pod three, get your butt down here."

Jeff could feel the resistance as his pod contacted the water and fell through it under the control of Pod One. The screen view already showed him that Diane was in the connecting tunnel and moving away from the staircase. He toggled his screen to a rearward view and watched the stairs recede. Then flipped it back to a forward view to keep an eye on their journey.

They had angled the pods' four engines slightly so they weren't firing directly into the pod behind them. Jeff felt a slight jolt, pulling him away from his seat, to mark the point where Diane had fired her engines to give the train some forward thrust.

"Next time, say something before you accelerate. Some of us are travelling backwards," Jeff complained.

"That's what seatbelts are for." He'd get no mercy from her.

They drifted towards the main chamber, Diane wasn't using continuous burns. Once she had her pod completely in it, she fired her starboard engines and made a left turn.

"Why left?" Jeff asked.

"Why not?" she responded. "We never established a protocol for this mission."

"Then left it is," Ahmed answered back.

"Once we complete the turn, I'm going to magnetize the cable and use Pod Two's engines for awhile."

Jeff flipped back to his own view and watched as his own pod made the turn into the circular transportation tunnel. A second later, he felt the jolt as the cable between the pods jerked straight. The cables now acted as rods between them and Pod Two would be pushing the train until it ran out of fuel.

He toggled back to a forward view as Diane accelerated the train slightly, they were making about three miles an hour so they didn't miss anything. And this time they brought enough light to fully illuminate the tunnel. They were able to see the sides of the tunnel as they travelled it at the pace of a normal walk.

"Clint, are you getting a video feed from down here?"

"It's a little intermittent."

"We'll have a better record when we get back."

"Hey, Jeff, do you guys see those cracks on the walls?"

Jeff looked over to the right side of his screen. Then toggled to a rear view to get a better look. "Some of them look like they're running from top to bottom here. Nope, not top," Jeff stretched into the pod bubble and tried looking straight up. "They keep going completely around the top. Some of them look to be an inch wide with large chunks of material chipped out of them. Diane, are you seeing these?"

Right about then, Jeff was pitched back into his seat. She had brought the train to a complete stop. As the shock passed, Jeff toggled back to a front view again. The tunnel in front of them was half filled with broken sections of the tunnel. The gap above the debris pile was not large enough for any of the pods to transverse.

Not only had some of the walls collapsed in, but there was a hole in the ceiling. Diane angled one of her camera towards the ceiling. The hole was only about two feet up, not enough to give her clearance to drive the pods through.

"Looks like we're heading back. You want to drive Jeff, or should I?"

He toggled his view screen rearward. More pieces of the larger cracks were beginning to break away from the walls and fall to the floor. "I will." He fired all four engines and brought the train up to ten miles an hour.

Before they could return to the main chamber they had started in, things had bounced off the top of the pods several times. By the time Jeff had brought the train to a halt in the chamber, five foot chunks of debris were falling from the tunnel they had just emerged from. Enough so that they were not going back that way again.

"Okay, decision time." Jeff began the radio conference. "Do we continue on down the other tunnel and hope it doesn't collapse also? Or abort and find another way to find those alligator men?"

"I'm for getting out of here," Logan said.

"It's too much of a coincidence that those walls collapsed while we were in there." Ahmed added.

"It had to be some turbulence we caused that brought them down," Diane concluded.

"So we call it a day?"

"It's just not safe down here." Diane turned the train to her left and headed back up the tunnel to the stairs leading to the surface.

Chapter 28

Difference of Opinion

Nancy was standing in front of the module hanger when they returned that afternoon. She'd been waiting in a chair on the porch of the maintenance building next to the hanger, but once she saw the shuttle approach, she got up to meet them. She had the hanger doors open by the time Clint was ready to back in.

Since the cargo module needed to be unloaded before it could be stowed away, Clint stopped in the middle of the hanger's work space, Jeff jumped out of the other side of the driver and began disconnecting the module. Diane and Ahmed came out the module's side door, while Logan lowered the ramp in back to begin unloading.

"What's up, Nan?" Jeff was at the side controls, lowering the module to the ground. After disconnecting from the now-leaving cockpit, all maneuvering of the module would be done from the module's controls on its right side.

"Are you finished with this foolishness?"

"By foolishness, you mean?" He kept dialing the gravitational units down until the module rested on the earthen floor of the hanger rather than floating above it.

"Chasing after 'Alligator Men'!" As Jeff turned away from the module's controls, she planted herself in his face, about two inches from his nose to her eyeballs.

It forced him to take a step back. "We haven't found them yet, if that's what you mean."

"I mean looking for them! I need every able-bodied person in this colony if I am to get enough housing built by winter. And you go dragging my best crane operator, my chemist, as well as two experienced laborers away from their duties. Not to mention the people you have trapped up north with the natives."

"What do you want me to do? These 'Alligator Men' pose a real threat to our community."

"Just like the Jabberwockies—oops, I mean Raffians—did?"

"Mike says they're more aggressive."

"And yet we haven't even seen one in the year we've been living here, until he went digging!"

"Yes, we have no idea where they're lurking."

"Housing, or lack thereof, is a much more urgent threat to our community. My God, Jeff, we still have people berthing on the Endeavor. Their only option, when we have to cannibalize their portion of it, will be to live in tents. I could throw up some apartment buildings for them, but they're willing to suffer it out until they can have the home they were promised on the trip here. You owe it to them."

"I owe them a safe community. I can't just ignore this new threat."

"Well, you, Ron, and a couple of the elders who are too feeble to swing a hammer, can keep chasing your bogie men. I'm taking Clint, Logan, Ahmed, and Diane; and putting them to some useful work."

"They need to help me unload."

"Do it yourself. The rest of us have real work to do." She turned and walked over to where the others were beginning to unload the escape pods from the back of the module.

"You three." She pointed in their direction. "Leave that. You're going back to work. Now, let's go get Clint." She turned and headed out the sliding door of the hanger, not waiting to see if they followed her.

Logan looked over to Jeff, who was now walking to the back of the module.

Jeff just motioned with his head that they should follow her. "I'll finish up," he said as he passed Logan and jumped up on the unloading ramp.

* * *

It was going on dusk by the time Jeff finished stowing all the gear they'd used and finagled the module back into its parking space. He headed over to the common mess hall to get his supper. He was also one of those without a home and the food stasis chamber in his cabin on the Endeavor was bare. The single bottle of beer wouldn't get him through the night.

On his tray he had a bowl of stew (made from edible native roots and wildlife), an individual bread roll, a plate of steamed green beans (part of their first crop from the seeds they brought from Earth), and a small bowl of pudding (he didn't ask). He found a table where several older individuals were having a card game and went over to it.

"Mind if I sit down?"

"We already have a full game here, son."

"I just want to eat." *And maybe talk,* he added internally. He picked a corner of the long table and set his tray on the end. Four men and one woman were playing a game he didn't recognize as he pulled up a chair and began to dig in.

"Don't eat so fast, son." The old lady looked over her cards and said. "You need to really chew that squirrel meat or it just sits in your belly spewing gas."

He remembered the last time he had eaten this type of stew and forced himself to spend more time chewing the bits of meat into smaller and smaller pieces before he swallowed. "Good advice, thanks."

"At least you get to do something, Harvey. All we can do is sit around playing Gin all day," the lady said while slapping a card on the central pile and pulling another from the deck.

"I didn't expect we'd travel all this way just to be put out to pasture," the man across from her said.

"I don't get to do a lot." Jeff recognized Harvey Frances, once he had a name to work with. "And what I do is constantly inspected by that Flannigan woman or her husband."

"Well, I can't even go for a walk," added the man now discarding a card and drawing another. "Without one of my kids telling me to go back inside and rest."

"We need something to do, move around more, get some exercise." As the man pumped his arms up and down for emphasis, the man next to him looked over at the cards he was no longer hiding. Then he pushed the card he had ready to discard back in his hand and drew a different one.

Jeff cut his roll in two and placed both pieces in his stew to suck up the remaining liquid in it. "If you guys are looking for something to do? Something that I think is important?"

"Just who do you think you are, young man?"

The man sitting across from Jeff took a hard look at him before saying, "That's Jeff Martin, McCurtel's colonial administrator." He set his cards face down on the table. "Just what do you have in mind, son?"

Chapter 29

Recruiting

"It was a boring trip," responded Nathan Reynolds. "What can I say? I specialized in playing video games. We didn't expect to land in my lifetime."

"Fortunately that's just what I need right now." Jeff was holding up a small radio-controlled platform. It had fans in all six sides of the micro-computer box mounted in the center. "I want to thank Jonathan Culpepper for designing this little beauty, that you, Mr. Reynolds, are going to fly down the underground tunnels."

Jon nodded acknowledgement. "I still have to seal the components against moisture," he added. "A little spray-on plastic should keep them working."

"And my son said I'd never amount to anything."

"How soon will it be finished?" Jeff handed their remote underwater vehicle back to its creator.

"I can spray it on the way up."

"Ron, you've got the control unit mounted in the cargo module and synched to the main computer so we can track its signal?"

"You'll have a complete map ready by the time you get back."

"I'm sure glad Nancy decided that weather prediction was important." He slapped Ron on the back of his shoulders and started walking to the door. "Let's get this show on the road."

"What about us?" Simon Brown asked. He was sitting on the far side of the central table, studying monitors with the satellite imagery of the clearings.

"Keep doing what you're doing." Jeff turned to talk to the parents of Carl—the Endeavor's engineer—while he held the door for the others leaving. "When the satellite goes over head, use whatever cameras you can to figure out the pattern of the buildings that had been built in those clearings."

Mary elbowed her husband in the ribs. "Just like astrometric navigation on Endeavor."

* * *

Jeff took a chance on the elderly gamer and after a few quick lessons on the shuttle's controls, let him pilot the already airborne ship. He took the controls back from the man as they began the trickier descent into the pit.

After he set it down, he released his straps and left the driver and entered the side door of the module. Nathan came in on the other side.

"Time to power it up and drop her off," Jeff closed the door behind him. The stairs leading to the tunnel were on the far side, the side Nathan had come in.

The fans on the little craft purred into existence. Nathan walked over to the control board mounted onto the floor of the module. He pulled the chair along its track until he was comfortably close enough to work the controls, then locked the chair into place.

Jon stepped out of the module.

Jeff called over to Nathan, "Don't forget to buckle in. We're going to follow this guy in the air. Expect the ride to get bumpy, I don't fly her as well as you do."

Over their radio, Jon called them. "I set the gravitational unit on the bottom of it for our current level. I am setting it in the water now and she is floating and waiting for your commands, Nate."

"Thanks. Dropping her into the water now."

Jeff walked over to the door, opened it and watched Jon work.

"She's descending. ... There come the lights. ... And now they've disappeared. How's she looking on your monitor?"

"Doing great, Jon."

"Come on back," Jeff hollered from the module's door. "We'll track her from the air."

"She's only got a twelve-hour battery," Jon said as he stepped back into the module.

"There's a series of clearings that we think connect to this tunnel system, starting about six miles from here. Hopefully, we can find somewhere to bring it up there and give her a recharge." Jeff pulled out a map Ron had prepared for them and unrolled it against the side wall of the module. "We're here and they start there. Assuming you turn right when you get to the main chamber, Nathan."

"Right, it is." Jeff just happened to be looking at his shoulder when he addressed Nathan and saw the forward light from their ROV make the turn he had suggested.

He rolled up the map and handed it to Jon. "I guess I had better get us airborne if we are going to follow it." He opened the side door and left the two men in the module. Then made his way to the cockpit and lifted out of the pit. "Give me new coordinates very five minutes, Nathan. Or would you prefer Nate?" he radioed the back section.

"Either one. As long as you don't call me 'sir'."

* * *

They followed the signal coming from the little drone for several hours. Jeff landed in one of the safer clearings and came back to check on his people.

"How are we doing?" he said as he entered the door. The blast of bright sunlight made Jon throw his hands in front of his eyes. Nathan had been keeping the inside of the module dark to assist him in seeing what the ROV filmed.

"Fine, as soon as I get my night vision back," Jon said as Jeff closed the door again. "I'm having Nate find a side tunnel and come up in a clearing." After rubbing his eyes one last time, Jon grabbed the map and held it to the wall. "We're thinking it should be this one," he pointed at a clearing on the map, "about a mile from where we are now. She should have plenty of juice for us to recover her."

"Want me to head for that clearing?"

"Let's wait for Nate to find the way to it. Or a way into whatever one we can get to."

"Have you been running into a lot of debris?"

"Nothing we couldn't get through. The system does seem to be collapsing, though."

"Have any of them been too small for a man-sized being to have swam through?"

"Man-sized?"

"Have any of the holes been less than two feet in diameter?"

"No, Nate's always found a spot near the ceiling large enough to get through with plenty of room to spare."

"Got one," Nathan called from off to their side. "Heading down it," he paused for a couple of seconds, "now!"

"Send me the coordinates and I'll fly us there." Jeff was out of the module and into the cockpit in under a minute. Of course, he had to fight against the bright light to do so.

* * *

"I'm staying just off the canopy of whatever is in this clearing until I can shove a pole into solid dirt," Jeff radioed back. "You guys stay put until I know if there is anything for us to walk on."

"There's debris at the foot of the stairs," Nathan radioed forward. "But I think I can see light coming from the top of them."

Jeff locked the gravitational units to hold the shuttle an inch off the ground and hovered there. He grabbed one of the metal poles that were now kept behind the pilot's seat in all five of the driver's cockpits, extended it to its full eight feet, and shoved it into the ground just outside his door. It went in as far as he was willing to shove it, with no resistance.

He squirmed over to the co-pilot's seat and tried that side with the same results. "We're not safe here. I'm moving the shuttle about ten feet to the right and trying again. Sit tight."

He had to repeat these moves four times before he found solid ground beneath the shuttle. He was on the very edge of the clearing when he set it down and went into the module.

"Okay, we're down. Now we just have to find where your ROV is in this mess of pits?"

"I've managed to fly her up the stairs and out of the water. There appears to be a lot of open space for me to fly through but I have to be more careful working in air than I was underwater. The resistance of the water actually helped me keep control."

Jeff opened the tool locker and took out a two foot machete. "Just let me know where you want a hole cut." He reached into one of the wall mounted cabinets and pulled out a hand held positioning device. "Give me the coordinates when you get them." He was out the door and circling the pit before the others could react to the bright, dark blink of the door.

"I've got it up to the top. The Z axis puts it inches below the surface. I'm sending you the X, Y coordinates now."

Jeff walked over to where Nathan had indicated and began hacking away at the roots making up the canopy for this pit. According to Nathan, the ROV was along one edge of the stone wall making up this pit.

Within minutes, Jeff had hacked open a hole large enough for Nathan to fly the little rover out. Jeff caught it and switched it off. He brought it into the module and plugged it into the shuttle's solar recharger.

"Give it a half hour and we can drop it in again."

Chapter 30

Drone Discoveries

Nathan maneuvered the ROV through another five large chambers before deciding it was again time to bring it up for a recharge. They had covered several more miles, getting further and further away from the Rockefeller River and Petersville.

He sent it down the tunnel that should lead them to another pit so they could extract it. The tunnel had its steps after the usual distance but they ran off to the side. The tunnel kept going straight ahead.

"This is weird, guys, the tunnel just keeps going. I almost missed these steps," he pointed at the video feed from the ROV, "here. What do you think, Jeff?" Nathan set the craft to hover while he looked over to Jeff for advice.

"How much power has that thing got?" He slid one of the tracked chairs to the station next to Nathan and sat down.

"I'd say we've used just under fifty percent battery power. Nothing we've run into so far has really put a drain on her systems." He rotated the ROV so that they could see up the stairs and the daylight at the top of them.

"We've got an out if we need it. Why is there a side tunnel here? Let's keep going." He watched the monitor as Nate swung the craft to head forward in the tunnel they were going down. After a few more minutes, it emerged into another of the large underwater chambers. This one a bit more broken up, with large chunks of the walls and ceiling laying on the floor. But not enough to obscure that it was another opening that one of the transport tunnels came through. To either side, they could see the round tunnel coming into the chamber and leaving again.

"Let's keep going."

"Which way?"

"Keep going south and east." Jeff pushed himself away from the weather forecasting station and spun the chair on its axis to allow him to use the communication's computer on the opposite side of the module. He touched his earpiece, "Ron, you still monitoring us?"

"I've been working the weather computer mostly. Nancy's been worried about the rain system coming in. There's an app analyzing your data as it comes in, so I really didn't have to. Oh, I see you've found a branching system."

"Yeah, could you send me the most up-to-date map the computer has drawn? I want to get an idea about what we've got here."

"Sure thing." Jeff heard the wheels of Ron's chair going across the floor as he was talking. "They should be on their way to you."

The map of what they had been surveying began to grow down the screen Jeff was looking at. "It's coming through now." As the image finished forming, "Thanks."

"No problem, anything else I can do for you?"

"Just keep Nancy happy."

He transferred the map, which was a line drawing of what they'd discovered, over to the large screen mounted on the front wall of the module and began studying it.

"This is looking more and more like that subway map you showed us, son." Jon walked over to the screen and began running his finger along one of the lines. "We've come this far. If this is a connecting subway loop, then it probably runs further south and east." He moved his finger along the path he was predicting.

Jon stepped over to one of the wall cabinets and pulled the paper photo map they brought out of it. He placed it against the projected line drawing. "Can you enlarge Ron's map to match, Jeff?"

"Sure." A few keystrokes later, the line map shined through the paper map, matching clearing for underwater chamber.

Jon stared at the map for a few minutes before announcing, "If we push, we should be able to get this clearing."

"Assuming that is the direction this thing goes."

"We both know there's only one way to answer that question."

"Everything looking good, Nate?"

"Right as rain, Jeff. But I could use another energy drink."

Jeff got out of his chair, walked over to the food stasis unit and pulled out the second to the last can of energy drink. "Make it count, you only have one more." He handed the can over to Nate's outstretched hand.

"Hey, pop the tab. I can't let this thing go."

"Sorry." Jeff took the can back, opened it and handed it back.

Nate took a large swig, "Thanks." It sounded to Jeff like he'd drank half the can in that swig.

The ROV powered its way down the tunnel. As it went further in, there was less debris that Nate had to maneuver around.

Chapter 31

Encampment Discovered

As Jeff brought the shuttle over the last stand of trees approaching the landing area, he could see over a hundred of the colonists waiting beside the hangers. He brought the shuttle down on Landing Pad Two, the same one he had used this morning. He stepped out to see what was happening.

Nancy strode out, with a few others to meet him. "I hope you've had your fun," she said on approaching. "But this snark hunt ends now!"

"We've gone over this, Nancy. You agreed I could keep looking for Mike's predators if I used people you couldn't."

She got right up in Jeff's face again. "But now you're taking essential people away from their jobs."

"Who?"

"Mr. Bales was unable to give us proper warning on the thunderstorm that hit our build this afternoon because he was uploading files to you."

"I let you know the chances it would hit your work area. It just came on faster than I predicted." Ron stood behind Nancy with several others.

"You were trying to work up to the last minute again, weren't you?" Jeff remembered this habit of hers. "Anyone get hurt?"

"No thanks to Mr. Bales."

"It's not his fault. You can't control nature like you could on the Endeavor. Ron can only give you the odds, then you have to decide what risks to take. Maybe you take too many?"

"He could keep an eye on things better if he wasn't fooling around with you."

"These predators could pose a real threat to us, but I won't know until I find and evaluate them."

"We left the jabberwockies alone and nothing happened to us."

"Other than two of our own being kidnapped. Granted, that turned out fine, but it could have gone the other way. I am not going to let something like 'alligator men' destroy this colony."

"Well, I say we put it to a vote and see if the colony wants your protection?"

"No!" Logan walked up to the front of the crowd and stood next to Jeff and Nancy. "One of the founding principles of this expedition was that the tyranny of the majority would not be inflicted on ANY of its members. AND Jeff is our leader, our duly elected leader."

"Leaders can be changed," Nancy challenged the two men.

"But even if they are, you still can NOT impose your will on Jeff Martin. Or myself. Jeff, I want to work with you on this project, if you'll have me."

"I can use all the help I can get, old friend."

"Then we'll help, too," about five members of the assembled crowd said also.

The side door to the module opened and Jon stepped down, one foot on the ground the other still in the module. "Hey, everyone. We think we've found where your boogie men are hiding."

Jeff and Logan rushed into the module, they were followed by Nancy, Ron, and Mike Black before Logan put a halt to anyone else. "There isn't room in here for everyone."

"Okay, what have you got, Jon? And it better be good, too many people out there are waiting for something." Nancy walked into the center of the room, daring the old man to have something worthwhile.

"On the way back, we mapped out the two subway circles we explored. Then, using the old Earth subway maps as a model, projected the courses of the subway here."

"So how does that get you to a location for the critters?" Mike asked.

"Since Ron gave us access to the satellite," Jon paused as Nancy growled, "we aimed its cameras at a few of our projected clearings. Ones that we hadn't already mapped out."

"No point in looking at what we already knew were there," Nate added.

"Right. On the far side of Buffett Bay, we found what looks like an encampment." Jon projected the satellite image on the wall monitor for everyone to see.

"You call that an encampment?" Nancy walked up to the monitor and scrutinized the image. "There's no houses, tents, not even lean-tos. And you think there is a community there?"

"If they are evolved from some type of reptile, and their escape from Mike's pit points in that direction, then their shelters would be that lake you see in the center of the image. What surprised me and drew my attention to this spot, is that fire a few feet away from the lake. It's controlled, those dark spots could be stones ringing it."

"Jonathan taught me everything I know about biology," Logan said. "If he says it's so, that's good enough for me to investigate the site."

"They're about two hundred miles away from us, with a projected access point to the Raffian subway," Nathan added when he saw heads nodding in agreement

"You're assuming the Raffians built it."

"And if they're flooded, what good is that?"

"Some Raffians had to." Nate said. "Maybe not the ones up north. But those tunnels are not natural, somebody had to have made them."

Jon added, "We may not be able to use them, but these creatures can. It's probably how they've been getting around without us seeing them."

"First thing in the morning, I'm taking a team over there." Jeff started towards the door. "Let's see how many people want to go."

Chapter 32

Not a Friendly Meeting

A people transport module was hooked up, despite Nancy's objections. Almost everyone from Nancy's rally volunteered for the trip. Jeff decided to hold the number to a dozen. Enough for a show of force without placing too many people in danger if the 'alligator people' were hostile. After all, they hadn't brought any weaponry with them from Earth.

"I understand the number of people, Jeff." Logan was riding as co-pilot on the first shuttle. "But it's kind of a bluff, isn't it. We don't have any weapons."

"If pressed, our machetes will do the job."

"Okay, any real weapons. I'm just saying these people aren't warriors. If attacked, they should run."

"Then we keep the shuttle powered up and manned while we're down there." Jeff leered over at Logan.

Logan's eyes sprung wide open. "Oh no. You're not keeping me behind as a pilot while you have all the fun."

"You agreed we needed a retreat strategy. You're it."

Logan was about to complain again, when Jeff pulled a hard right turn and pushed him deeper into his seat. They were staying over land, adding about fifty miles to the trip, rather than risking flying directly across the bay.

"And who can I trust with people's safety more that you? Logan, you can have the next one."

"There are more natives on this planet? Why did we land here in the first place?"

"Orbital surveys told us this planet was devoid of intelligent life, you know that."

"I'm beginning to doubt the analysis of the AIs we had."

"It's not going to be easy, but we're going to have to find some way to live with the Raffians without forcing our lifestyles on them. Too many indigenous cultures have died because of a more advanced invader."

"Yeah, it's just hard to think of ourselves as invaders."

"But that's exactly what we are."

"So what are we going to do about this group?"

"We were wrong about the jabberwockies. Maybe this is just another descendant culture."

"Then I hope they're as peaceful as the ones up north."

"So keep our escape route open while we find out if this is another indigenous culture; we can't risk contaminating it also."

* * *

Jeff took the shuttle in two circles around the area Jonathan had indicated was the settlement. They could see the fire pit and the lake. A mound of garbage about ten yards from the pit and several large sheets of something laying around the encampment. On the northern side of the clearing was an opened hole into an underground pit. But they could see none of the inhabitants who should be living down there.

"Attention, please," Jeff radioed the module. "I'm going to be setting down. I want two, and only two, people ready to help me see what reaction we get. If it's safe, you can bring the rest of you out. Logan's going to stay here and keep the engines warm."

"Roger that." Mike Black's voice came back.

Jeff spiraled his shuttle down to the clearing, keeping the lake between it and the pit. "Something is odd about that lake," Logan commented as they got lower.

"You mean how square-ish it is?"

"Yeah, makes me think they've cleared out one of the pits and filled it with water somehow."

"Maybe it's a swimming pool. Reptiles like water."

Jeff hovered the shuttle inches over the place he wanted to land. Logan opened his door and poked the ground to see that it was solid. He nodded at Jeff as he sat back into his seat, keeping the pole on his lap, and Jeff finished his descent.

"Switching controls over to you," he turned to Logan and dramatically lifted his hands away from them.

"You owe me."

As he stepped to the ground, he thought he saw ripples in the lake. He reached behind the pilot's seat and pulled out the other ground testing pole to carry as a walking stick. "I wish I had trained on stick fighting," he said to himself.

He turned to the side door of the module, tapped on it twice with his staff to let the people who were going to come with him know they could come out. "Stay close and keep this door open. If I say run, you high-tail it back immediately, no questions asked."

"I'm ready for those things now," Mike said as he twirled his machete around his hand as he stepped out.

"Put that thing away. You're more likely to hurt one of us than the creatures, the way you've been handling it." His wife, Mary, emerged right after him and dropped her hand on his to stop his playing around.

"She's right, Mike. Keep it on your belt where you can get to it in a hurry, but be prepared to run rather than fight, if we need to."

"You guys take all the fun out of life."

"Must be my day for doing that. Logan said the same thing." After Mary emerged, Jeff held up his hand to stop Francois and the rest from coming out. "Give us a second to look around. Three can jump back in faster than a dozen."

The three of them walked over to the lake and looked down. The sides were the same as all the other pits they'd investigated, with none of the debris removed from the bottom. Mike pointed to almost the center of a large mound where some of the silt was drifting down to the pile. "Does that look like settling to you?"

"I thought I saw a ripple when we landed," Jeff replied.

"But I don't see anyone in there."

"Let's get this place assessed. Our friends want out of that box." Mary turned and walked over to the fire pit. "Mostly charred wood." Holding her hand directly over a foot-long branch, she then reached down and picked it up. "Barely warm. Whoever lives here had a fire going at one time, but it must have been out for quite a while."

She handed the branch to her approaching husband. He turned it over and looked at the end. "This looks like cut marks. Granted a dull blade, but definitely not broken." He held it in both hands and brought it over his knee. It snapped in two. "Though they could have broken it."

"Not if it was still green when they prepared it." Jeff reached down and started spreading the charred bits of wood aside. He felt the pile get warmer as he did. Finally he had to draw his hand away from the heat building up. He took one of the cooler sticks and began stirring the ashes. Some of the smaller twigs burst into a small flame.

"Yep, it's still active. Someone just banked it for later use. We'd better put this thing back out." Jeff took his water bottle from his belt and doused the small fire. "Somebody built this." He turned around and looked over the encampment. "Let's spread out and look for any signs of where they might have gone."

They stepped away from the fire pit, Mike heading towards where they thought the subway entrance was. He had gone several feet when his foot kicked what he had thought was a large leaf. It rang out like it was made of metal against the steel that protected his toes.

Jeff turned at the sound. He saw his friend reach down to look under the object. "Mike, no!"

More than a dozen similar leaves were thrown over, and creatures jumped out from under them. One grabbed Mike's right arm immediately, another quickly grabbed the other. Jeff punched his radio, "Logan, get everyone out of here. Now!" A large hand with long, pointed fingers grabbed his hand away from his ear and pulled it to meet his other one behind his back.

Jeff turned his head just enough to see the shuttle lift away from the encampment.

While not as long as Mike had described them, these creatures had snoots on them three times the length of the Raffian filter masks. But they had every bit the scales of the Earth creatures Mike had claimed they resembled.

They stood on their hind legs, and while not completely upright, they were over waist high. Except for a few of them that held sticks in one hand to push them fully upright and to the same height as Jeff. One of them picked up the metal pole Jeff had dropped when he was grabbed and handed it to another. The second one accepted it and gave his stick to the first.

With one on each side holding the humans, they whipped their tails against the human's legs, driving all three of them towards the surrounding forest.

Jeff was spun around and shoved against a tall tree. They wrapped native vines several times around him and tied them off. From a pouch on a belt Jeff hadn't noticed before, one of the creatures produced a sharpened hand stone. It cut the vine off whatever it was growing from.

The same thing happened to Mike and Mary.

The creatures all stepped back as another, the one that now had Jeff's metal pole, approached. It stood looking at them for a moment then raised its hands—Jeff saw they were flexible paws with very sharp claws—to the sky and barked something. Jeff turned to look at his companions; both were tied to trees on his right. They both shook their heads in incomprehension.

"Jeff, Mike, Mary. If you can hear this, nod."

Jeff turned his head skyward to see if he could locate where Logan was calling him from. Sure enough, the shuttle sat stationary about 100 feet above the encampment. He turned his head back to his fellow captives, he started to nod before they followed suit. Then they nodded vigorously enough that Logan would be able to see them without binoculars.

The one that had spoken—at least Jeff assumed that's what it had done—now walked up to Jeff and grabbed his chin with its right hand, stopping his nodding. It growled at Jeff, then turned and barked at its companions, before running one of its claws down across the shirt Jeff was wearing. It tore the fabric for a few inches, then it pulled its claw back and checked on its instructions. Two of them had gone up to the Blacks and done the same, minus the ripping of their shirts.

"Okay, no more asking you to signal back. We're going to sit tight up here. We'll find a way to get you out of there. Just don't provoke those guys any further," Logan radioed.

It wasn't easy. Looking over the two foot snoot of the creature standing in front of him, Jeff stared straight back at it. The creature opened its mouth displaying a full set of teeth. Jeff found himself counting them to keep himself from reacting to the primal fear building inside him. And there was the reek of the creature's breath. He got up to fifty-five teeth before it snapped its jaws shut and turned around.

These weren't masks they were wearing, these things had somehow evolved from a reptilian species. Evolved enough to have discovered how to use and control fire, use speech and walk upright. As the leader stepped away to talk with other members of this community, Jeff looked around at the weapons each of them were carrying. Everyone seemed to have a vine belt tied and looped over their shoulders. In that belt a few of them had hatchets sitting in thinner loops. Hatchets made from pieces of stone that appeared to have been chipped into sharp edges and imbedded on wooden handles. A stone dagger was in another loop, almost as long as the hatchets were. The staffs most of them carried ended in a sharpened stone head mounted on the end.

"Hey, Bozo, what're you going to do with us?" Mike hollered at the lead lizard.

"Mike, don't," Jeff said in a quieter tone.

The leader turned and stared at Mike for an instant. Then walked over and roared a challenge back while poking Mike in the chest with one of its claws.

It turned back to its followers and barked something else. Then it pulled its claw away from Mike and sliced through the top strand of the vine holding him to the tree. The vines fell to the ground at Mike's feet. Others came over and did the same to Mary and Jeff.

Again the three of them were grabbed by their arms and this time lead to a covered pit, where the tarp of vines was pulled back and the three of them shoved in. While their falls were broken by the debris in the bottom, something scraped against Jeff's leg. He winched and rolled away from it. As soon as he did, he rolled back to cover up whatever it had been.

Seconds later, the 'alligator people' covered the pit back up with the tarp, cutting off most of the light. Jeff felt for whatever he'd scraped against. It was the edge of the construction stone used in making these pits. He brought his hands down to it, pulled them as far apart as he could get them and began rubbing the vines binding him against the stone.

"Jeff, you okay?" He heard Mike call out.

"Hold your voice down," he replied. "We should be able to talk down here if we keep it down."

"Mike, those are the things that tried grabbing you." Mary announced.

"There," Jeff pulled his hands away from each other and brought them in front of himself. He scurried over to the others, pulling a stone chip from the rubble. He found Mary first. "Turn over, I'm going to cut those vines off." As she complied, he added, "Pull your hands apart, keep the vines tight."

They broke. "Thanks, Jeff."

But he was already on his way over to where a dark shape announced itself as Mike. He repeated the process.

As the Blacks were rubbing their wrists, Jeff pressed his earpiece. "Logan, can you hear me?"

"It looks like they threw you guys in a pit. Want us to come get you?"

"Trying to uncover the tarp would take too long, put you guys at risk. No, wait until nightfall."

"If you think you'll be safe?"

"After dark, Logan."

Jeff dropped his hand to help Mary up. "We need to start finding our own way out of this place. Start looking for any chinks in the walls we can climb up with."

"It's odd that they only took your pole, Jeff."

Jeff thought about that for a minute. "I think it was because I dropped it." Then his hand flew to his machete, it was still mounted on his belt. "They might not have any idea that these things are tools. They don't have anything made from metal."

Mike started rummaging through the pockets of the cargo pants he was wearing. "Oh, here's a flashlight." He pulled out of his pocket a three-inch long, inch-wide tube and turned it on. "Let there be light."

"What else?" Jeff asked as he patted down his pants, hoping he had forgot to remove something important.

"I've got a handful of nails Nancy had us keep with us at all times," Mary added. "I don't even have a flashlight. Why were you carrying that?"

"She had me in pockets of homes you don't want to think about." He ran his hands over the lower pockets of his work pants. "Oh, I still have my plastic wrapped sandwich."

"Put that sandwich away and give me that flashlight. We need to find an escape route." Jeff took the offered light and began examining the walls that ran straight up on the sides of the pit.

"Hey, Jeff, if we climbed on the top of that pile over there and reached up with a machete, you think we could cut one of the vines and get it to fall down here? Then use it to climb out."

"We're fifteen feet underground." Jeff spun to face Mike and look at the pile he was talking about. It looked like it might have about six feet of debris on it. After running the numbers in his head, Jeff announced, "Not high enough."

"Jeff Martin, it's not like you to give up so easily," Mary scolded him. "If I sat on Mike's shoulders, while you supported the two of us, I could easily reach the canopy above us."

"You know, that might work." He started scrambling up the mound of stuff, some slid down as he climbed, but enough supported him. His fingers were able to get within four feet of the canopy. "Yes, I think that might work."

He reached down and helped Mike climb to the top of the pile. Mike dug his feet into the shiftable material until he felt he was solid enough.

Jeff then reached down and helped Mary up. Then he grabbed Mike as he bent over and let his wife climb onto his shoulders. As he stood up again, Jeff had hold of his belt, giving him a third anchor point. As they moved around, the debris shifted again, but not enough to destroy the pyramid they'd built. Mary was scraping her head against the vines covering the pit. She stabilized their position by grabbing one of the thicker vines.

Rather than risking their balance by having Mary pull her machete, Jeff passed his up. It took about five minutes of sawing before the vine she had been holding parted. She swayed a bit before grabbing another one. Both of her support posts quickly recovered and she began work on the next one. She cut four more, making a tear in the canopy about three feet long. She passed the machete back to Jeff. He dropped it point first into the debris.

"I'm going to see what's happening." Mary pulled apart the tear she'd created and stuck the top of her head up, just enough to get her eyes outside. She had to wait a few moments before they could adjust to daylight.

"It's quiet again. No one's about."

"Hiding under their metal sheets," Mike whispered back.

"Okay, Mary, grab one of those strands and pull it down with you. Just squat, Mike, and I'll catch Mary." Jeff moved behind the couple, keeping a hold on them while he did. "Okay, I'm ready."

Mike slowly bent his knees and brought his wife straight down. Jeff grabbed her around her chest, just under her armpits, and pulled her away from Mike, allowing him to duck out from under her.

As he set her on the mound, he took the vine she'd held on to and pulled it as hard as he could. When it wouldn't come any further; he jumped up, grabbed hold of it slightly higher and fell back down. He came within inches of the mound, but wouldn't go any further.

He started climbing up until he could reach the severed vine next to one he was on. He grabbed that vine and let go of the one he had climbed. With both hands on the new vine, he fell all the way to the debris without the vine stopping. He handed it to Mike, "Pull this down as far as you can." Then he climbed the first one again to grab a third vine.

Eventually they had all the vines Mary had cut pulled into the pit and sunlight was pouring through the rent they had made. "Logan, we're climbing out of the center of the pit. Be ready to drop and retrieve us."

"Roger that. I'll land on the south side."

"Okay, now we climb." Jeff took hold of one of the vines and again climbed his way up. When he got to the top, he pushed aside the diagonal vines and squeezed his way through them. He pulled himself up and rolled on the canopy away from the hole.

"I see ya," Jeff heard Logan.

Mary was the next out, followed by her husband. Then all three crawled their way across the canopy until they reached solid ground. There they stood up and waited as Logan brought the shuttle down a few feet away. The side door of the module opened up and the three of them ran over to it and jumped in.

"Go," Francois hollered into the radio, sliding the door shut behind them.

Logan lifted out of the clearing to the sounds of things banging against the hull. He set a direct course back to Petersville, not caring if they flew over water.

Chapter 33

The Big Question

"That didn't go well," Mary said as they walked over to Town Hall to discuss things.

"Unmitigated disaster would be a better way of putting it." Mike dropped his tool belt outside the door and walked across the entry way and into the Situation Room.

"Hey, everybody got out okay." Ahmed grabbed the first chair he could find, spun it around and sat in it backwards, facing the Big Board table.

"What is going on on this planet?" Jeff walked to the far side of the table and keyed satellite cameras on the encampment they had just left, patching it into the table's monitor. The image started to shimmer, the satellite was moving away and losing the image. Jeff froze the picture before the satellite completely moved out of range.

"From orbit, we detected no signs of intelligent life. Then almost a year into our colonization of it, we find that there had been a sentient race inhabiting this planet after all. A very advanced race, but that has de-evolved into a stone age culture, doing so in the last couple of hundred years. Now we find a race of alligator creatures who appear to be evolving right before our eyes."

"We don't know they are evolving that fast."

"The Raffians have no knowledge of these creatures. Either they are really, really good at hiding or they have done so after the original Raffians began their downward trek. If the latter, that's really fast."

More of the people from the shuttle came in and sat around the central table. Logan, as the last pilot, had to park the shuttle in its hanger before he could join them.

Ahmed leaned over the picture. He enlarged sections of it for a moment then restored them before moving on to other areas of the picture for similar enlargements. "I'm not a biologist like you, Frank, but don't reptiles like to bask in the sun?"

"Normally speaking, yes." Francois stood up to lean into the enlargement Ahmed still had up. It was off to one side of the pond and showed several of the structures like the natives had hid under before jumping Jeff's crew earlier.

Ahmed enlarged that portion of the picture to its maximum. While it was starting to get grainy, he pointed to something sticking out of the cover. "Then why are they hiding from the sun under these... You said they were metal, right, Mike?"

"That's what they sounded like when I kicked one."

"Okay, why are they hiding from the sun?"

"They should be cold blooded. They should like to bask in the open sun. Unless..." Francois stood back, rubbed his chin and looked at the ceiling.

"Spill it, Frank." Jeff leaned back in his chair, waiting for the biologist to answer.

"Large brains usually need a warm-blooded circulatory system to maintain them. This village shows signs of advanced brain activity, not something a cold-blooded system could support. The creatures must have evolved with a warm-blooded system. Hence, they prefer the shade."

"Then why be out in the sun at all? They could easily get into the shade of the forest."

Diane decided to offer her opinion. "Instinct. If these animals started with the usual cold-blooded system found on Earth, they would instinctively want to be in the sun."

"But if they are now warm-blooded, they can't do that anymore. Their scaly outer skin wasn't evolved to shed heat."

"But their instincts haven't caught up."

"So you guys are saying," Jeff paused to encourage them to continue their explanations.

"Something is pushing these creatures' evolution," Francois said.

"Something outside the natural evolutionary process."

The two biologists looked at each other, then turned to Jeff. "And somehow that something is de-evolving the original inhabitants at the same time," they said in unison.

"So what do we do about it?" Jeff asked.

"I think the first question is should we do anything about this?" Logan was standing just inside the door, Jeff hadn't seen him come in. "I mean this isn't our planet. Do we have a right to interfere with its natural development?"

"It's our planet now," Diane said. "The Endeavor is in no shape to take us anywhere else."

"She's right," Jeff added. "For better or worse, we have to find a way to live on Belenius 3. Whether it's as good neighbors or conquerors, we're here to stay."

An elderly voice from the back of the room added, "First, we have to find out what is happening." Everyone in the room turned to the old man standing in the corner of the room. "It could be happening to us." Nathan Reynolds sat back in the chair he'd been sitting in since before everyone else had arrived.

Chapter 34

Military Raid

"Have you thought this through?" Logan walked across the landing field with Jeff and had one foot on the step into the passenger module. Jeff pulled on the handle of the co-pilot compartment; Clint was flying this time.

"Is there any part of this plan you question?"

"You're better at this than I am. I just want to make sure you've thought of everything. This is our first military raid, after all."

"We're only attempting to capture one of the alligator men for testing. If we can find a dead one, it would work just as well." He looked back at the module, imagining the twelve people inside who had volunteered even after seeing the video of the creatures. "We should have enough people to overpower any single creature. I have no plans to engage a pack of them."

"It's not one or two that I'm worry about," Logan opened the side door and started to step in. "Just hold back and make sure your plan stays on track. Let us do the work." He stepped inside and closed the door. Jeff waited for it to lock before opening the cockpit and climbing in.

Clint was finishing his checklist when he noticed Jeff's arrival. "Got everything covered?"

"Not you, too!" Clint lifted off the pad and veered northwest, around Buffet Bay.

* * *

It was a three-hour flight to the clearing just north of the creatures' encampment that Jeff had planned on using as a staging area. Four of the men took the cargo net out of the storage locker and began looking for a wide path to the other clearing. Diane led them through the water-soaked forest; not quite a swamp, but everyone's shoes were getting thoroughly soaked today. Logan led a crew to modify the module; removing the side door, slinging safety belts to the inside rails, assembling the makeshift steel cage.

As a last resort, Dr. Parker had a tranquilizer blow gun ready. He was practicing with an inert dart on one of the trees while everyone else got things ready. At least until he missed and lost it in the inch-deep water.

They picked an alligator hiding under one of the metal sheets closest to the treeline. As quietly as Diane could keep them, they strung the net between two trees that were spaced almost five feet apart, wide enough for someone to run between. After which they withdrew and waited for the sun to reach its zenith, to drive every one of the creatures into hiding.

Jeff crept up to look at the progress and assess their timing. Logan was right at his elbow, having finished the setup work to the module. "I'm going to make sure you're leading from the rear," he had told Jeff before leaving their staging area.

The net was up, Jeff gave it a tug to make sure it was secure, but not too secure. The encampment was quiet. Everything was ready. Jeff was about to give the 'Go!' command when Logan dropped a hand to his shoulder and pointed off to their left.

One of the creatures crawled out from under its sheet and walked over to the far trees. It crawled on its four legs, not standing up like they had when they had captured Jeff earlier.

Jeff turned and looked at Logan, then gestured to return to the staging area. Logan waved his right hand above his head and gestured everyone follow them.

"Okay, this changes things," Jeff began. He paced along the left side of the shuttle, hands clasped behind his back. "They're not going to run into the net like I thought."

"Alligators are also quite fast on all fours," Francois offered. "Your video showed them with unsteady gate on two legs. My opinion would be that they would revert to using all four in an all-out chase."

"We rigged that net to catch someone walking into it," it was Diane's turn, "not to capture a scurrying prey. I need to re-rig the thing, make it a floor mounted trap."

"That might make it less visible with all the water around here," Logan observed.

"How long?"

"The five of us could re-rig it up in about ten minutes, if we didn't have to worry about making noise." She gestured to the men who had done the initial setup. "Give me a good hour." They left to begin work.

"Logan, I'm putting you in command of the retrieval team. You get that thing caged when Diane captures it. Doc and I will be with her."

"Nope! I told you, lead from the rear. Your place is in the module, making any changes we need to the plan. I'll take Doc to the capture zone."

"When did you get all military like?"

"Too many war videos, I guess." Logan shrugged, then walked off to find Doctor Parker. He grabbed the middle-aged man by his shoulder and said something Jeff couldn't hear. They followed Diane's team towards the creature's encampment.

"Okay, if I'm going to stay with the shuttle, I'd better get the containment team prepared." He walked over to the cockpit, where Clint was still sitting inside and waved the other six members of the team over.

"Keeping dry?" He said as he popped open the door. Strains of disco music blasted from the cockpit, dropping in volume as Clint turned down the dashboard player he was listening to.

"I hate soggy socks."

"Everyone, its time. Get into the module and change into whatever fresh clothes you brought. At least get dry socks on. Then get yourselves belted onto the safety lines. This is a doors-open mission. No one is falling out of this bird on my watch. Clear?" *Damn, now I'm talking like Logan,* he mentally scolded himself. "Frank, Carl; you're the wrangling team. Keep its jaws shut, it's harder for an alligator to open them than to close them."

"I'm aware of that, Jeff." Francois said. "I'm the one who told you that."

"Good, then you'll be the first to grab it when we bring it aboard. Get the band on that snoot and get it into the cage. Use your Kevlar suits, those claws are extremely sharp.

We've got three suits with us, so who wants to volunteer to help them?"

"I'll help." Victoria Notski raised her hand.

"Are you sure you're up to this?"

"Why, because I'm a woman?"

"No, because of your stature."

She grabbed one of the poles mounted on the side of the module behind her and spun it around to smack Jeff upside his head but stopped her strike less than a inch from his cheek.

"Damn, the women of this colony are scarier than their men. Okay, you've got the job. Just use that pole on the creature, not me. The rest of you stay out of reach of it. Zero injuries this trip, people, zero injuries."

They stepped inside the module. All the seats had been folded into the walls to make room for the fight to come. The cage stood open against the rear cargo door, so it could be dropped overboard in case the creature threatened to get out. Poles with machetes taped to their ends were racked against the left wall. Everything loose had been stowed away, making the open space as free of obstacles as possible.

The two men and one woman were helped by the others to buckle into their Kevlar suits. First the pants, then the neck collar, followed by the torso shirt, finally the upper arms and lower arms were snapped on separately. Their headgear was kept ready so they wouldn't overheat in the now-not-air-conditioned module.

"Clint," Jeff pressed his ear radio, "I think it's time to get into position." Then he turned to everyone else. "Clip your lines onto the safety poles. Good luck!"

Through the open wall of the module, Jeff watched the ground, water and trees fall away as the shuttle lifted up. When they were about fifty feet above the trees, the shuttle turned and started moving south towards the next clearing. As it came into view a few minutes later, Jeff put his index finger to his lips, not that anyone had said anything on the trip here.

Jeff could see the break for the clearing ahead of them, when the shuttle stopped its forward movement. "We're here," came through his ear radio.

He motioned Peter and Colin to start winching the line down to the capture team. After a moment, "Got it." He held up his hand for the winch to stop. "Ready," Diane whispered into the radio.

Jeff pulled a pair of binoculars over his head and made his way to the open door, switching his line between safety poles as he did. He leaned out against the pull of the line, holding his safety belt inside the module, and looked down.

He could make out Doctor Parker and Logan standing just beyond where he assumed the far edge of the capture net was. Diane was just stepping out of the water onto the raised ground of the encampment and approaching the closest of the metal sheets. She grabbed the metal sheet and ran back amongst the trees dragging it behind her.

The creature that had been under it was facing away from her. It had to turn around to see what had happened. When it did, Jeff could hear a growl over Logan's open mic before the creature rounded on the fleeing human and gave chase. As they suspected, it ran after Diane on all fours. She veered close to the net trap, close enough for the creature to see the two humans standing in the trees.

Logan's waving had caught its attention, Doc had his hands on the blowgun poised before his mouth. The creature turned and came at the two men. It was making an amazing speed. If they hadn't diverted it, it would have caught Diane in a matter of minutes.

It slowed down as it began stepping on the water-covered net but kept coming until it hit the trigger wire and the net's corners jumped out of the water.

Jeff turned to the men on the winch, "Now!"

The motor started pulling the cable they had earlier dropped, back into the module. The shuttle leaned to the right side a little with the increased weight. But not enough that Jeff couldn't move his safety lines back to the other side of the module.

"Doc, hit it!" Jeff heard Logan over the radio. "It's fighting the net."

"Faster, Peter, faster. Get that creature up here. Frank, Carl, Vicky; get ready."

The three of them moved over to either side of the door. Victoria held one of the few poles without a machete mounted to it. The two men grabbed the net and pulled it into the shuttle, which righted itself as the weight of the creature shifted its balance.

It was still thrashing about, but not as vigorously as Jeff had been worried about. The dart in its belly must be working. They pulled the heavy load to the back of the module, directly in front of the cage door. They opened the net and Victoria nudged the creature inside with strong prods from her staff. They got the door closed and locked without the creature taking a single swipe at any of them.

"Clint, get back to the staging area quick. The rest of the village spotted us," Logan panted.

Jeff saw the shuttle turn around, losing altitude as it headed for the original clearing. It sounded like it was going to be a hurried pickup.

Clint was barely over the treetops when he passed into the clearing. Before he even set down, members of the capture team were jumping into the module. Jeff and Colin pulling each one in. They could hear the noise of the approaching alligator men.

Logan threw in the doctor and jumped after him. Jeff grabbed the sliding door and closed it. "That's everyone. GO!" he yelled into the radio.

"Take a long way home," Ahmed said. "They know what shuttles are now. They'll be watching for us."

Chapter 35

The Storage Room

"I think we have just enough power to make one more report." Clarence sat on the log bench staring at the recorder that he was turning over and over in his palm.

"And the recharger is out on the shuttle, isn't it?" Howard dropped onto the same log, staring into the fire burning in front of them.

"They've got to be getting fresh air from somewhere. If only I had thought to bring the portable solar charger with us."

"If only we had thought to make this trip a week earlier. No point in beating ourselves up about things we can't control." Howard put his arm around the amateur archeologist. "We've got a couple more months, think of all the stuff we'll know about these people when we return to Petersville."

"I'm barely beginning to learn how to communicate with them."

"You're doing better than me."

"But your kids..."

"What about our kids?" Marsha sat down next to her husband.

"They're picking up the Raffian's language and customs at an exponential pace," Clarence explained. Then after a minute added, "But what do we want to send Jeff in this last transmission?"

"Last transmission?" Marsha looked from Clarence to her husband.

"It's all the power we have left. Even my recorder died last week."

"If we keep the transmission short, how long can we extend the batteries in your recorder?"

"I've thought of that, but the radio system and the recorder use different types of batteries. There's no way one can power the other. Maybe it's time we invented paper and pencils?"

"Well, we came here to investigate their climbing claws and we didn't have a really good answer last time. Have we learned anything more about them?" Marsha reminded the two men.

"Then we'd better dig into that more and stop sitting on these logs feeling bored all winter." Clarence started to rise from his seat. "How's you guys' Raffian?"

"About the same as yours," Howard answered, looking over to his wife.

"Not as good as the children," Marsha said, rising also. "But if I don't practice, I'll never get any better. Are you coming, Howard?" She reached her hand down to help him up.

"If I must." He reached up his hand and let her pull him to his feet. "I was really starting to enjoy this boredom." He smiled at his wife but directed the words at Clarence.

They scanned the open area looking for Lerick. He was over with the two boys, building new clay pots for the nightly kiln firing. The three adults crossed the central area and walked over to almost the most northeasterly corner of the cavern where the ground was soft enough still for clay deposits to be dug out and worked.

"Hi, Mom," Billy said as they got close.

Tommy jumped up when he heard his brother, ran over to the approaching adults and gave his mother a hug. "Mom, come see what I made." He grabbed hold of her pants pocket and pulled her over to his pottery wheel. He pointed to the drinking mug he was working on, which was not ready to be removed yet. "Like it?"

"It's wonderful, dear. Are you boys having fun?"

Lerick grunted a couple of sounds Clarence didn't understand.

"Um," Billy replied.

Then Lerick added something else.

Clarence looked over at the elder boy and asked, "What are you guys talking about?"

"He wanted to know if Mom liked Tommy's mug. I told him she did. Then he said that parental approval helps motivate learning."

"Impressive concepts for their limited language."

Billy stopped pedaling his wheel, stood up, and wiped his hands on the skin apron he was wearing over his clothes. "They're all recorded on the wisdom scrolls behind the artifacts."

"Scrolls? What are they made of?" He looked over at the room storing the items left by the Raffian's ancestors.

"I'm not sure."

"I'd love to see these, if I could."

"Won't do you much good. I can't even read them. Some of the other kids have tried teaching me their meanings, but the sounds and symbols just don't go together for me. Oh, and they're in another artifact room, not the one you're looking at."

He turned back to face Billy. "If they still use writing, that's important." *And they may have something I can make notes with,* he said to himself.

"Clarence." He felt Howard touch him on his shoulder. "We can worry about that later. We wanted to get something new to report to Jeff before your batteries go dead."

"Right. Thanks, Howard. Squirrel moment." Clarence shook his head, then brushed the hair out of his left eye. He normally kept his hair long, just not long enough to fly into his eyes. "Marsha, can you ask Lerick if we can see the claws again?"

Marsha grunted a few words. Lerick's eyes squinted in a puzzled look before he responded.

Tommy was chuckling into his project and Billy hid his giggles behind his clasped hands.

"Okay, you two. What's so funny?"

"Mom," offered Billy. "You asked him if you could burn the walls. To which he responded, 'You can try, but we aren't able to'."

Lerick leaned over to the elder boy and said something none of the adults understood. Billy said something back and they both laughed.

"Okay, young man," Marsha said in a harsher tone. "If my dialogue is so hilarious, you can translate for Clarence."

"What do you want to know, Mr. Knowles?"

Clarence placed his hands on the boy's shoulders, squatted down slightly and looked Billy square in his eyes. "How do they construct their climbing gloves? Where do they get the claws from?" He let the boy go and stood up as Billy turned back to Lerick, who was pulling a piece of string under the bottom of the pitcher he had just created. Billy asked him Clarence's question in Raffian.

Lerick held the pot above his head, staring at it. Then he set it down, turned to Billy, then looked at Clarence and answered the young man.

Billy gave Lerick a quick reply before turning back to Clarence. "They don't. There are a few more in cold storage," Billy pointed over to a dwelling a few doors down from the shrine, "but once those are gone, they will have to find a new way to climb trees."

"Cold storage?" Clarence asked. Then formed another question. "Can we see this cold storage area?"

After a quick exchange with Lerick, the tribal leader led them across the cavern. They entered another unmarked dwelling—Clarence again wondered how they knew which building was which around their village; they all looked alike to him. They walked to the back, where a large animal skin rug hung from ceiling to floor. Lerick brushed it aside and they all walked through another door into a much colder room.

Lerick pointed at what looked to Clarence like a white, metal box. It was as tall as the room and had two three-foot sections. Lerick pushed one edge of the double doors but nothing happened. Then he shoved his fingers between them and pried the door open, saying something to Billy in the process.

"He said the doors used to push in and open out until a few years ago. Now they have to pry them open."

A blast of cold came from inside the next room. Lerick lead them in, followed by Billy, then the adults. The door swung shut and Clarence heard the clack of two objects smacking into each other.

On their way through the door, Clarence couldn't stop himself from have a look at its mechanism. There was a plastic tube mounted to the top of the door frame with a rod of similar material inside. The rod moved in and out of the tube quite easily, too easily to hold the door closed. On the end of the rod—Clarence held his wrist ID bracelet up to it and felt the pull—was a magnet. "A spring mechanism could have held the door shut and allowed Lerick to push it to open the door. It must have busted years ago. Still, this is pretty advanced for a stone age tribe." He continued on after the others.

Floor to ceiling shelves ran from front to back in the room, with an aisle on the near wall to go between them. On the shelves were various items they had seen the Raffian use since they had been with them. And some they had not.

Clarence pulled down a four-inch metal tube, about a quarter inch in diameter, with a point on one end and a dial on the other. He could see markings on the dial; when he covered the pointed end with his hand, the dial moved slightly.

"A thermometer," he said under his breath, which condensed in front of him.

"What did you say?"

"Billy, ask Lerick what this is?" He handed the tube over to the boy.

After a brief exchange. "He has no idea. Those have been sitting on that shelf since before he was born."

"Can he read the markings?"

Another exchange. "He can read, but not those symbols. He also asks that you return it to its shelf when you are done."

Clarence was reaching to put it back with the dozens of similar devices on the shelf, when a thought occurred to him. "Would he mind if I worked with this a bit? I might find a use they could make of it."

After Billy talked to Lerick some more, "Just make sure you mark it off when we leave."

"What?"

"On the wall behind you," Billy pointed back the way they had come, at the wall with drawings and marks all along it.

"They have an inventory system," Clarence exclaimed.

"Isn't the concept of recording things a bit advanced for these people?" Howard asked as they went back to the wall and studied it.

"So is a pottery wheel and kiln. They should be sun drying their ceramics," Marsha added. Clarence looked at Howard and saw the same astonished look on his face, Clarence knew he was sporting. "What?" Marsha continued. "I thought you guys had already realized that, so I didn't say anything."

"We 'squirreled' again, guys," Clarence turned and began catching up with Billy and Lerick. "Billy, can you guys lead us to the climbing claws?"

At the end of the row, the shelves from floor to ceiling contained the gloves they were looking for. "There must be hundreds here."

"Three hundred forty-one, according to the chart on the wall, Lerick says."

"And he doesn't know anything about how they were made?"

After another brief discussion, "No, they have always been here."

Howard was staring all around the storage locker they were standing in. "Just who built this place?"

Billy asked. "It too has always been here. Lerick's father showed it to him, like his father before that."

"Well, maybe there's a clue in here," Clarence said. "Ask Lerick if there's any problem with us looking around in here? We promise to make sure everything gets back in its proper place."

After another exchange, Lerick offered Clarence his hand. After a handshake, he walked past the humans and out of the room. They heard the door open and close.

"He trusts us, but he needs to get back to his pottery. I'd like to stay and help, but I promised I'mac a dinner set for tonight's firing. So, if I may be excused?" Billy walked past his parents and out of the room also.

"Three hundred forty-one to look through. I'm glad the shelves across from them are empty; otherwise, we wouldn't have a place to put them after we examined them."

"What was on those shelves?" Howard looked at the four levels of empty shelves. "Honey, could you take a look at that inventory thingy and see what they had stored there?"

The two men started on the top shelf, they had to reach up slightly as it was at eye level. They pulled the claws down one at a time, examined each and passed them over to the other shelves. They'd completed twenty-five each when Marsha returned.

"Just more of the claws," she examined the rapidly filling empty shelves. "But I don't see the lacings that should have been next to them." She sat down on the floor facing the bottom shelf of claws to go through them. "Damn, that's a cold floor." She got back up and headed back to the front of the row they were in. "I'm going to find something to sit on."

Clarence was just setting down a claw, "Why would they store lacings next to the climbing claws?" He picked the claw he had just looked at back up for a closer look. He turned it inside out as much as the glove would allow him. There was the seam. He looked at the outside again, keeping his fingers on the seam he had found. The seam was just under the last row of top scales.

"Hey," they heard Marsha shout. "Look what I found." She came down the aisle holding a tanned animal skin, a tanned alligator skin.

Chapter 36

The Test

"William, translate this exactly." Howard stood across the pottery wheel from the Raffian leader. "If you have never seen nor heard of alligators, just what is this?" He held the alligator skin up by its neck as high as he could reach and still the tail drug on the floor.

"Dad, it doesn't work that way. They don't have words for a detailed inquiry."

"Son, these are the creatures we came up here to find out about. We need to know what they know."

"I'll do what I can."

Sarah and Tommy heard the angry tones and came up to stand on either side of their mother. Other Raffians heard the tones also and were coming to investigate.

Billy said what he could to Lerick, who rose from his log stool and addressed Howard.

"What did he say?" Howard waved his son to translate.

"He asks what has angered you? They know nothing of the pelt you took. He didn't even know they had one."

"They have a three foot pile of them," Marsha added. She had her hands on each of her two younger children.

M'cron walked up next to Lerick and spoke to the humans. Billy translated, "Those are armor pelts. They were used in the days before we shut ourselves off from the dangers outside. I'mac wore a suit made from such pelts when he walked down to where you villaged."

"What, where did you get them?" Howard asked.

Billy translated, "They have always been here. They were gifts from the gods. Like the stores where you found them, they were here for us when we arrived."

Clarence placed his hand on Howard's shoulder and pulled him over enough so he could whisper in his ear. "Whoever built this place left these things for the Raffians to use. If we assume that this is a descendant race of beings, then they must have seen what was coming and created this sanctuary for their descendants."

Billy spoke again, "The gods knew. The gods protected. They will protect us even from you, if they must."

"What?" Howard looked over at his son. "Did you just tell them everything Mr. Knowles just said to me?"

"You said to translate exactly."

M'cron banged the end of his staff on the dirt floor and spoke again. Billy again translated, "The gods require you be tested. You are to be taken to The Chamber to see if you are smart enough to open it." M'cron turned and the humans were immediately surrounded by natives urging them to follow the shaman.

They were led to a dwelling a few doors down from the one the store room was behind. M'cron and Lerick entered, then waited as the rest of the villagers urged the humans in also. The villagers did not enter, but stayed in front of the door, blocking any exit, chanting "urgron".

"Billy, what are they saying?" Howard asked.

"Test."

M'cron turned to face the line of humans. Clarence was the furthest in, followed by Howard, Billy, Tommy, Marsha and Sarah. Marsha was still holding her youngest children tightly. "Luk," M'cron said and pointed his staff at the back wall. A foot-long rectangular object was mounted to it about chest height.

"He said "open", Dad." Billy looked up at his father, hoping he had the answer.

Clarence walked over and grabbed the handle. He gave it a pull and nothing happened. He ran his fingers from the top of it, where it was firmly affixed to the wall, all along its length. At the bottom, he found a hairline gap between the handle and the wall.

He placed his hands on the door and pushed it like he had seen Lerick do earlier. Nothing happened.

He ran his hands over the door's surface, looking for any holes that might indicate a key hole. There were none.

He found a gap between what he assumed were two swinging doors but was unable to get his fingers in it enough to pry either door open.

He looked around the room to see if there was anything he could force between the doors. Other than the people, the room only contained two separate piles of stones, one pile on either side of the door.

Clarence looked over to the McCurdels for help. His eyes fell on the medallion that M'cron wore. Lerick didn't have a similar one. "Ceremonial?" Clarence said under his breath. It was a small metal plate with a strap strung through a hole in the top, on that plate sat a rock attached to it, the rock clung to the plate.

Clarence looked at the two piles of rocks again. Then he passed his bracelet over the one on the right side of the door. Nothing. When he passed it over the left pile, several of the stones leapt up and clung to his bracelet.

He heard a gasp coming from the dwelling's entryway. He took one of the stones, shook off the others and placed it on the top of the handle. Nothing happened even when he tried to turn the handle.

He passed the stone over the entire door, hoping to move some mechanism on the other side. But still nothing happened.

As soon as he moved the stone to the other door—about handle height—and pulled it upwards, he heard a slight click. He tried the handle again. This time, it turned to the right, away from the other door. When he had turned it parallel to the ground, he pulled the door outwards.

He heard a cheer emanating from the assembled Raffians. Howard walked up to the other side of the door to help Clarence by pushing from the inside.

Billy turned to listen to the shaman for a minute before going up to his father. "M'cron says you may find the answer you seek in there. While they knew there was a connection between the stones and the door, they didn't know it could open it. Mr. Knowles would have passed the test if he had simply found the stones that stuck to the door."

"Let me out of here," Howard pushed his way past his son, gasping for breath.

Clarence stuck his head around the door to see what the room contained. He pulled his head back quickly when he too starting gasping. "I think we'll need to air that place out before we can go in."

"Why?" Howard panted out.

"Take deep breaths. In fact, everyone get out into the main room. We've just opened a chamber devoid of oxygen, its why you can't breathe."

"Why?" Howard straightened himself up, gathered Billy and headed for the exit to the room.

"There's a nitrogen blanket on the things in that vault. I think someone wanted to springboard civilization once they figured out what was happening." Howard shooed the rest of the people in the room out. "Billy, tell Lerick we need to air that room out before anyone goes near it."

"Is it really that dangerous, Mr. Knowles?" The boy asked after relaying Clarence's instructions to the tribal leader.

"Tomorrow. We just have to give the room time to get enough oxygen in it to allow us to breath." He stopped a few feet outside the room and turned to address Billy face-to-face. "Do they even understand the concept of breathing? Do they know what oxygen is and what it is for?"

"Sure they do, something as simple as that."

"It's not that simple, Billy. Oxygen and nitrogen are both colorless, odorless gases; so we normally don't perceive them. It took mankind several millennia before he understood the relationship between breathing and atmospheric gases. Not a simple idea at all."

"Ruum is their word for the part of the air that supports life, aruum are those gases that mix with the breathing gas but don't support life and kruum is their word for toxic, poisonous gases."

"These people amaze me more and more. Let's go outside. I have a data dump to prepare for Petersville." He led the boy over to the logs where he had left his stuff. He sat down, pulled over his pack, opened it and pulled out his hand computer. He spent the next hour dictating notes into it, getting ready for the satellite flyover at 1900 hours that evening. At least his watch's batteries should keep running for the rest of their time here.

Chapter 37

Signs of Trouble

"At least we hadn't taken this room apart," Logan said as they closed the crew quarter's hatch, then dropped the newly welded bar across the door. They could tell that the creature they'd captured was waking up by the noises it was making against the bars of the cage holding it prisoner.

"Yet." Jeff swung the hasp over the bar and pushed the restraining pin in to secure it. Then jerked up on the bar to make sure it wasn't moving. "Francois has his DNA, even clipped part of the thing's claw. Ahmed is working on the bandolier we took from the thing, to see what it's constructed of. The dang thing even had pockets on its underside, there were small stone knives in them.

"We split the creature's tools between Bill Flanigan and Al Notski to see what construction guys could make of them. Doc shoved it into his auto diagnostic unit and took the samples it directed him to. We've got cameras mounted inside there to monitor the thing round the clock. We have it in a cage; behind a steel hull. I think it's time for a beer."

"I concur." The two men stepped down the metal walkway of the Endeavor's corpse until they came upon a section of the hull that had been removed and walked out of their old ship.

"Unless Nancy sees us coming," Logan pointed down the hill at the approaching figure.

"She's seen us!" Several steps below them and climbing, she pointed her finger directly at them. "There's no ducking for cover now."

"If you two are finished playing your alligator games," she began. She stopped two steps below Jeff and Logan, blocking the log steps that had been constructed to make climbing up to the plateau, where the Endeavor rested, easier. They thought about jumping onto the packed dirt ramp that was built alongside the stairs to facilitate the removal of the useful parts of the ship and sliding away from her. But she would give them hell when she caught up with them again if they did, more hell than she was going to lay on them now.

"We still have to wait for the lab results," Logan began.

"And study the reactions of the beast, determine how intelligent it actually is," Jeff finished.

"We still have a community to build." she finished her sentence like she hadn't been interrupted.

"And you're doing a magnificent job of it." That wasn't going to work on her, but Jeff gave it a try anyway.

"And just what the hell have you got my brother playing at? I need him on the Simmons home. Ahmed says he has tests you ordered him to run and can't work on the batches of adhesive I need. When is this game of yours going to end?" She planted her fists on her hips, feet wide, and scowled at the two men. Jeff felt she was daring them to make a break for it.

"I gave him the creature's hatchet. He's an engineer. I wanted to see what he would make of it. How it was put together. What level of intelligence would be needed to design and build the thing. I need to know what we're up against. There's over a hundred of those things in that one encampment alone."

"So we drift further and further behind schedule?"

"If we have to. Security is important. Right now everyone has some form of shelter, cramped but still shelter. I'm not going to let anyone get killed so we can hold to some arbitrary schedule."

"McCurdel's back in a couple of months. We'll see what he has to say about this." She turned and marched back down the stairs, leaving the two men breathing heavily.

"That went easier than I expected," Logan said.

"I'd better forego the beer and see what people have found out." Jeff quickly caught the breath he hadn't known he'd been holding during the encounter. "Why does she scare me more than our alligator friend up there?" Jeff jerked his thumb in the direction of the ship.

"Probably because you know what action you can take with them. You gotta live with whatever you do to our Nancy. I'll grab a couple and join you."

"Not in the Situation Room, Logan. But you go have one for both of us, be there in half an hour." He took off down the stairs two at a time, quick stepped over to Town Hall and marched into the Situation Room where Ron was on monitor duty.

"How soon can I get current satellite imagery on the alligator village?" Jeff dropped into the control chair of the Big Board and called up the last photo they had taken.

"The satellite will be in position in about twenty minutes."

"Just off the top of your head like that?" Jeff turned and looked at the meteorologist, who was still in the back of the room on the weather computer.

Ron turned to look at the colonial administrator. "I've been paying special attention to those pass overs since your first mission to that area." He walked the three feet to the central table and dialed up a different image to the one Jeff pulled up. "This one was taken yesterday just after you guys pulled off that raid." He changed the image and pressed the large arrow in it. "And here's the video."

As the video started playing, the encampment was empty. A few seconds in, dozens of the alligator creatures walked on two legs out of the woods. Several more came out on all four. A minute later, they all turned their attention skyward, then the shuttle came into the frame. As the satellite passed from one end of the village to the other, Jeff could see the largest creature take out its axe and violently chop into one of the logs piled by the fire pit.

"I was right," Jeff said as the video ended. "They know what shuttles are now."

"So what're we going to do about them?"

"Get hold of Ahmed, Bill Flannigan and Al. Tell them to bring whatever they have here in half an hour. We need to think tank this." Jeff was out of his chair and headed for the door. "Doc doesn't always wear his earpiece. I'll go get him myself."

* * *

Jeff walked into the clinic, through the waiting room and into the back examination area. There he found Doc Parker and a chair he could sit down in.

"You sick?" Simon finished putting the newly sterilized tray of instruments away and turned his attention to Jeff.

"Nope." Jeff put his hands behind his head and leaned back into the chair. "I just want to find out what you've discovered about our new friends."

"The blood analysis shows it has an increased protein content in its blood plasma. It's getting very close to the same as ours. If you check out that book I have open on the table to your left, cold-blooded creatures typically have a lower protein content. Their sodium, potassium and calcium contents are shifting around also."

Jeff was trying to make sense out of the book Simon had pointed him to. He closed it and set it back down. "So?"

"Whoever suggested that these creatures were evolving into warm-blooded versions was right." Simon rolled up another chair and sat in front of Jeff. "I don't know how it's being accomplished, but it's happening. I need to see Frank's DNA analysis when he's finished."

"That's another reason I'm here." Jeff looked over and saw the Doctor's earpiece sitting on his exam table. "I'm scheduling a meeting," he looked over at the clock on the wall, it read 1345, "at two o'clock in the Situation Room. I want you there."

"Okay, let me get cleaned up."

"And from now until then," he pointed at the exam table, "could you keep your radio in your ear?"

A ding sounded from the other side of the room. "That's the spinal fluid analysis. If you'll excuse me?"

"See you at two, Doc." Jeff left and headed back to Town Hall.

* * *

On his way back, Jeff ran into Harvey Fenderman. He was not in his usual suit and tie. He had a flannel shirt and overalls on, both showing signs of dirt and mud caking. With his boss gone, Jeff had heard that Nancy'd reassigned him to crop duty, since he couldn't swing a hammer safely.

"Jeff, you've got to help me."

"Harvey, it's Nancy's call. Until the housing shortage is over, she directs our labor resources." *Even I have trouble dealing with her about that,* Jeff kept to himself.

"It's my mind. I'm having trouble remembering what Mr. McCurdel looks like."

"I can't blame you." Jeff delved into his own memory and found an image of the Colonial Governor, but it wasn't easy, nor complete. The only memories he could recall were the fights they had gotten into after landfall.

The man was still speaking when Jeff pulled out of his trance. But Jeff hadn't caught what it was. "Harvey, two o'clock, Town Hall. Be there." He stepped around the man and ran back to Town Hall.

* * *

Logan, Ahmed and Ron were already waiting when he burst in the room. "Hey where's the fire?" Logan asked as he stood up.

"What were you doing when they announced we were approaching the Belenius system?" Jeff blurted out.

"I was, huh, er. Damn, I can't remember."

"Ron, your first date with Sandy?"

"What's this about, Jeff?" Logan asked.

"Ron, do you remember?"

Ron leaned forward in his office chair, turning his head from side to side. "I should remember something as special as that. But, Jeff. I don't."

"Harvey just told me he was having trouble remembering what Howard looked like." Jeff looked over at the clock. "When are those others going to get here?" It was one minute until two.

The door opened again and Bill walked in holding the axe they had been studying. He held the door for Al, who followed him in.

"Bill, what did you have for breakfast this morning?" Jeff fired rapid questions as they entered.

"Rye cereal. Why?"

"Al, supper, yesterday?"

"Let me think, Maggie's stew in the dining hall. Why?"

"What's the last thing you remember about Clarence Knowles before he got trapped up north?"

"Clarence's up north?" Bill answered.

"Who's Clarence Knowles?" Al responded.

The door opened again. Harvey preceded Simon into the room. "You're not going to believe this," Simon began.

"We're losing our long-term memories," Jeff finished for him. "I ran into Harvey on the way here."

"It's after two o'clock," Ron announced. "Where's Frank?"

"Now he's got short-term memory problems." Logan bemoaned. "I'll give him a call." He reached for his earpiece when the door opened again.

"I'm not late, am I? The sequencer took a little longer than I thought."

"Everyone have a seat," Jeff began. "I think our problem just went from serious to critical! Ron, is the satellite still over the encampment?"

"For about another ten minutes."

"Put it on the Big Board."

The old image from the raid was replaced by live feed from the satellite cameras down on the encampment. It showed the fire pit, the pool, but all the metal sheets appeared to be in a single stack. There were no alligator-men in the area.

"Ron, re-angle the camera. Are they heading our way?" Jeff was out of his chair and leaning over the table monitor.

"I can't find them heading either east towards the bay or north around it," he announced after a few minutes.

"Widen the search!" Logan exclaimed.

"I'm getting a heat trail heading southwest," he pointed at the red dots appearing on the new map. "And there goes the satellite. It won't be back over this area until this time tomorrow."

"Why did they leave their encampment?"

"They stacked everything like they were coming back."

"Clint," Jeff said into his earpiece. "Come to the Situation Room, immediately." Then he went back to addressing the people in the room. "Ron, you've got your spare survey equipment mounted in one of the modules, right?"

"One of the early cargo units we built."

"Is it equipped with Infrared sensors?"

"Yes."

"We saw that the beasts were showing up as warm-blooded, just as your tests said, Simon."

"You want to track them from the sky?" Logan asked.

"They have to be going somewhere. It might be a clue to what is happening to them."

"And to us." Frank finished. "Something is rewiring the alligator DNA. It doesn't look like the usual viral agent." He opened the pouch on his belt and started pulling out plastic sample tubes with swabs mounted inside their lids. "I want a sample of each of your DNA. We need to see what's happening to us."

Chapter 38

The Hot Pool

"There, I've got them." Ron pointed at the infrared image on his screen. Almost a hundred different red blobs were moving from left to right, occasionally concealed when they passed under more dense foliage. Jeff could tell, since Ron also had a visual camera pointed at the same area. Ron touched his earpiece to contact the cockpit, "Clint, about ten degrees more to the south."

Logan was upfront in the copilot seat, since Jeff had chosen to ride in the module and monitor the equipment with Ron and Francois. The red images moving through the forest below appeared to be walking upright, they were a bit too short to be crawling on all fours, and they were occasionally using the trees for support.

"Is it my imagination," Jeff pointed to one of the creatures' tails, "or are their tails growing shorter?"

"I'll have to defer to your judgment," Francois said. "You're the one who saw them up close."

"It's probably just the angle you're looking at them," Ron threw in.

"Could they, though?" Jeff ignored him in favor of his biologist's answer.

"Usually, no. They would keep growing with the rest of the creature. But we don't know what the changes in their DNA will result in. We still haven't learned how to really read DNA, just compare it."

"It could be some ritualistic mutilation ceremony," Logan offered over the radio.

"Or it could just be the angle you're looking at them," Ron continued.

"Yeah, it could just be the angle," Jeff said as he stared closer at the image.

Ron kept the camera focused on the center of the migration. "Where ever they're going, they aren't in any hurry to get there."

"Clint, pull up a little bit." Jeff dropped his hand to his side. "Ron, angle the visual cameras forward. Let's see if we can find out where they're going before they get there." Jeff went over to the wall-mounted cabinets and took out one of the fist-sized drones they had put in there before leaving Petersville. He set it on top of the banks of four monitors they were using, pulled down one of the control units. He switched on the power to the drone to make sure he had the right control. Then he activated the drone's camera and linked it to the fourth monitor, which was currently blank. When he got a visual of the interior of the module, he set the gravity control on the drone to their current altitude, opened the side door and flew it out and ahead of the shuttle.

"That's far enough, Clint," Ron radioed the pilot. The red blobs on his screen were falling behind, he'd stopped Clint before they'd all disappeared. "We don't want to lose the pack." He switched the magnification settings. "Just a couple of clearings coming up, nothing unusual about them."

"Wait, that clearing goes on and on." Francois turned to Jeff, "There's no vegetation in it, just a rocky strip running from the Carnegie Ocean northward as far as we can see. With a couple of streams running down into the ocean. That's steam coming off them when they hit the ocean water. That has to be some really hot water. Can we land?"

"That's out of the question. We're here to follow the creatures, find out why they abruptly left their homes. To make sure they aren't heading our way." Jeff angled the camera back to match the infrared one still tracking the creatures. They could follow them by their heat signatures but the trees obscured any visual sightings. "But..." He handed the drone's remote control over to the scientist.

Francois grinned, sat down in front of the monitor the drone was feeding and flew it over the streams. "Damn, I wish Jacob was here. We need a geologist for this." He brought it down as close to the ground as he could.

They hung about a hundred yards above the treetops and slowly paced the alligator-men migration. It was a couple of hours later that the creatures broke out of the woods onto that rocky slope Francois kept his drone over. He had been climbing the drone up the hillside in an effort to find the source of the streams when Ron called out that the creatures were climbing onto the steeply rising slope. He took the drone vertically up one hundred feet before they broke out.

They began climbing but not on the rocks. They stayed just past the trees, on the grass-covered ground running on the side. Two streams cut their way down the slope about six feet apart. Each of them registered as hotter than anything else present on Ron's infrared.

Clint stopped the shuttle over the trees. Jeff thought that might keep the alligator-men from spotting them. The human's cameras did an excellent job of following the climbers, they didn't have to stay in the creatures' line of sight. If necessary, Jeff had a couple more drones he could toss out of the module.

The creatures climbed the slope for another half hour, just over another mile. Then stopped, sat down and waited until everyone had caught up, before they crossed the hot rocks to a central pool. Francois ran the drone a little further up and it looked like the two streams emanated from that pool. In the downward edge of the pool was a large pockmarked stone, about two yards in diameter. The streams flowed around the sides of the stone before heading down the hill.

Ron made some adjustments to his infrared camera, all the colors blue shifted slightly. "Those rocks are hotter than the creatures." He pointed at the image.

"Am I reading this right? The pool is hotter still?" Jeff stared at the image.

"With all that heat, they're taking seats around the pool." Francois ran the drone directly over the pool but high enough and quiet enough that it did not disturb the assembled creatures.

They sat around the top of the pool, encircling it from stream to stream, though they stayed a good distance from the hot water flowing down. The one with the ceremonial staff stood at the top of the partial circle and held that staff up in the air. He waved it around before bringing it down and striking the stone in the pool.

Sparks flew from the stone at the point of contact. But a faint blue light shot away from it spherically. The light registered on the visual cameras but not the infrared. The alligator-shaman did this four more times before motioning for everyone to rise. Then they turned around and with their backs to the pool, they allowed their tails to enter its waters.

Some of them screamed in pain but the majority of them just stood there, moving their tails back and forth in the water. After a few minutes, the shaman took two steps forward and turned to say something to the others assembled.

The humans were too far away to pick up what it was saying, but watched as its entire congregation took a step away from the pool, pulling their tails free of it.

"Are they standing up straighter?" Jeff said in a low voice.

"You're imagining things again." The radio system had been on so the cockpit could hear what the back section was doing.

"Jeff," this time it was Clint. "Something's wrong. I'm feeling a little off. I'm heading back to Petersville before whatever this is gets too serious for me to get us back."

Jeff put his hand to his forehead, thinking he felt tingly all over his body and a fuzziness was muddling his brain. "Just get us home safely."

Ron and Francois had dropped into their chairs with their arms hanging at their sides. The remote for the drone sat on the floor under Francois' right hand. As Clint turned the shuttle around and headed back to their base, no one recovered the little drone.

The last thing Jeff saw, before falling to the floor and losing consciousness, was the auto-return light go on. Knowing the shuttle would get back to Petersville on its own was enough relief for him to fall into a deep sleep.

An hour later, the drone went into power-saver mode and just hung one hundred feet over the pool as the alligator-men began their march back into the woods.

Chapter 39

Addled Brains

Alarms howled throughout Petersville. Nancy dropped the hammer she had been using to install the floor boards of the Carlton home. It was the shuttle's distress frequency. Something had gone wrong with Jeff's damned field trip.

Her brother, Ahmed, and the Blacks met her at the Town Hall to find out what had happened, too. She had waved Carl Brown, Sandra Bales, and Doc Parker to head out to the landing pad, to meet the shuttle in case of injuries, as she passed them on the wooden walkway.

On the Alarm Board, the auto-return sequence light was glowing red. She had tried calling everyone who had gone out with Jeff, but no one was answering. She activated the camera above the pilot's seat in the shuttle. Then fed the image into the monitoring station. The image was the top of Clint's head looped over to the side, leaning against Logan's shoulder. Tilting the camera, she was able to see that Logan had his head resting on the door. Returning it to forward view, outside the windshield she could see the waters of Buffet Bay as the shuttle sped over it. In the distance, Petersville's dock came into view.

She pressed her finger to her ear to address the people she had sent to the landing field as well as those in the Situation Room. "They should be here in a couple of minutes. She walked over to the remote shuttle controls. "I'm taking remote control of the shuttle, now!" Her finger fell away from her ear, she was going to need both hands for this.

As the shuttle cleared the dock and moved north towards the landing field, Nancy got visual feeds of its descent on the bench-top monitor she sat in front of. Where a driver pilot had a single joystick, Nancy had to work with a pair of them. The remote station didn't have the foot pedals of an actual shuttle.

She maneuvered her virtual image of it into the red circle on the monitor. Once it was properly centered, the circle turned green. She killed the forward and lateral momentum of the craft, and allowed it to sit directly above Landing Pad Two. Next, she set the gravity units to decrease slowly to zero elevation and the shuttle landed on the dusty surface, without throwing up any of the loose dust under it.

She shut off all power inside it, followed by switching off her remote station, got up from her chair and ran for the door. "Bill, you stay here and monitor." She touched her radio earpiece as she pushed apart the Town Hall doors that weren't opening fast enough. "She's ready to open up."

She was halfway across the open space to the landing pad; Doc Parker was just entering the side door of the module, followed closely by Sandra. Carl was already pulling Logan from his seat and setting him on the ground. She sprinted around to the pilot's door with Ahmed close behind her. As she pulled the door open, Ahmed grabbed

Clint and began pulling him out. They worked him around until Ahmed could drag him over to the unconscious form of Logan, already resting.

Nancy left him to it and opened the pilot side door of the module. Mary and Mike Black were jumping in. Simon had managed to revive Jeff slightly. He was trying to sit him up when Mike grabbed Jeff by the shoulder Simon was trying to hold up and minister to his patient. Nancy jumped in and got on Jeff's left side. They lifted Jeff to his feet, but he was too groggy to support himself. They carried him out on Doc Parker's instructions.

As they were setting him on the ground, Jeff groggily swatted off their attempts to lie him down. Nancy looked into Mike's eyes and left him to handle Jeff. She jumped back into the module. Mary and Sandra had Ron in a two-man fireman's carry and were carrying him out, Doc Parker had given up trying to rouse him.

"Come on, Frank." The Doc was gently patting the laying man's face with his right hand and holding a stinky vial under his nose with his left. "Frank, wake up."

He looked over his shoulder as Nancy's step into the module shifted it slightly. She got on the other side of Francois and started lifting him with the doctor. They moved the biologist out into the open air and laid him down with the others.

"Jeff, you just sit still." Doc Parker leaned over his moving form and barked. Nancy could see him trying to stand up. Obviously against doctors orders, as he was putting his hand on Jeff's chest to hold him down. Doc Parker put his finger to his ear, then grimaced and dropped his hand. "Nancy, see if you can get some stretchers out here."

"Anyone near the clinic, we need five stretchers out at Landing Pad Two immediately." She said into her radio. "I repeat. Anyone..."

* * *

An hour later, Doc Parker was giving his patients the all clear to get out of the beds he had been keeping them in. "I still don't know what happened to you all," he said offering his hand to Clint. He had been the last of them to awaken naturally and was still the most groggy.

"Those creatures did something to that stone out there and it put the whammy on us," Francois said.

" 'Whammy'? That's not a very scientific term, Frank." Nancy gave the scientist a puzzled look.

"Well, it's what happened."

"You sure we're all right, Doc? I'm still having trouble finding the words to des... tell what happened out there." Jeff looked at the rest of the expedition's members. Some getting up, others staying flat on their backs. Bales even threw his arm over his eyes against the lights shining down on him, while his wife sat next to his bed. "Anyone else feel strange? Foggy-headed?"

"You probably all just need a good night's sleep. You're overwrought from your exertions."

"What'd you say, doc?" Logan asked.

"I said you're tired, Mr. Rogers. I prescribe at least eight hours of slumber for each of you."

"Eight hours of what?" Clint used his elbow to lift himself off the mattress to ask.

"Everyone get back into your beds. No one is going anywhere until you get the rest I just prescribed." He finished putting away the items he'd been using to examine everyone and locking the cabinets he'd placed them in. He turned down the lights, left the room, shooing Nancy ahead of him, then closed the door to the only ward this fledgling hospital had so far.

"In the morning, I'll have to run more tests. Whatever's going on, I need to understand it or I can't treat them." He walked over to his diagnostic equipment and powered them down for the night.

"I'll go over the shuttle's logs. Maybe there's something in them." As she walked into the clinic's waiting area, she touched her earpiece. "Ahmed, meet me at Landing Pad Two. We need to find out what happened out there."

"It'll be about a half hour. I'm finishing that batch of roofing adhesive."

"Can you put it on hold?"

"Yes, but you said you needed it yesterday."

"It can wait. Meet me at the shuttle."

"On my way."

"Damn, but he's eager to get out of that lab," she said to herself.

But Doc Parker had heard her. "Scientists thrive on a mystery. Mixing a batch of chemicals is nothing compared to playing with a good puzzle. He'll thank you for the break."

She walked out of the sliding hospital doors and across to where the shuttle still sat on Landing Pad Two. Ahmed came running to catch her before she could open the side door and climb into the module.

"We might want to open every door in this thing," he advised as he placed his hands on either side to the door frame and stepped up and in. "Ventilation. If it was something airborne, we don't want to fall victim to it ourselves."

"Good idea." She stepped across and opened the other side door and popped it into the latch to hold it open. She heard a similar sound and knew Ahmed had done the same on the side they came in.

Then she went to the module's control panel and dropped the loading hatch in back to completely open the box up. A slight breeze came from the back end and circulated out the side doors.

"I didn't smell anything," Ahmed said as he passed his small atmospheric detector through the air in the module. "And neither does this thing. But better safe."

"Yeah. Let's see what these guys were looking at before they went on auto." She stepped over to Ron's mobile meteorological equipment and powered it back up. They replayed the last several minutes of the visual feed; from the time the creatures started sitting in front of the stone until the wave of blue emissions hit the shuttle. After that the visual feed stopped.

"Doesn't that indicate a drone feed?" Ahmed pointed to an icon on the lower left corner of the image. "Can you pull up its file?"

As she was doing that, he went over to the cabinet storing the drones. "Hey, one of them is missing."

"I'm getting the drone's recorded feed now." The video playback switched angles on the scene they had just witnessed. But this time, the drone kept recording. "It looks like it kept going for another hour." Nancy pointed at the time marker at the bottom of the video. "I'm scanning ahead to see what happened." The video went into a rapid viewing mode. They watched the creatures continue sitting for several minutes until they all got up extremely quickly and walked very fast back down the hillside before disappearing into the woods. A few minutes later, the drone appeared to cease functions.

"What was that blue light?" Nancy spun the chair around she had been sitting in to face Ahmed.

"I've never seen anything like it before. Let's slow down that section of the videos and maybe we can spot something we missed."

They ran the videos again. They ran the videos frame by frame. They ran the videos split screen with the infrared feed, where the blue light didn't even show up.

"Let's try something else," Ahmed suggested. "Let's see if that blue light is in the background before and after the stone gets struck."

"You mean lose all the other colors and isolate that wavelength?"

"I'll make a scientist out of you yet." He pushed her chair away from the station, selected a frame where the blue light was the most intense and captured its wavelength. Then he told the computer to remove all other wavelengths from the image until only the blue light was left. As expected, a moment after the shaman had struck the stone, the light filled the screen.

With the color he wanted chosen, Ahmed backed up the video. The color faded away until it was extremely faint before the shaman first struck the stone. Ahmed dialed the video ahead. The light again faded to mere background a few moments after the shaman had stopped striking the stone. But it didn't go away, even after the creatures had left and the drone powered down.

On a hunch, Nancy activated the outside cameras on the module and feed them through Ahmed's filter. The faded blue light was everywhere around the module, everywhere around Petersville as she angled the camera.

Faded, dim, but present. Everywhere.

Chapter 40

Research Adventure

"I'm just asking, Nan. Do you really think this is a good idea?" Bill turned to his sister from the pilot's seat of the same shuttle Clint had taken Jeff on his expedition in earlier.

"We need a sample of that stone and its water supply if we want to figure out what's happening to our people." She stared straight ahead as the tops of trees whizzed past just a couple of feet below them. "But I do think you're flying a bit low, so could you please keep your eyes forward?"

"There's the clearing now." Bill pointed with his free hand. "It looks like I have to go north from here." He pivoted the craft and followed the rocky waterfall up until they finally got to the stone Nancy and Ahmed wanted a piece of. The waterfall ended at that point.

"It's like that stone impacted the earth and opened up a hot spring just underneath," Nancy commented as she activated the radio link with the back of their module. "We're here."

"Better not set down," Carl radioed back. "I'm getting readings from the surrounding rocks of over one hundred fifty degrees Fahrenheit. It could play havoc with our circuits, should be safe to walk on, though."

She could hear the module's side door close through their radio link. "The ground's too steep here anyway, I'll have to adjust the height of the gravitational units separately. It'll keep the shuttle level, but while we'll be a foot off the ground on the right, I'll be too high up to get down and help you guys."

"That must really break your heart." As the shuttle stabilized its position, Nancy opened her door and climbed down. Glad that her hiking boots had an inch-thick leather sole, she could feel the warmth coming through them.

Ahmed had already emerged from the module, carrying a large, sealed bucket. On his belt was mounted a ripping hammer and metal chisel on his right side, and his machete on the other. "Carl, grab my testing kit, would you?" he called back.

He walked up to the top edge of the pool, above where the stone sat inside it, about six inches from the edge, initiating the double streams of super-heated water that cascaded down the hillside. He removed the cover from the bucket and took out his thermometer gun. The water was reading over one hundred and ten degrees Celsius. Ten degrees over the normal boiling point for water and it wasn't even bubbling, simply steaming. He pointed the gun at the middle of the stone, it was eighty-four degrees Celsius. "No one's grabbing this baby." Then he aimed it at the top, only eighty degrees. "It looks like the hot springs here is what's heating the stone up."

"Hot springs?" Carl asked before Nancy had a chance.

"Grab my dip sampler and collect a few water samples. Store about four containers for analysis when we get back . Then run some of the water through the mineral analyzer." Ahmed pulled a foot-wide metal box from the bucket and handed it to Carl. "Check the Calcium, Magnesium, Sodium, and Potassium levels; hell, any soluble metal it can find." He turned to Nancy to answer Carl's question. "Something in this pool is raising the natural boiling point of this water. Usually that's the minerals I just asked to be tested for. There's probably some other soluble anions to go with those metals, but I have to get samples back to the lab to test for them."

"Are you planning to chip off a sample from the stone?" Nancy pointed to the hammer and chisel on his belt.

"That was my plan."

"Wasn't it the pounding the shaman gave the thing that caused the blue light to emanate from it? The Blue light that seemed to cause the problems Jeff and the others are now having. I don't think hitting it with a hammer and chisel is such a good idea."

"But I need a sample to figure out what it is and why it gives off that light." He scratched the stubble on his chin for a minute. "Stones don't usually emit that kind of light when struck." He straightened up and thought for a couple of minutes. "Something in that rock could be being catalyzed by the water or, more likely, the heat of the water? Can we pull it out of the pool?"

"You said the water's superheated."

"Come on, you're an engineer. Engineer something! If we can take it back to Petersville, we can put it under controlled conditions. Run proper tests. Under strict safety precautions. Figure this thing out."

"Bill," she hollered over to the shuttle. She waved him to come down when he turned to look at her. As he opened his door, she hollered over, "I need you out here."

He looked down at the six feet he was from the ground. "Give me a minute, I'm climbing out the other side."

"Damn, that's a thick soup," Carl said as the analyzer dinged it had completed its tests. He handed the machine over to Ahmed, who sent the numbers to the module's computer, which in turn sent them to Endeavor's computer memory core, where Ahmed had a folder for chemistry results.

Ahmed clipped the unit to his belt using the carabineer mounted to the back of the unit. "Carl, I want you to go downstream and collect another series of water samples and fill the vials in this rack. Let them cool to fifty degrees Celsius before attaching their caps. Then seal them tightly. The resulting vacuum will preserve them until we get home. Whereas if you cap them right away, it could implode the sample containers."

"You want to do what with that stone?" Bill was asking Nancy, but when he saw Ahmed walking their way, asked him the same question. "Are you crazy? You know how hot that thing is?"

"The rope we have in the back of the module will be able to handle the heat if you two can rig a way to pull the stone out. Just don't let it roll down the hill."

"And why not?" Bill asked.

"Cause then you'd have to go chasing after it. I mean to take it back to Petersville for study."

"Well, let's see how much rope we have and if there are any pulleys we can use. How much do you think this thing weighs?"

"I've no idea. That's one of the things I need to get it out to determine: What's its density? What's its composition? Just what is this thing made of?"

"Okay," Bill turned to his sister. "You got any ideas?"

She was already heading around the shuttle. "The first thing we have to do is see what we have to work with. C'mon." She hopped into the right side door of the module knowing Bill would grouse for a moment, then follow her.

By the time he finally got into the module, Nancy had pulled open one of the six foot tall cabinets and was dragging out a large web net. "This must be the capture net Jeff used when he brought in the alligator-man. It's going to be more than adequate for carrying that stone." She did a quick look around. "The rope should be stored in the middle left cabinet in the back."

He started walking over to the pilot's side of the shuttle. "No, my left. I'm pointed in the wrong direction. The co-pilot's side."

* * *

"That should do it." Nancy said as she admired her and her brother's improvisation. While there were no actual pulleys stored on the module, something she would be addressing when this was all over, there had been several dozen carabineers.

They had rigged up a pulling system that connected several of the nearby trees, the ones over two feet in diameter, and the net they had draped over the stone. They had hooked the whole thing up to use the shuttle to pull it out of the water. Once the stone was moving, they could disconnect all the carabineer pulleys and use the power winch to pull it up under the shuttle for a ride back to Petersville.

That is, assuming it was round, like they expected.

"Bring up the tension on this section," Nancy shouted to Carl at the tree with the first pulley/carabineer. He and Ahmed pulled on the rope that tightened one of the lines running from the net and into the balancing blocks Bill had bored out for them to get the four lines coming from the net equally tightened.

"Good, now tie it off." She walked over to give the next line, the one on the bottom left side, a tug. Since it was tight enough, she moved on to the upper right line and checked it. "Now bring up the tension on this one."

After running through another series of line adjustments, Nancy scrambled out of the lines and called to her brother standing under the module on the pilot's side. "Okay, Bill, tighten everything up with the winch." It pulled the rope an inch or almost two, forcing one of the trees to bend slightly. "Okay, stop." Nancy went over to it and looked at the tree. Once she was satisfied, "Okay, lock it down."

He came out from under the module, stretched himself erect again and began climbing the chain ladder they had mounted by the pilot's door so he didn't have to crawl through the cockpit to get back to the controls. "Ready when you are," he radioed everyone after he got himself belted in.

"Take it slow at first," Nancy said into the radio. As the shuttle started to move to the left side of the clearing,

"Slowly!" It stopped its forward motion as the rigging snapped a musical note of tension.

"Back up slightly and try again," Nancy suggested.

Bill backed the shuttle up about an inch, enough to relieve the rigging's tension, then pulled forward again.

Nancy watched the stone shift slightly to the right and stop.

"One more time. This time at full power!"

He backed up again and set the drive motors on full. He moved the inch he backed up plus an inch more, then came to a stop again. A third try produced no further results.

Nancy and Carl untied the lower two ropes connecting to the net and pulled them deeper below the stone. After they got them retied, she had Bill give it one more try to move the stone.

When he backed up a foot to get a better run, the stone stayed in place for a couple of seconds before it rolled back into its original resting place.

"We need to get some gravitational units to place on that thing. Just to lighten the load we're trying to pull." Ahmed bounced his finger off one of the still-tight ropes.

As the noise from the rope's vibration died out, Nancy heard a rustle coming from the woods. She jerked her head around to make a quick count, pulled her machete and cleaved the line running from the shuttle through their improvised block and tackle arrangement. "Everyone in the shuttle, NOW!"

Seconds after they had sealed the doors and Bill had lifted them straight up from the stone, the creatures emerged from the woods. They climbed the hillside to the pool and defensively surrounded the stone. One of them had the ceremonial staff Nancy had seen on the videos.

"That must be their shaman." It shook the staff over its head at the retreating humans. Then started spinning the staff while turning to face the stone in the pool.

"Bill, get us out of here fast!" Nancy hollered over her radio.

As they were leaving their camera's range, Nancy saw the shaman bring its staff down, striking the stone as she had seen in Jeff's earlier video.

"Bill, set this thing on auto-return." She tapped her radio for another channel, "Command Center, Nancy Flannigan calling. We are setting our shuttle on auto-return. If you don't hear from us in an hour, assume control of it and bring her in." She tapped her earpiece to repeat her message three more times.

Chapter 41

More Added Brains

"Control, this is Flannigan. I am directly over the landing pad. Ah, how do I bring this thing down?"

Simon stopped his chair from swinging. He'd come to Town Hall to be on hand for the shuttle's return after their distress call came in.

James Matthews, who was currently in charge of the Situation Room, gave Simon a puzzled look. "Bill, could you please verify that request?"

"We're over the landing field, I can see one of those ringy things directly under us. But this thing is just sitting here."

"You said you were putting it on auto-return. Is it still on that setting?"

"Auto, auto, oh auto-return. There's a light on directly above that label."

James jumped out of his chair and over to the remote landing console. He activated the connection to the shuttle and was getting ready to bring it down.

"I flipped the switch under the label and the light went out. Hey, this thing's wobbling up here."

"Damn," James said. As the controllers released their grip on the shuttle, he dropped into a chair nearby and pulled it up to the console. "Bill, you've got to reengage the auto-return. I was just about to bring you down."

"How do I do that?"

"That switch you just flipped, flip it back up."

"This one? Hey, we stopped wobbling."

When the two controllers in front of him snapped to life, James grabbed the pair of them and stabilized the shuttle. He thumb-locked the left joystick and set the gravity units on a descent path until they gently brought the shuttle down onto Landing Pad Two, the same one it had left from. When all six units acknowledged ground contact, he cut the power to the driver's cockpit.

"I think they may be in trouble, Doc." James was out of his chair and heading for the door.

Simon pushed himself out of his chair, not being as spry as James, and radioed a couple of the people he had medic trained to meet them at the landing field with stretchers. The sliding doors of Town Hall closed behind him as he headed across the compound.

James was already opening the pilot's door and pulling Bill from his seat by the time Simon got close. He went over to the module's side door and opened it. Peter and Mildred, two of the teens he had trained, were coming up behind him, kicking up dust with the two stretchers they were pushing.

Inside, Nancy was leaning against the back wall and Ahmed was helping Carl to his feet. "Hey, Doc, glad you could meet us," Nancy turned and walked over to the door he held open. "You won't believe what we've been through."

"Can the three of you walk?"

Carl's knee didn't engage as Ahmed pulled him up the first time. But the chemist caught him before he could actually fall. He then tried a couple of steps. "Yeah, I think so."

"Then get over to the clinic. Nancy?"

"I'm a little woozy, nothing I can't deal with."

"Then get over there also." He got away from the door so the three of them could leave and headed for the cockpit. "Millie, bring that stretcher over here."

James had Bill out of the cockpit and was laying him on the ground. The engineer was mumbling incoherently as he lay there reaching for the controls he had left in the driver.

"Peter, get over here. We're going to need your help getting him onto the stretcher."

James and Simon took his shoulders, while Mildred and Peter grabbed a leg each and lifted him up. They gently set him on the gurney stretcher. "You two, get him into the examination room. Stat."

They spun the stretcher around, Mildred took the guiding end and Peter provided the push. Then they hurried off to the clinic, going around the slowly advancing party that came from the back of the shuttle.

"I'm going to run out of bed space with this lot. You'd better try and roust me up some more beds." Simon turned and started off for the clinic before James replied.

"I'll do what I can. No promises."

* * *

"Keep those three in the waiting room." Doc Parker said as his sliding doors closed behind him. Peter had returned to the waiting room with the three ambulatory victims. Mildred was obviously with Bill in the exam room. Before he walked through the doors to the exam room, "Keep them talking. See if you can find any lapses in their memories." He pushed aside the swinging doors and walked in to exam the worst of his new patients.

"Bill, can you hear me?" Simon leaned over the top of the stretcher and motioned Mildred to get to the foot. "We're transferring you over to the exam table." They lifted the sheet Bill was on and set him on the exam table. "Okay, how do you feel?"

He mumbled something.

"I said, how are you feeling?"

"Fine, just fine." came back to him. Bill looked like he was ready to fall asleep.

"You can't sleep now. I need you awake to run a few tests. Then you can sleep." He lifted his head. "Millie, 5 CCs of pseudoaggressite."

She mixed the drug with the carrier solvent, put on a pair of latex gloves, soaked a cotton ball and rubbed the mixture on Bill's upper left arm. Seconds later, the arm was dry as the two chemicals had been absorbed through his skin.

Bill's eyes opened wider a minute later. "What's going on?" He tried to sit up, but Simon pushed him back to the table's mattress.

"We're thinking you got hit by the same thing that got Jeff and his party. We still don't know what it is. What can you remember?"

Bill related everything that happened in minute detail before Simon finally held up his hand for him to stop. "Whatever it is, it's only messing with people's long-term memory." Simon reached up to the auto-doc controls and requested an analysis. "After I run these tests on you, I want a complete audio record of your adventures." As Bill rolled into the diagnostic tunnel, "Before you lose those memories."

"Milly, go out into the waiting room and check on everyone. If they are able, send them over to Town Hall and ask them to make a similar statement before their memories fade."

Seconds after Mildred went into the other room, Peter came into the exam room. "Hey, Doc, Ahmed said something about water samples he needs to run. He says they're in the module."

"He's got an intern. You help Millie get those people over to James in the Situation Room and I'll have Lamar run the samples. Ahmad's got to record his memories before he forgets them."

Simon touched his ear to call Lamar just as his eyes saw his radio sitting on his desk. "One of these days I'm going to have to remember to wear the damned thing." He went over and twisted it into his ear, then pressed it again. "Lamar Crawford, please report to the examination room of the clinic."

Once he got the boy's acknowledgement and as he was checking the readouts of the auto-doc, the machine dinged that it had finished its analysis and began rolling Bill out of its tunnel.

"Just as I expected. It can't find anything wrong with you, just like it couldn't with Jeff, Logan, Clint and the others." Bill started to sit up, Simon helped him down from the exam table and over to his desk. "Everything you told me about your trip, I want you to record it into this file on my computer." Simon leaned over the man, opened his voice recorder and transcriber, then started the two of them for him. "I'll leave you to it."

He was finishing up getting the auto-doc ready for the next patient when Lamar came in. "What's ya need, Doc?"

"Ahmed said there were some water samples in the back of the shuttle that needed analysis."

"Probably in his sample case. I'll get right on it." He hesitated for a moment. "Ah, do you know what he wanted them tested for?"

"Find them and set them up. You can call him when you're ready."

"Will do," Lamar said on his way out.

"How're you coming?" Simon asked as he walked over to his desk and Bill.

"I'm finished, but I think there is something more I need to do?"

"Something about the expedition?"

"No. Or I'm not sure."

"Did you save the file?"

"Nooo. How do you do that?"

Simon leaned over Bill's right side and told the computer to save both files as 'Stone Expedition-Bill'.

"Let's get you into the ward. That aggressite should be wearing off soon." He helped Bill out of the chair and into the next room. Two beds were still free, so he guided him to the closest of them and helped him lay down.

As he was leaving, Simon turned to check on everyone. Bill rolled onto his side, the rest were all asleep. He turned down the lights some more and closed the door to the room.

He set the ward's security suite to notify him of any of them got up and left the room to go back to, well, to wherever they remembered to go.

* * *

Simon found James and his wife Susan the only occupants of the Situation Room when he arrived.

"Where'd the others go?"

"In back," James threw his thumb towards the lunch room in back. "You told me to find somewhere for them to sleep. Sue got three cots out of the warehouse and set them up in the lunch room."

"Did they get their transcriptions done?"

"Mostly. They started falling out of their chairs, asleep. Ahmed was the last one to give up, but I don't think any of them really finished. I saved what they had completed in different files."

"Can you pull everything we have found out about this condition into a single folder?"

"Everything?"

"What we have on the stone, the alligator-men, the various descriptions of the expeditions and Lamar's analysis. Plus what I have on this chip, then copy it to my chip and everywhere else you can think of."

"Everywhere?"

"If we don't solve this quickly, someone else is going to have to find this information and solve it for us. This may give them the head start we need."

Chapter 42

Not the Home They Left

Howard, Tommy and Lerick waited at the entrance of the village cavern as I'mac and a couple of other Raffians worked their flint knives into the frozen-over gaps between the snow blocks that had protected the entrance all these months. M'cron had tested the air coming in the cavern's vent holes and decided that the season of growing had begun. Two weeks late, but it had finally begun.

"I like it up here, but it will be nice to get back to my friends in Petersville." Tommy looked up at his father.

"We've been out of touch with them for the last couple of months, I hope they remember we're still up here." They stood to the side as the Raffians began removing the frozen blocks back to their village. Plastic drums were waiting for them to allow the blocks to melt into stored water.

"I just hope we've got battery power in the shuttle." Clarence came up the tunnel and joined them as a hole was broken through the barrier and outside air flooded into the musty atmosphere they had been breathing. "I'd forgotten how good fresh air smelt."

They didn't bring in the ice bricks that were part of the outside layer but pushed them outward. As they picked away the layers of bricks, they would always push out the outermost ones. Never taking any of them back to the water cisterns.

"What's the matter with the outer bricks?" Clarence asked Tommy.

After a quick conversation with Lerick, Tommy responded, "The blue dust is not good for drinking. They discard the outer blocks where the dust accumulates, to avoid its evil spirits."

Finally, they had removed enough of the inner layers and pushed aside enough of the outer ones so the humans could squeeze through. They made their way out to the greening tundra where they'd left their shuttle.

Almost all of the snow had melted and run off. Even the ice blocks that had been thrown out were rapidly disappearing once they were in the Beleniusen sun, Only small patches of it remained, mostly in the shade of rocks and trees. Clarence could find no traces of the blue dust Tommy had talked about. The ground was moist with the melted snow, so they had to tread lightly getting to the shuttle, lest they slipped and fell in the mud.

Clarence opened the side door to the module. Inside the lights flickered to life. "We've got power." He climbed in enough to check the module's batteries. "We've got full power back here." He pushed his way past Howard and into the cockpit. "Full power to the engines also," he called out. "We can go home whenever we want.

Howard came up to the door Clarence had just climbed in. "Radio Petersville. Let them know our status and that we should be home by nightfall."

"With pleasure," Clarence took his earpiece from his pocket, dropped it in the charger box, then picked up the shuttle's headset. "Knowles to Petersville Control. Knowles to Petersville Control; come in, please."

Howard took the five earpieces he was carrying and dropped them in to charge also before heading back to his son in the module.

"Tommy, get your brother and sister." He said as he stepped into the module. "Start getting the stuff we're taking back with us ready to go."

"Sure thing, Dad." The boy ran out of the module, almost knocking his father over in his hurry, and dashed back for the cave entrance.

After he was gone, the hatch between the cockpit and the module opened. Clarence shouted between the two compartments. "I can't raise Petersville. I think we'd better get going as soon as possible."

Howard reached for his radio to call the others. He stopped his hand before it ever made contact with the earpiece. "They're charging," he muttered on his way out the door.

He banged on the door to the cockpit for Clarence to open it. "I'll get things loaded up. You get this thing ready to head back."

* * *

It took the five of them plus several of their Raffian friends about an hour to get all the stuff they had acquired over the past few months stored away. After a few final goodbyes, they were strapped in and on their way south.

Howard sat in the co-pilot seat and kept trying to raise the Situation Room, a place that was supposed to be continuously manned. Clarence pushed the engines to maximum, worrying about what they would find. The normal five-hour trip down from the Raffian settlement took them an exhausting four.

As they circled the landing field, Clarence pointed at the shuttle already occupying Landing Pad Two, the newer of the pair. "Guess I'm going to have to set down on one. Still no word from Command?"

"None, just set her down and we can start looking for everyone."

The ground on Landing Pad One wasn't as tightly packed as it was on Landing Pad Two; as the shuttle's feet set down inside the circle, they kicked a little fine dust into the air. Nothing any of them noticed, though.

Howard was out the door, stuffing an earpiece into his ear as he ran across the field to the Town Hall. He pushed the sliding doors open, since they barely moved as he approached. They stayed open after him.

He shoved the door open into the Situation Room and found it empty. Most of the monitors were dark and the Big Board was shut down. Then he noticed that it was the light coming in through the windows that illuminated the room. The internal lighting system wasn't powered up.

"Marsha, you and the kids split up. Try to find anyone." At least his earpiece had power and would work at this short range without having to go through the central computer. "Clarence, I think something is wrong with the electrical generator. Meet me in the Power Room."

Marsha ran up to him as he emerged from the Town Hall building and wrapped him in a frightened hug. "Howard, what's wrong?"

"I don't know, it's why I need you and the kids to find anyone who can explain things to us." He broke the embrace. "I need to see if I can get the power on again." He walked around the side of the Town Hall and over the three blocks to the edge of the woods where the solar energy converters and batteries were housed.

The concrete block building was dug into the side of the hill to prevent natural catastrophes from interrupting the colony's power supply. The building was undamaged, but its door stood open.

"Okay, what's up?" Clarence quickly caught his breath after having run the last several yards. He placed his hand on the outward-opening door. "Hey, this thing ain't moving."

They bent down enough to see the mud that had pooled and hardened under the door. Clarence pulled hard on it and broke the door free. "How long's this thing been open?"

It was dark inside, where banks of lights should have brightly illuminated the interior. Howard produced a flashlight from his pocket, one that he had charged up on their flight down, and illuminated the power station's interior. "Let's get the power on and see what the computers can tell us."

They walked into the massive battery room. As they walked past each of the racks of storage units, Howard pointed at their green lights. Clarence nodded to acknowledge each one. At the back of the room, "Okay, they're all powered up, or at least have enough charge to function."

Clarence ran his hand over the last of them. "But their power isn't getting out? Besides, don't most of the buildings use their panels' power directly before sending it here?"

"Find one of the lifts. We'll see if there's a problem on top of Town Hall. It's those computers we need." He slapped Clarence on the back and headed out of the building.

While Clarence was off obtaining a lifting basket, Howard examined the connections coming out of the ground that should have been supplying the power to each of the buildings in Petersville.

Each of them had a small rodent laying dead next to the wire they had chewed through. He was going to have to close the breaker on all the homes before he could repair the wiring and restore power to any of them. "The Situation Room has its own solar panels." Howard said to the no one who was there. "Once we get them active again, the computers can tell us what happened." He moved away from the back of the building and headed directly to the center of the town.

Clarence came floating up to the side of the building. He stood at the controls of a six by three foot plasti-steel tube box. He settled it on the ground, Howard opened the gate and stepped in. Then he took one of the safety belts hanging from the top rail and wrapped it around his waist. Clarence adjusted the gravitational units to lift them to the top of the two-story Town Hall.

He angled the gate towards the roof, then locked the controls. They opened the gate and stepped out onto the very slightly-slanting surface. In the center were the seventeen solar panels that were angled to catch sunlight no matter what time of day it was. They inspected each one, finding nothing wrong with them.

Next they went over to the lowest corner of the roof where the drainage line was and checked on the converter box. The lid wasn't on tightly like it was supposed to be. Howard pulled it the rest of the way open. Inside, the metal adjustment screws for keeping the box level had corroded through, and the converter had fallen enough to pull the power lines leading from it out of the unit.

Clarence reached around the outside of the box and cut the power coming from the solar panels to it. "You should be safe."

"Thanks." Howard pulled the cable leading into the building and reconnected it to the converter. Once it snapped back into place, he closed the lid and stood up. "That should do it. We can get a real repair team up here later to do a proper job."

Clarence pushed the switch back into position and the building began to hum again. "I think we have power."

"Let's get down and check those computers." Howard headed back to where they had left their lift waiting.

Once back in the Situation Room, everything was running again. The two men walked from terminal to terminal checking to make sure they were all functional. Clarence, who had gone to the left and was working on the bank of them in the back now, called out. "Howard, over here. Doc left us a note."

"To whoever finds this:

"Something is happening to the members of our community. Long term memories are either being made inaccessible or erased. I do not have the equipment to determine which. I believe this may have been what happened to the original inhabitants of this planet.

"Before I forget, members of our party have been trapped up with those inhabitants up in the mountains to the north. Please try and find them or their descendants.

"I have set up a folder in main memory core of the colony and this computer as backup, labeled **'Disaster'**. All of the findings and data we have collected about this phenomena should be stored there. My hope is it will give you a leg up trying to figure this thing out.

"But if you can't, get off this planet before the blue light gets you."

"Find that directory." Howard stood up as Tommy beeped him on their radio link.

"Dad, I've found everyone. They're in the Endeavor's cargo hold. Something's wrong with them, none of them recognize me."

"Tommy, get back to Town Hall at once. Marsha, Billy, Sarah, all of you. Get back to Town Hall now."

* * *

Howard pulled a chair up to the Big Board's table. "Clarence, feed whatever logs you can find over here. Then pour over whatever other data you're comfortable with. When the family gets here, parse as much as you can to them." Howard turned his attention to Jeff's last video recording.

"Something is happening to each of us. Ron and Francois have already passed out because of the blue light coming from the alligator-men's stone. Clint's getting us back to Petersville. I feel a tingling all over my body and my brain is trying to shut down. I really, really want to fall asleep right now. There's something about that stone. The large one, it reminds me of a meteor, the way it's pockmarked. Their shaman struck it and..." The video play-back ended a few minutes after Jeff fell out of his chair.

"This is Nancy Flannigan recording. I have instructed our pilot—okay, it's Bill, my brother—to set the shuttle on auto-return just as Clint had done when Jeff came back. At least we'll get back.

"There is something about that stone. We managed to move it, but not completely out of the pool it is sitting in. The water in the pool is heating it up. I don't know if that interaction is the cause of the blue light that permeated the area. Jeff had described a visible blue light that shot from the stone when stuck by the shaman's staff. But when we filtered all the other colors out of the surroundings, a faint blue glow remained. Striking the stone intensifies the emission, but it is happening all the time from that thing. Ahmed has water samples from the pool, but we didn't dare crack off a piece from the stone itself.

"I can feel my mind getting fuzzy, like it wants to fall asleep. I hope whoever sees this can do something about what's happened to us." That was the end of Nancy's report.

Marsha, Billy and Sarah came into the Situation Room and huddled around Howard. Resting her head on his shoulder, Marsha asked, "What can we do?"

She had meant it as more of a general question but he gave her specific actions instead. "Clarence has divided up the last known files they collected. You and Billy see what you can make of them. Did you see Tommy on the way back?"

"No, I assumed he'd beat us here."

Howard got up from his chair. "I'm going to look for him. Give me something I can use when I get back." He was out the door while Clarence was setting Marsha and Billy up at their own terminals. Marsha got Doc Parker's medical files and Billy the chemical analysis from Ahmed's lab.

Howard had just started up the log stairs leading to the Endeavor when he caught sight of his son. "Tommy."

"Dad, turn around. Run." Tommy was running down, taking the stairs two at a time.

Behind the young McCurdel were about two dozen of the alligator-men chasing the boy.

He ran two steps up, grabbed his son's hand and turned as his son arrived at the same step he was on. He guided the two of them to the back of Town Hall, where the lift was still waiting for them. Tommy jumped the railing while the elder McCurdel had to open the gate to get in. Tommy already had the unit moving upwards by the time his father latched the gate shut.

They dashed across the roof to the skylight. Lifted the window open and dropped onto the second floor of the structure. "Get downstairs and lock all the doors before they figure out how to get in."

"Okay, we have a problem," Howard burst into the room. As everyone turned their heads to him, "We weren't the only ones heading here. This place is about to be surrounded by Mike's alligator-men. Tommy's getting the doors locked, but we need to find anything we can barricade them with. We have to buy ourselves enough time to figure out what to do."

"Billy, come with me," Marsha was out of her chair and heading for a side door. "The metal tables from Endeavor are in the meeting room, once we lock down the front doors, they can be our barricade."

"Clarence, you keep parsing those files. Sarah, darling, find as many cameras as you can and put them in the second story windows, pointing down. Clarence, link them in so we can see what our friends out there are doing." Howard ran to the other side of the Situation Room before Clarence could complain about double-tasking him. Then into the hallway and down to the emergency storage room. He threw open the door, jammed a hammer into his belt, a box of nails into his pocket and leaned the storage racks to one side, dumping everything off of them. He pulled first one then the other into the hallway and over to the side door of Town Hall. He checked to make sure Tommy had already locked it, it was. Then he pushed the first metal shelf against the door frame and pounded nails through the open screw holes and into the wooden door frame. He repeated the process after placing the second set of shelves on top of the first.

All the windows were transparent plasti-steel, if the creatures could break through those, they were in real trouble.

"Howard," Clarence called to him as he entered. "Check out that monitor." Clarence had moved over to the long bank of terminals on the north wall to the one Clarence had been pointing at.

"Okay, you've found a picture, no wait, that's a video. Okay, you've found a video of Jeff's rock?"

Clarence finished adjusting the sixth of the monitors on that bench and came up behind where Howard was standing. He reached over to the touchpad on the right and slid his finger across it. The stone moved to the left of the scene. Howard stood up and looked at Clarence. "It's a live feed. Apparently, they left a drone hanging two hundred feet above the thing."

"Can you filter out the light like Ahmed did?"

"Not in the drone. Let me run the feed through the main computer and see what I can do."

Marsha came into the Situation Room with her two sons. "They didn't skimp on that table. If those things get through those doors, they'll have a dilly of a time moving it."

Howard touched the hammer still hanging from his belt and patted his pocket to find the box of nails still there. He pulled the box out and the hammer off. "Billy, take these and nail that table across the door. Every few seconds may count."

His son took them and headed back into the entrance. Seconds later, Howard could hear him pounding.

"There," Clarence announced. He pointed over to the screen with the drone feed. Everything else had been removed from the image except a faint blue haze all over the screen. "What's really odd," Clarence rolled his chair across the floor and back to the monitor. "This wavelength is unique to this haze. There is nothing else in the picture that contains that exact wavelength."

"Then that's the cause of what's happening," Howard announced. "Now what do we do about it?"

"If we reviewed all the recordings, we might discover what triggers its bursts. Likewise see if anything decreases the intensity," Marsha suggested.

"Good idea," Clarence said. "But there's a lot of footage to go through."

"Well, there's six of us and over a dozen terminals," Billy suggested. "Can you divide up the assignment and have each of us looking?"

Howard looked over at his son. It took him a moment to realize his son was smiling at the pride Howard was radiating at him. He put his hands on his son's shoulders and said, "Clarence, do what he says. Let's crack this thing."

Chapter 43

Release the Prisoner

Within the walls of Town Hall, silence reigned. Every few minutes a loud banging was heard against the outside wall. Every time he heard it, Clarence checked the outside monitors again. It was why early on he had moved his viewing station to within eyesight of the bank of them.

Outside, the creatures were mostly finding a slightly shady spot to take an afternoon nap, some even pulling sheets of plywood from the storehouse to lay under. A few were walking around the perimeter of the building on all fours, occasionally swinging their tails into the side of the structure when they turned around. Clarence had to keep reassuring himself they weren't breaking in.

"Clarence, look at this," Marsha broke the biologist out of his worries. He stepped over to her console. "Am I right in assuming there is no difference in these DNA results?"

He spent a few seconds going over the computer's write up of its analysis. "No. These are two separate individuals." He looked at the file name. "Alligator-men."

She pulled up a different file. "And what about these?"

"Those are identical." He looked at the file for a moment. "Because you have two samples of Jeff Martin's DNA."

"Except that the one on the top is from when we landed on this planet and the bottom one was run over a month ago."

He pulled up a chair and sat down. "Let me see that first slide."

As she pulled it up, she explained. "The top sample appears to have been taken from one of the climbing gloves. I remember Sarah saying she'd given one to Jeff before we went north for the winter. They took the bottom one from the creature they captured. they held it in the Endeavor for about a week before Simon wanted it back in the clinic for more—" She stopped talking for a second, then called over to her husband. "Howard, they've got one of those things imprisoned in the clinic!"

He jumped from his chair, "That's probably what drew those creatures here. We need to free it."

Clarence was a little slower getting to his feet. "Assuming it's still alive." He headed for the second story stairs. "We can take the man-lift across and see."

"Honey, you and the kids keep searching that data." He was out the door, down the hallway, passing Clarence and taking the stairs two at a time.

Clarence reached the top stair as Howard was pushing open the skylight. "Grab that box over there," Howard instructed.

"Be careful," Clarence said, pushing the box under the open window. "It's that light plastic."

As Howard stepped up on the two-foot-tall box, it started to crush under his weight. He launched himself as best he could before the plastic finally gave out. He caught the edge of the window and pulled himself out. Then he swung around and stretched his arms back down to get Clarence.

While Clarence was too short to reach him, he was able to jump high enough to grab hold of Howard's arms and be pulled out of the building.

The man-lift was still where they had left it. It was a matter of moments to get in and across to the roof of the clinic. They watched the creatures below, who swarmed around the building like they were looking for a way inside. Clarence found himself hoping they weren't looking up.

They searched the few storage rooms on the second floor, then made their way down to the main area. In the back of the main ward, they found the creature. Still caged, it lay on the floor of that cage. Awake, it offered a weak growl at the two intruders.

"It's starving," Clarence announced.

"We have to get it out of here." Howard walked over to the cage. Staying about three feet away, he looked in on the creature. "Let's find some way to move this thing."

The cage was not equipped with either gravitational units nor rollers, inertia would keep it in place. "Damn, Howard look at this." Clarence pointed to the floor. Several inches behind the cage were scratched up. "It looks like it was hitting this thing hard enough to move it."

"Let's see if these IV pole are strong enough?" He pulled out a couple of the poles attached to the beds and threw one to Clarence. They got behind the cage, braced against the back wall and pushed using the metal poles.

It moved, not easily, but it moved. The two men found the more they got it going, the easier the going got. It took them about ten minutes to get the cage out of the twenty-foot-deep ward, but out the door and across the waiting room was only a few moments' work. They got it up to the sliding glass of the front of the building. Before they got close enough, "Howard, stop."

Breathing heavy, Howard leaned on his pole. "It's going to be hell getting this thing going again."

"We have to unlock it before we push it out the door." He walked to the front of the cage, then ducked back when he saw one of the creatures crawl past the glass doors. "Once we do, we're going to have to run to get out of here. Those things will get around the cage and, well, I don't want to think what they'll do to us."

There was a key lock on the front of the cage. Neither of them had the key, so they had to remove the hinge pins. Once the three had been pulled, the door could be pulled open.

They pulled it open an inch, then went behind the cage again and pushed it right up against the sliding doors. Clarence flipped the switch activating the door mechanism. As they started to slide apart, the two men ran for the stairs leading up.

Clarence turned to see a couple of the creatures pulling the cage door off its frame and a couple more crawling around the cage to head in his direction. "Howard, quickly." He held his hands in position for the governor to climb out onto the roof.

"We may need these," Clarence tossed up the two metal poles they'd recovered, then jumped up to catch Howard's hands and be pulled out of the building.

Even standing on their hind legs, the creatures were not tall enough to reach the skylight as Howard dropped it shut.

* * *

"Dad, I think I've got it," Billy swung around in his chair as the two men walked back in.

"Watch the intensity." As the video ran forward, the top of the stone lost some of the blue light's intensity. He had all the other colors removed, so only that wavelength was being visualized and measured. "Note the time index," he pointed to the counter embedded in the video. "And watch what happens when I replay this scene in the infrared spectra." The video ran itself back, the image shifted to the infrared, and Billy ran it forward. As the stone began moving out of the heated pool of water, the top shifted from a bright red to a slightly duller version. Billy froze the image and pointed at the time index, one that was exactly the same as the earlier video run.

"Could it be as simple as temperature?" Howard looked from the monitor to their resident scientist.

"It could be superheated on the inside and every time it's struck, it releases whatever is inside of it. Cooling it down could work." Clarence sat back in his chair and stroked his chin. "Yes, it's got to be the answer. The cold of the Raffian cave kept it at bay during our winter stay with them."

"Kept what at bay?" Marsha asked. "They found no difference in the DNA from before we started being exposed to that light to afterwards. And I've looked through all the DNA tests they did."

"Did Simon do any scans? Have we found his data yet?

Tommy turned back to his computer and searched for the colony's medical folder in the main memory. "Dad, I've got it." He opened the first folder in the directory, one labeled '_a Open me first.'

"Clarence, Howard, or whoever finds this. The files in the folder labeled 'Disaster' will contain all the evidence I've collected to back up this diagnosis. Something in that blue light is physically affecting the brains of the Raffians, the alligator-men and, heaven help us, ourselves. It is shutting down our higher reasoning centers and I have to assume raising the rest of the fauna on this planet until I suspect all life forms will have the same level of intelligence. But that level will be no higher than what the Raffians have now.

"It's the stone. You have to do something about the stone. Destroy it somehow, before you succumb to its effect.

"I wish you luck."

"How the hell do we destroy something that if we hit it will emit even more of what's effecting us?"

"We cool it down," Clarence went over to the Big Board and started pulling up a video. "We have to not only cool this thing down, but freeze it."

The table was now showing the scene where Nancy's team was pulling the stone out of the pool. Just as the stone began moving, Clarence froze the picture. "There," he pointed to the carbineer rigging that was pulling the net containing the stone. "The rig they were using wasn't very efficient and," he pointed at the connection to the shuttle, "shuttles don't have a lot of pulling power. We use the winches on the crane module when we need to move heavy stuff."

"So you're saying with better equipment, the six of us can move something two engineers couldn't?"

"The right tools for the right job. They didn't have the right tools."

"Okay, let's give it a try."

"Howard, dear, there's only one slight problem," his wife began. "We have the wrong module hooked up to either of the drivers. I doubt our friends out there are going to be nice enough to just let us walk around freely and change them out."

"I hate it when you're right. Clarence, how do we get around that obvious problem?"

"Dad."

"What, Tommy?"

"Couldn't we remote one of the shuttles and get the alligator-men to chase it?"

"It's not like they're drones, son. We don't have remote controllers for them."

"Wait a minute, Howard. If we reverse the auto-return program, they might think someone was flying away. We can't precisely control the craft, like flying it over to the hanger, but we could send it back to its last location. If they think we're aboard, it might draw them away long enough for one of us to run out there and fly the other unit over to the hanger."

"And if someone uses the man-lift unit to get to the hanger, they could have everything ready for a quick change out."

Howard smiled at his son's idea. "Okay, let's do this before we become imbeciles ourselves."

Chapter 44

Escape

"Clarence, why does it have to be our son running across the field?" Marsha asked.

"Because he's the best pilot here." He brushed past Howard and leaned over Tommy's shoulders at the settings on the auto-return program.

"It's set for the shuttle on Landing Pad Two, Mr. Knowles. That's about five yards further out then Landing Pad One."

"That'll give your brother a better chance of getting to it," he replied. "Can we tell where you're sending it?"

"The starting coordinates it had match the area where that stone is."

Howard leaned over Tommy's right side. "That'll give us two platforms to work from when we get out there."

"But first we have to get out there. You three get up to the roof and have the man-lift ready, Tommy and I will join you as soon as Billy's made it to the shuttle." He leaned the second IV pole against the computer bench for Tommy to use after he'd sent off the shuttle.

As Sarah, Marsha and Howard headed for the second floor, Clarence and Billy went into the lobby of Town Hall. There were more creatures crawling around in front of it now since they had released the creature from its cage.

"Are you ready for this?"

The young man nodded.

"Watch out for their tails, alligators have very strong muscles in them and can move them quickly. Their jaw muscles are stronger for clamping down on something than for opening them again, so it's safer to run near the ones with their mouths already closed. But they can turn quickly. Pick your path and keep moving."

"Thanks, Mr. Knowles, I'll do my best."

Clarence clipped a small box onto Billy's belt. "If you get into trouble..."

"A rescue field! Thanks, Mr. Knowles."

"Just in case. You ready?"

"I'll get scared if we don't get this started."

Clarence pressed a finger to his radio. "Tommy, launch the shuttle."

From the door they couldn't see the shuttle on its pad, but as it rose and headed southwest, it came into their view. They turned their focus on the creatures. Some of them spotted it taking off and started following it. One of the larger ones turned back. Clarence and Billy ducked out of sight. Then the creatures growled something that sounded eerily like the Raffian speech. More of the creatures turned and went along with the ones that already left.

A couple of them stayed in front of the building, just off the wooden sidewalk, using its shade as cover from the direct sunlight.

"Take this." Clarence handed Billy the other metal IV pole. "Good luck."

The doors slid open as Clarence pressed their open button. Billy took off at a sprint. He jumped over the creature closest to the door. Then stayed three yards away from another two who were sunning themselves on the dirt tarmac. From there he had a clear dash to the shuttle.

One of the creatures hiding under the sidewalk, made a dash to catch the McCurdel youth. Clarence could tell Billy was not going to reach the shuttle before the creature would catch him. He pressed his earpiece. "Billy, behind you. Use the rescue field." But Clarence knew that once he did, Billy would have to roll over to the shuttle and deactivate it before opening the door.

Billy turned and saw the approaching creature. His hand started reaching for the activation button, then paused.

The creature got closer.

Billy pulled the device off his belt and readied it for use. Then he underhanded the device at the creature.

It hit with its front side down, on the creature's back. One of the spines pressed the activation button in and the field sprang to life. With the creature inside.

Billy didn't wait to see his results of his handiwork, he ran even faster for Landing Pad One. A minute later, he had the door open and shut again, with himself inside. As some of the other creatures started heading his way, he lifted the shuttle off the pad fifty feet and turned it towards the module's hanger.

"He did it!" Clarence shouted. Then when he saw the rest of the creatures react to his voice, "Tommy, it's time to get upstairs."

"Already there," Tommy called from the second floor. "I brought this." He held out the pole towards Clarence as he got to the top of the stairs. "But I don't know what you wanted me to do with it."

Clarence took the pole and tossed it through the skylight. Then he boosted Tommy up to the arms of his father. Finally, he jumped after him.

He heard noise from the first floor that told him the creatures had broken in. "Let's get over to the hanger," he said, latching the man-lift gate shut.

Clarence turned around and found Sarah, four-foot-tall Sarah, was at the controls and lifting them off the roof. He looked Howard and Marsha in the eyes and pointed at the child.

"She wanted to drive and Carl told me she was fully qualified before we went north," her mother said.

Clarence set his pole on top of the upper rail and wrapped both hands around the two pipes. He kept his gaze forward as the box swung around, pointed to the hanger and crossed the tops of the several buildings needed to get to its roof.

"Stay in the basket," Howard said as he opened the gate and jumped onto the roof of the hanger. He looked below. Seeing no creatures, he jumped down and ran inside. A minute later, the entire roof of the hanger began to retract.

Sarah lowered the basket next to the crane module. Everyone exited the man-lift before she shut everything down and got out herself.

Billy brought the shuttle over the top of the open hanger a few minutes later and set it down on the opposite side of the crane. "Nice thought, Dad," he said, getting out of the cockpit. "Unfortunately the hanger isn't large enough to disconnect this cargo module and attach the crane. We'll still have to open the main doors for that."

"I see another problem," Clarence was patting the side of the crane module. "There's only a single seat on the crane for an operator. The cockpit can hold two, three if we pack people in. That leaves two people behind."

"Not acceptable," Marsha burst out. "No one gets left behind."

"Sarah and I could drive the man-lift," Tommy began.

"NO," Marsha didn't even let her son finish the thought.

"It doesn't have enough power to make the trip," Howard explained to them. "Nor does it have the ability to recharge itself."

"But we could secure the basket to the crane's arms. A couple of welds should do the trick," Clarence speculated. "Then Howard and I could strap into the basket and ride in it to the site." He looked over at Howard, who was now holding his eldest son. "Assuming Billy can find his way there?"

"I want to ride in the basket," Tommy announced.

"No, son," Howard knelt down in front of his other son. "The smaller the people crowding into the cockpit, the easier it will be for your brother to drive. I need you and Sarah in there. Your mother can ride in the crane operator's compartment."

"Howard," Marsha began.

"It's the best we can do. Unless you want to duct tape me to the roof?"

"No."

"Then let's get this thing modified and that module unhooked from the shuttle."

"There's not enough room in here," Billy repeated.

"We can have it unhooked, ready for you to pull away from it before we expose ourselves to those things again," Clarence said. "Okay, who knows any welding?"

"I assumed you did. It was your idea," Howard said.

"Okay, so that idea is out. We could hook the man-lift to the lifting ball on the crane. Even if we shorten the cable tight, we'll still swing some. Howard, we'll have to get two points of contact on our harnesses."

"If the crane lets go?"

"Then we'll sit there until Billy comes back to get us. The box has its own gravitational units, after all."

It took them another hour to get everything ready. Billy sat at the controls while his father pulled the chain to open the hanger door. They didn't want to risk any delays with stopping and restarting the motor.

Clarence stepped outside and kept an eye on the remaining creatures. The chain pulley made a little noise as it got started, it hadn't been used since it was installed, but quieted down after a moment. Moving the doors caused a bit more noise. When Billy fired up the drive motors of the shuttle, its noise, added to the rest, began drawing the sleeping creatures' attention; they turned towards the hanger.

"Get that thing out of here." Clarence waved at Billy to urge him to get moving.

The shuttle pulled away from the cargo module. The creatures began turning towards the hanger and walking towards the noise.

Billy slid the driver five feet to his right and instructed the computer to dock with the crane module. Then the slow process of backing the shuttle into the hanger and connecting it began. Clarence twirled the IV pole he still had, to loosen his muscles up in case the creatures got too close.

It took about the time for Clarence to watch the alligator-man to crawl within six feet of where he was standing for Billy to back up enough to slide the driver's stem under the crane. Clarence took a step back, the creature a step forward. Marsha and Tommy connected the circuits of the crane into the cockpit and drove home the magnetized connective bolt.

Clarence planted his back foot and drove the end of his pole into the open jaws of the beast. It tried shaking its head to dislodge it, but Clarence pushed down as hard as he could. Then the creature snapped its jaws shut. A crunch ensued, and Clarence had to stop himself from pitching forward. The front end of his pole had been severed. He dropped the pole and sprinted to the back of the crane. He dove into the basket and latched the gate. Everyone else was already secured.

"Go, Billy, go," he radioed. Fumbling for the safety straps, he tried to clip his harness into place as the cage he was in passed inches above the creature he had tried to fight off.

It flipped over and grabbed for the bottom of the cage. It got a grip on the back of it as it passed over its head. The normal paws of alligators had been transformed on it into hands with sufficient hold on to the man-lift's bars. It was pulled off the ground as the shuttle lifted away from the landing field.

The creature started to climb up the four bars that made up the vertical sides of the cage. Clarence, facing in its direction, watched the creature climb. Howard faced forward and couldn't see it. Realizing there was no way he could bring his feet around to kick the creature off the cage before it had climbed in on top of them, Clarence stood up against the flow of wind. He activated the controls of the lift and swung it from side to side.

"What the hell are you doing?" Howard shouted against the wind.

Clarence used his left hand to point behind him. "Kick it, Howard. Before it gets in, kick it."

Seeing the creature grabbing the top rail and placing its foot on the bottom one, Howard allowed himself to slide backwards and kicked out at the thing through the second and third rails of the cage. It caught the beast in its underbelly hard enough to loosen its grip on the cage. A second quick kick sent the creature falling back to Petersville, now fifty feet below them.

"This isn't getting any easier," Clarence said against the wind. He slid back down to the bottom of a cage that was swinging side to side.

Chapter 45

Catching the Problem

"Son, lower the shuttle to twenty feet." Howard lay on the bottom of the man-lift staring through bars at the large pockmarked rock, still sitting in its pool of steaming water. He removed his finger from his ear. "Clarence, have you got the controls?"

Using the bars to pull himself up, Clarence worked his way to the control panel of the man-lift, disconnecting one of his safety lines to be reconnected forward before doing the same with the other. It took him a couple of minutes to cross that six foot cage. "Everything's powered up."

Howard pressed his earpiece again. "Marsha, release the hook. We'll take the man-lift down and assess things."

Against the wind, Howard heard the sound of the cock-pit door opening and closing. "Billy," he quickly repressed his earpiece to change connections, "what's going on up there?" Neither man could see the doors.

"Tommy jumped over to the other shuttle."

"I've taken it off auto-pilot, Dad," Tommy said over Howard's earpiece. "Want me to come pick you up?"

"You stay right there, young man. Howard, did you give him permission to make that dangerous jump?" Howard could hear the tremble in his wife's voice. The control cab for the crane was behind the pilot side of the cockpit and she couldn't see what her children were doing, either.

"Mom, it had to be done. Sarah hasn't been trained on the shuttles yet."

"Well, you stay right where you are."

"Marsha, he's safe now. Probably safer than the rest of us once we put this crazy plan into motion. And Tommy. You do what your mother said and sit tight until we finish, understand?"

"Yes, Dad."

"Thunk" came from near the cockpit door, then again a couple of feet away. The second occurred just as Marsha was releasing the man-lift.

Howard was hanging on to the side of the cage despite the two straps connecting him to it as the small cage fell about six feet.

Clarence, who was working the controls, was ready for it. He'd dropped them just enough to get away from the hydraulic lines that controlled the crane's arm and the ball. "We're clear," he said into the radio.

"Run this thing over so I can see what those kids are doing now."

Clarence maneuvered them across to the gap between the two shuttles. Howard watched the side door of the module finish closing and pointed to Clarence to take them up there.

The man-lift fitted between the two shuttles snuggly. Clarence had to block the cockpit door in order that Howard could gain access to the side door.

Which he was now banging on.

The door swung open away from the man-lift and Sarah stood inside. "Hi, Dad. The computers in here still have power."

"What were you thinking, young lady? We just scolded your brother for taking dangerous chances."

"He didn't use safety lines." She lifted the strap still connected to her body harness, touching the release button and pulling hard enough to dislodge the magnetic clamp on the end from the floor of the module. "I stuck one on each of the shuttles before pulling myself across."

His daughter had done the right thing, but he still didn't like it. And Marsha... "Tell your mother that we brought you over to this shuttle when she asks how you got here, you hear? Do not mention you jumped."

"I understand."

He opened the gate and stepped over into the module to see what was available. There were a couple of cameras focused on the area below, but only on the infrared was there signs of movement. Red images were coming their way.

"Honey, you keep an eye on those red spots. Radio me when they get to here," he pointed to a spot on the screen that was ten yards from the stone. "Okay?"

"Those are the alligator-men, aren't they?"

"Yes. I hope Clarence and I can get done before they get here." He went over to the door and stepped back into the man-lift. "And keep this door shut."

"Let's go take a look at what's left down there." Howard snapped his safety line onto the cage bar next to Clarence as he spoke.

Clarence dropped the basket, at a much slower rate, until he was inches above the ground. Then he moved it over to where the stone was, parking it just over the two running streams the stone created. They could feel the heat from below and the wetness of water condensing on their bodies.

"I don't think it's completely under the stone." Howard looked at the metal cable netting Nancy had constructed and tried to place.

Clarence reached out to grab the cable. He jerked his hand back before touching it. "Damn, its hot!"

"The ends run half way to the tree line. Maybe we can snag the four of them without actually having to touch them."

"Anything to get out of this steam room."

Clarence moved the lift over to the tree line and set down where the four lines were connected to the improvised wooden block.

With this section not being as hot as the cables over the stone, Howard attempted to pull the wooden block up. It splintered in his hand from the weight of the cables.

"There goes that idea." Howard brushed the remaining wood fibers from his hand. "Too bad Nancy didn't put any loops in them."

"Yeah, it's not like we can tie them together."

"Then how did Nancy hold the net strands together?" Howard looked back over to the exposed netting around the stone. "Clips. She used clips to hold the cables in place." He placed his finger in his ear. "Sarah, look in the cabinets up there. Can you find any metal clamps or clips?"

After a few minutes. "Dad, it looks like about a dozen of them. Should I toss them down?"

"No," he responded as Clarence was already raising the man-lift. "Clarence is on his way to get them."

* * *

The metal clips he returned with were two metal tubes, welded together at right angles, that had a screw tightening them down on whatever was slid into the tube. In the case of the cables Nancy had used, right through the wire strands that made them up. They slid them over the warm, but not overly hot, ends of the cables. They pulled them down about nine inches then looped the end back into the second tube of the clamp. Tightening the screws down, they soon had four loops.

"Marsha, lower the ball down," Clarence radioed after they had finished. Then watched as it played out the fifty feet needed to reach the loops. One by one they fed the loops over the hook on the end of the crane's lifting ball.

"Okay, honey, take it up a little." They were too far away for Howard to use hand signals. After all the slack was taken out of two of the cables, the others having a shorter trip to the stone, "Stop. Lock it off there until we're ready for the lift."

"I found a couple of branches we can use to push this guy into the net as it gets pulled up." Clarence emerged from the tree line that Howard hadn't seen him go into with a pair of ten foot long, three inch thick, wood branches. He dropped one next to where Howard was standing and went to the left side of the pool. He looked over to Howard to see if he were ready.

Howard lifted his branch, placed it into the pool as far under the stone as he could, just as Clarence was doing. He could feel the mud on the side of the stone give way until he had it right up against the hard side of the rock. "Ready?"

Clarence nodded.

Howard touched his earpiece again. "Marsha, slowly raise the stone."

"Okay." The tension on the cable increased. The two men pulled down on their branches to roll the stone more securely into the net.

Everything was slow to move, when Sarah came over the radio. "Dad, those red spots are getting real close."

He reached up and double tapped his radio. "Marsha. we need to pull this thing a little faster."

The stone moved slightly, trying to roll out of the net. But the efforts of Howard and Clarence forced it back the other way. After a few minutes, it rolled back into the net enough that water started spouting out of the hole it had been sitting in.

Both men had to move to the side to keep from getting burned by the superheated water. But the stone moved upwards and centered itself in the net pulling it up.

"Marsha, take it up."

"Howard, behind you!" Clarence shouted, as the stone began to move into the air and the pool formed a six foot geyser, spewing water in a ten foot radius. Both men moved, as much as to confront the creatures that were emerging from the forest cover, as to avoid the scalding water fountain.

Howard went to his left, drawing the first of the creatures towards him. He leveled his branch at the rising creature's underbelly and charged into it. He managed to pin it against a tree trunk, then leaned into his branch to hold it.

The second one to emerge was already on its hind feet, which slowed its charge out of the woods. As it waddled as fast as it could, Clarence swung his weapon around and caught the thing on the side of its head. The creature dove head first into the rocky landscape. He stared at it for a second; since it appeared to be stunned, he started over to help Howard.

"Clarence, look out," Howard yelled.

When he looked, the creature was shaking its head. After a second, it started charging on all fours towards him. Jaws opened to show its full spread of sharp teeth.

Clarence jammed his branch into the opening, driving the bottom jaw against the rocks. The creature snapped its mouth closed and severed the three-inch-thick stick like it was a toothpick. Clarence stepped back, but the hot water spewing from the geyser caught him on his shoulder, and he flinched forward.

The creature was starting to reopen it jaw.

He kept going forward and ran over its half-opened upper jaw, driving the whole thing closed again. Clarence got behind the thing. Planted himself, raised the remainder of his weapon. And was promptly swept off his feet by a swing from the alligator-man's tail.

He dropped his branch and duck-walked backwards away from the creature until he was up against a tree. He pushed himself upright using the trunk until he was standing again, banging his head against a low branch on his way up.

The creature turned around, looked at the branch laying on the ground and slowly stalked its prey. When it was within three feet, it opened its jaws once again. Wider than Clarence had previously seen it do.

Then the pain in his head made him look to the branch he had hit. He grabbed it and tried to break it off. He couldn't. So he swung up as far as he could, got on it and climbed into the tree.

The alligator-man roared at its missed opportunity. It stood up and tried to grab Clarence as he scrambled higher up.

As he went from branch to branch, he was turned to face deeper into the woods. He could see several more of the creatures coming. "Howard, get out of there."

Howard leaned harder into his branch and looked where Clarence had called from. He stepped back, holding the creature against the tree. He got his feet planted with his right leg forward and his left carrying his weight. He rapidly raised the branch from the creature's chest and brought it back down on its head as the creature was dropping to face him on all four legs. He drove its head sharply against the rocks.

Howard then dropped his branch and made a dash for the man-lift. He was raising it off the rocks as both creatures grabbed the railings of the lift. He got it ten feet in the air before the first one let go and fell. But the other one had climbed up to the top railing and would be over it into the basket in a moment.

Howard grabbed several of the extra cable clips he had and slid them onto his right hand fingers. Then pushing with his left hand and punching with his right, he attacked the soft underbelly of the creature.

As it got its head over the top, Howard slammed his right fist into one of the creature's hands, smashing it against the top rail.

The fingers opened slightly, so Howard drove his fist into the other hand and pushed even harder. The creature fell, landed on top of the other one, back to back as several more surrounded their fallen comrades and roared at the retreating basket.

"Clarence, there's a bare spot a few feet further up, climb up to it. I'll pick you up." He worked his way back to the controls, removing the clamps so he could manipulate them.

"I don't know if these branches will support me."

"Give them a try. I'll get as close as I can."

Howard maneuvered the lift into a gap created by some fire years ago. Stubs of branches still sprang from the tree but they weren't growing. "It's like a fireball came through here," Clarence had observed when they had first arrived. "It's at the same level in all the trees of this clearing. From the rate of growth, I'd say this happened about a couple hundred years ago."

He opened the gate. Then brought the cage against the tree with the opening for Clarence to get into the cage off to the right side of the trunk. Finally, he lowered it as much as he could, breaking the dead then living branches out of his way.

He locked the control, got into a prone position and stretched his arms out as far as they would go. "Grab hold."

"It's not going to work. You're too far away. I can't work my way around to your side. Leave me, get that stone outta here."

"No, people are the most important thing we have in this colony. I'm not leaving anyone behind." He unhooked one of his safety straps and stretched further out.

Then he pulled himself back in the cage. He stared at the strap. It had a carabineer on each end, one to attach to the person's harness and the other to attach to the safety rails. But...

"Clarence, take one of your safety straps off. Link them together by their carabineers and throw me the line."

A minute later, Howard had a safety line to Clarence that he clipped over one of the main rails of the basket. It still wasn't long enough to reach a safety rail and Howard wasn't going to risk his friend's life attaching it to the gate.

"Now jump. If I miss, I can pull you back up."

Clarence stood on a solid branch slightly away from the trunk, bent his knees and the branch some, then jumped over to the basket. The spring from the branch gave him enough push to catch the bottom of the cage with one hand and Howard's arm with the other.

Clarence quickly pulled himself into the cage. As he unclipped his extension strap and clipped his safety line onto its rail, Howard maneuvered the cage away from the tree. Clarence pulled the gate shut and reattached his secondary line.

Howard brought the lift up towards the shuttle Tommy was piloting. "Marsha, get that thing up. Billy, how much power have you got left?"

Clarence opened the gate again as they approached the side of the module Sarah was still in. "I don't have enough power to get back north with this thing," Billy finally answered.

"Take it about a hundred yards off shore and dunk the thing overnight," Clarence suggested. "We can at least cool the thing off while the shuttles recharge."

"Billy, you catch that?" Howard asked.

"Yes, sir."

"Get going, then. Marsha, you sit tight. Once we've got things locked down here, we'll pull the two of you out. We can't have you guys sleeping there for the couple of days it'll take to charge these things." The two men climbed into the module. They turned the cage on its side and pulled it through the door after them.

"Tommy," Howard radioed the cockpit. "You okay up there? Want one of us to relieve you?"

"I'm fine, Dad. Want me to go after Mom and Billy?"

"If you feel up to it." They watched the shuttle turn around and head after the other shuttle on the forward camera. Marsha had pulled the stone up until the swivel ball its hook was attached to met the pulley that raised and lowered it. The stone swung only slightly. Tommy kept the distance between them constant.

As the first shuttle started to slow down. Howard watched as Tommy brought theirs off to the side so he could line up the doors and allow Marsha to leave the crane control box.

Billy brought his shuttle to a stop, Tommy pulled up alongside. Howard opened the module door to see how his wife was holding up. When she gave him a thumbs up, he pressed his radio link to her. "Okay, let her down slowly. How much cable have you got?"

"About two hundred feet."

"We can't dangle the stone that deep unless we can set it on the bottom," Clarence said. "It'll swing the shuttle around or break away."

Howard turned to his daughter on the computer terminal. "How deep is the ocean at this point?"

"One hundred and ninety feet," she replied.

"Billy, do you copy? We need you to bring your shuttle right down to the water's edge."

"Can do, Dad. Are we in high or low tide right now?"

Howard looked over at the other two manning the computers. "Low," Clarence said.

"Well, let's see how high I can place this thing and still hit bottom."

The shuttle dropped from the fifty foot above the waves it had been. The stone was going down on its own and sizzled slightly as it plunged into the cold ocean waters. Between the shuttle's descent and the crane's cable being played out, the stone quickly dropped to the ocean floor. When Billy got the shuttle on station, they were about five feet above the churning white caps.

"That's it," Marsha announced over the radio. "I'm played out. I guess I didn't have as much as I thought."

"Billy, bring the shuttle closer to shore. Let's see if we can make that enough cable."

Howard watched the other shuttle retreat from where they waited. They only had to go a yard before the cable bent back.

"Marsha, pull the stone up and re-drop it."

Howard watched the spool turn, collecting its cable until that cable again straightened. "Good, let's see if we hit bottom this time."

The cable played out less than a quarter of the line it had retracted before going slack. Marsha fed out another five feet, then radioed Billy to raise the shuttle by that amount.

They both locked down their systems and transferred over to the other module. "Do you think we need to keep someone in the other driver to keep it out of the water?" Billy asked.

"That might not be a bad idea," Clarence began. "We've put a lot of work into this. I'd hate for it all to be washed away."

"We'll all stay." Marsha announced. "We can monitor the ocean level in here, or up another twenty feet, and wait until these things are charged enough to get this rock up north." She dropped to her knees and started crying. "We can't go home anyway, those creatures are there."

Chapter 46

Putting the Problem Away

They spent twenty-four hours hovering over the same spot in the ocean and measuring the heights of high and low tides. The two separate moons orbiting Belenius 3 gave them a very strange schedule, but never anything that came close to where they had parked the crane. Late afternoon of that second day, they headed back to Petersville to see if they could get into the hanger and swap their cargo module for the extra battery one.

As they approached the still-open hanger, dusk was descending on them. With their infrared camera, they were able to pin-point the remaining creatures. Only twenty were still in the area. Some taking shelter in the clinic, where they had pulled out the cage used to hold the captured creature and pulled apart anything that hadn't been welded together. A couple were inside Town Hall, where the front door had been pulled from its hinges and lay trampled just off the sidewalk, shards of its glass scattered about. They got the clearest view of the couple that were in the hanger, as nothing was restricting their heat signatures.

Howard had taken over the controls of the shuttle and positioned it between the hanger and the machine shop before beginning his descent. This allowed him to come down almost silently.

Once Howard cut the gravitational units upon landing, he and Clarence went over to the machine shop. They grabbed a welding backpack and attached the welding lead on a ten foot metal pole. Clarence slipped the pack on and carried the pole like a medieval spear. Once back outside, Howard got back into the cockpit and Clarence went through the open hanger doors to find the creatures.

As he entered, the two turned, stared at him, then stood up and started walking towards him. They both carried metal poles they must have found in the tool racks. They pointed those poles directly at Clarence.

Clarence powered up his welder and charged the two of them. He used his longer pole to sweep aside the first attack, then plunged his welding lead into the belly of the other creature. It screamed in pain, fell over, and stopped moving. "Damn, too much power," he said under his breath. With no time to make an adjustment, Clarence quickly turned back to the other one. It was again holding the pole straight at Clarence.

This time Clarence aimed for the metal pole. The electric arc surged across from the welding lead to the creature's pole. It dropped the pole and ran to the back of the hanger, as far away from Clarence as it could get.

Clarence stepped back to the door and motioned for Howard to bring the shuttle in. It took them five minutes to switch the modules out. Clarence climbed into the back of the module with the battery banks, Tommy and Marsha.

"Let's get out of here," Clarence radioed up to the cockpit.

* * *

Three days later, after some negotiations with and promises to the Raffians, they were guiding the stone through the library entrance to the former Raffian cavern village. Billy and Clarence had attached gravitational units to lift the stone so it could be easily pushed into the cold vault in the back of the cavern.

Howard ran a spectral analysis on the surroundings after the door was sealed and found none of the blue light that had been pervading the planet earlier. He even flew down to Buffet Bay and ran the test to make sure.

The Raffians had packed everything they could out of the vault before the stone was placed inside, which included a couple of vehicles that they could pack a lot of the heavier stuff in. Unfortunately, they couldn't get the machines to work. So the tribe packed up what it could carry, stowed what they couldn't, and began marching south to Petersville, where Howard had promised to build new lives for them.

But first, he had to find the people he had come to this planet with and drive the alligator-men out of their colony.

"I just hope we can find a solution to the problem they pose without resorting to genocide," Clarence said as he got in the long-range shuttle's cockpit to fly home.

"I don't see one. But Jeff has been known for showing me better ways. Let's hope he has some ideas. Sentient life is too precious to waste." He buckled his belt and checked on the people in back. Which included Lerick, M'cron, I'mac and Ank in addition to his family.

Clarence was in the air and headed south as soon as Howard said they were ready.

Chapter 47

New Neighbors

Setting the shuttle on hover at fifty feet above Petersville gave them line of site on the entire town. Not all of the planted crop land, but anywhere the creatures or their friends could be hiding.

When they didn't see anything, they landed by the hanger. Marsha and Sarah went into the cargo module that still contained the scanning equipment, changed out the camera in a drone, launched it over the city and initiated an infrared scan of the area. But there were no heat signatures coming from it, either.

"This thing is scanning all the way to the Endeavor, isn't it?" Howard asked.

"The ship was too well insulated," Marsha answered. "As are most of the homes we've built."

"Okay," Clarence turned away from the monitor screen. "It looks like we'll have to do a house-by-house search."

"Can we get one of those stun rods you built?" Tommy asked.

Howard keyed his radio. "Billy, take us down next to the machine shop." He looked over at Clarence, who nodded agreement. "In front. Let's draw them out if they're down there."

Clarence went into the shop first to make sure it was clear of creatures. Sending the infrared drone in first, Sarah verified the building was clear. Then everyone piled out of the module, to at least stretch their legs, and into the shop.

"Remember to step the voltage way down this time," Howard said as Clarence set another unit on the bench behind the one he was working on.

"Let's just hope I didn't push it too far down." He turned back to working on the fifth and final one he was making.

He turned to the waiting crowd, "Alright, here's the drill." He explained the workings of the units to the Raffians through Tommy, as his Raffian was still poor.

Clarence clamped a thick wood beam to another workbench and let each of the Raffian adults practice with it.

"Alright, let's load these things up," Howard said. "And widen our search."

They were airborne again in ten minutes. The Raffians were again glued to the visual monitor of the areas they were flying over.

The fields were clear, as was the area surrounding the Rockefeller River. Clarence sat in back going over the notes that Doc Parker had left them on the tablet computer from the clinic.

"Hey." He looked up from the device. "Jeff apparently found the location of the alligator-men's village, nest, whatever you call it."

Howard stood up from staring over his daughter's shoulder and turned to him. "Sounds like a place to start."

He radioed the coordinates up to Billy and felt the shuttle change direction.

Less than an hour later, Sarah announced that heat signatures were appearing on her screen. Howard radioed the news to Billy, who took the shuttle higher and slowed down to around twenty knots.

As the clearing came into view, images of different intensities appeared. The visual camera showed those bodies to be both the alligator-men and the humans. There was no mistaking the fact that Jeff and his party were building structures for the creatures.

"We've got to come in discreetly," Howard said. "Quietly get someone to tell us what is going on there."

"There's a clearing," Marsha pointed at the upper portion of the screen.

"Looks like it's about a tenth of a mile away." He touched his radio. "Billy, bear north about 2 degrees. Set down in the clearing up there."

"Roger, Dad."

"Tommy, tell our guests to wait here. Clarence and I will go out and bring someone back."

He nodded and explained to I'mac while the other two watched the monitor.

"We're down and clear," Billy said over the radio.

The two men headed for the door; Lerick and M'cron started to get up. "Tommy!"

Tommy placed his hand on Lerick's shoulder and guided him back to his seat, re-explaining things to the two of them.

It was a short walk to the creature's clearing, made longer by the need to move quietly through the underbrush. When they got there, they crouched behind two trees to assess things.

The humans appeared to be cutting down nearby trees and using them to build log structures over the existing pits in the ground. Using axes from Petersville, not the creatures' stone ones.

They didn't get a lot of time to watch, Bill Flannigan began heading over to one of the trees next to where they were hiding. He walked around the side of a tree and raised an axe. Howard and Clarence worked their way over to him. Before he could bring it down on the tree, Clarence grabbed the axe, Howard placed his hand over Bill's mouth and the two of them pulled him deeper into the forest.

Bill struggled for a few seconds, then his eyes went wide and he relaxed.

Clarence put a finger to his lips as Howard released Bill's mouth and whispered, "What's going on?"

"Hey, guys," Bill said in his normal voice. "We can use..."

Howard slapped his hand back over the man's mouth again. "Bill, we don't want the creatures to know we're here."

"This is a rescue," Clarence whispered.

Bill's eyes squinted in confusion and he tried to stand up. The two of them could hear him trying to say something under Howard's hand. Howard lifted it again.

In the same loud voice. "...rescuing. Our new friends..."

"Let's get him back to the shuttle and sort this out." Clarence took Bill by his arm. Howard took the other and they began walking him backwards away from the clearing. Every time Howard tried to remove his hand, Bill tried to shout back to the village. It took them even longer to get back to the shuttle than it did to get to the clearing.

Billy had gone back into the module with everyone else by the time they got back. He helped them pull Bill into the compartment and close the door.

"You can stop shouting now, Bill," Howard said as they dropped him into one of the chairs and spun it to face the semicircle they formed around him. The Raffians pulled themselves away from the video game Tommy left running for them to watch and stood off to one side.

"No one can hear you." Clarence added,

"What do you guys want? I thought you were our friends?" His voice dropped back to a normal tone.

"We are," Marsha said. "Which is why we want to understand what's happened to everyone."

"How did the alligator-men enslave everyone?"

Bill Flannigan looked from one person to another with a dazed look on his face. "Enslave?"

"Aren't they forcing you to work for them?"

"Did they threaten to eat you?"

"I don't understand." Bill started sobbing. "Who is enslaving us?"

"The creatures out there."

"They're our friends!"

"Your friends?"

"Like them," Bill pointed at Lerick standing behind Tommy.

"Can you talk to them?" Tommy blurted out.

"Well, we kinda point at things. But we make ourselves understood."

"Why did you leave Petersville?" Howard waved down his son and continued the conversation.

"The Aquaks needed our help."

"Who are the Aquaks?" Clarence asked.

Bill just pointed in the direction of the alligator-men's clearing.

"Okay. What did they need your help with?" Marsha followed up.

"Building their homes. They saw what we'd done and wanted some themselves."

"We are under no obligation to these creatures." Howard exploded at the man. "We have to take care of ourselves."

"They're our neighbors, Mr. McCurdel. We have to look after our neighbors."

"They are not," Howard began.

But his wife turned him to face her. "Remember what Jeff said the night we lost our home?"

"But these creatures are not even human."

"They're sentient, if they can ask for help. And unless you plan on genocide, they're going to be our neighbors."

Clarence took a step and got behind Marsha. "I hate to admit it. As scary as those things are, they're evolving into something like the Raffians, and us. It's a big planet, maybe we can build a three-way culture here?

"Let's see what Jeff has to say."

Marsha continued the thought, "I think it's time to introduce ourselves to our other neighbors."

Epilogue

Jeff, Howard, Lerick, M'cron and three of the Aquaks—Jeff thought that was a better name than alligator-people—sat speeding down the newly-cleared transit system. It was only a mile long, but it was a start.

The train reached its station, and the doors opened. Well, almost. Jeff and Lerick had to push on them to get them to fully open. When his door clicked, Jeff gestured for Lerick to proceed him onto the platform where dozens of citizens of Belenius 3 awaited them. "It's your system."

"No, friend Martin, it's our system."

"Please, Jeff. Martin is my family name." The Raffians had amazed him by their rapid return to the thinkers who had originally built this planet. And, too, how fast the Aquaks had evolved into the purely bipedal, sentient species they were.

In less than a month, the humans had regained their facilities. A year later, the Raffians were studying their ancient texts, as well as learning English and human construction techniques. This, the second year after the meteorite was placed in storage, the Aquaks were attending classes right along with the Raffians and human children.

"Friends," Lerick stepped onto the middle of the raised platform set up for this celebration. Howard stepped up on his right side and Ashsor, the Aquak cleric, on his left. "I welcome you. Humans, Aquaks, and Raffians working together. Together we will build a strong society here on what was called Raff, then Belenius 3, and now Hope. For this planet offers all our species hope going into the future. Hope for better lives. Hope for contact with other races. And hope for understanding each of our strengths, weaknesses, fears, and dreams.

"I pronounce this spur," he turned to Howard, who nodded at his use of the word, "open for business. Now let's get going and connect every part of our grand experiment together.

"Thank you. Now back to work."

"Slave driver," someone jovially called from the crowd. But most of the crowd had turned and were walking out of the new station, back up to the daylight that awaited them in Watersberg. What had been nothing more than an encampment for the pre-evolved Aquaks, now had dozens of homes ready for Aquak families.

The other end of the spur was connected to the outskirts of First City. The Raffians had an advantage in building, they still had repairable foundations that could be built upon. Three times the number of homes had already gone up. And the foundation restoration techniques were quickly adapted to restoring the underground transit system.

Jeff stepped back into the transit train for the trip back to First City, to oversee the construction of a tunnel to Petersville. As he took a seat—alone, as everyone else was headed to the celebratory party—his mind wandered. *If we could build another shuttle? I could explore the rest of this planet. We had no idea what was here when we landed. Maybe there's other wonders out there.*

The train began moving.

The End

Books by John Lars Shoberg

More books by John Lars Shoberg:

The Waste Gun - Dr Von Scorio has developed a way to permanently dispose of radioactive waste. Others see it as threat to the Earth. 247 pages

Time Off - A washed-out seal decides to take a vacation on an interstellar cruise. Somehow, he can't quite shake the feeling that somebody is trying to kill him. 277 pages

The Stone Builders - Tension simmers in a colony shared by 2 races. It explodes when they discover the remains of an earlier colony by a third, unknown race. Even worse, something on the planet seems to have declared war on this colony. 273 pages

All available in hard copy from MoonPhaze.com

Books by Other Authors

Books by Other MoonPhaze Authors:

Cali - by Trudy V Myers - Sidek rescues a woman from a spring flood, and gets swept up in her search for revenge. 240 pages

The Secret in Morris Valley - by Linda (NMI) Joy (AKA Trudy V Myers) - Ondrea arrives to conduct a study on the unusual wolves reported to be in Morris Valley. Barry Morris has plans for her. So do the wolves. 60 pages

All available in hard copy from MoonPhaze.com

www.ingramcontent.com/pod-product-compliance
Lightning Source LLC
Chambersburg PA
CBHW070048120726
47909CB00002B/320
* 9 7 8 0 9 8 6 3 3 0 1 5 5 *